About the Author

Fran Pickering is a London-based British murder mystery writer who's travelled extensively in Japan. Her experiences there provide the inspiration for the Josie Clark in Japan mystery series.
She writes about London art and events with a Japanese connection on her blog, Sequins and Cherry Blossom.

COPYRIGHT

ISBN-13: 978-1500961923

ISBN-10: 1500961922

Copyright © Fran Pickering 2014

First published 2014

The right of Fran Pickering to be identified as the author of this work has been asserted in accordance with sections 77 and 78 of the Copyright, Designs and Patents Act of 1988.

All rights reserved. No part of this publication may be reproduced, stored in a retrieval system or transmitted in any form or by any means, electronic, mechanical, photocopying, recording or otherwise, without the prior written permission of the author.

This is a work of fiction. All characters and events, other than those clearly in the public domain, are fictitious and any resemblance to actual persons, living or dead, or actual events is purely coincidental.

The Haiku Murder

A Josie Clark in Japan mystery

Fran Pickering

Also by Fran Pickering

The Tokyo Karaoke Murder (Josie Clark in Japan #0 novellette)

The Cherry Blossom Murder (Josie Clark in Japan #1)

The Bullet Train Murder (Josie Clark in Japan #3 - coming soon)

The Haiku Murder

ONE

'There they are,' said Ken. 'Over by the group check-in sign.'

Josie craned her neck to see over the heads of the queue of passengers at the economy class check-in desk and spotted an alert young woman with red lipstick and a professional smile, clipboard at the ready. She wore a smart blue suit with a jaunty yellow scarf at the neck and the little group of people behind her had labels in the same zinging shade of yellow tied to their luggage.

'Yes, that's them,' Josie said. 'I can see Mr Kimura standing behind the tour guide. What's her name?'

'Hina. She's nice, you'll like her.'

Josie took a yellow scarf like the one Hina was wearing out of her bag and tied it around her neck so the blue logo and the words *Haiku Country Tours* were visible. She hoped it looked natural and casual, though she suspected it actually just made her look sallow and western. Ken didn't have a scarf, but he was wearing his Haiku Country Tours tie, which was blue with a very small logo in yellow. Josie wished she could have had a tie too instead of her all-too-noticeable scarf.

They made their way across the departure hall towards the waiting group, dodging through the ever-moving mass of families, business people and tourists trying, like them, to get from the top of the escalator from the monorail to the right check-in counter with their luggage and their sanity intact. A group of uniformed school children sitting cross-legged on the floor blocked their way, but the teacher obligingly opened up a pathway through, like Moses parting the waves. His eyes rested briefly on Josie and flicked back to his charges. Haneda airport on a Monday morning was not a place where people took much notice of how you looked, even if you were, like Josie, a tall skinny foreigner with untidy hair and an unflattering scarf.

As they reached the other side Josie's boss, Mr Kimura, detached himself from the yellow-labeled group and came to meet them. His Haiku Country Tours tie hung limply around his thin neck and his long face looked even more lugubrious than usual, as though he'd rather be safely at his desk than about to set off on a haiku adventure.

'Mr Ueda,' he said to Ken. 'Thank you for picking Miss Clark up and ensuring she got here on time.' He glanced severely at Josie. 'I know she does struggle with timekeeping sometimes.'

Josie bristled but restrained herself from replying. She'd had to set her alarm for four thirty in order to meet Ken at Tokyo station by half past six. Why couldn't they have got a flight at a more sensible time? It was only an hour and a half to Matsuyama – not exactly a trek to the Arctic.

'Think nothing of it,' said Ken. 'We're both really looking forward to the trip. And the haiku, of course.'

'Fortunately you're not the last to arrive,' said Mr Kimura, mollified by Ken's show of enthusiasm. 'Mr Ando has just texted to say he and his wife will arrive just before take-off. But the rest of the Ando Investments party are here. You know Hina, of course.' He turned to the woman with the clipboard who had been hovering behind him.

'Yes,' said Ken. 'We've been liaising over the tour arrangements.'

'This is Josie Clark,' said Mr Kimura to Hina. 'She works in Corporate Support with me and this is her first experience of haiku writing. But I'm sure she will turn out to be very talented, despite not being Japanese.'

Hina turned to Ken with a worried expression.

'Don't worry, Josie speaks Japanese,' he said.

Looking relieved, Hina bowed, smiled and handed Josie a large pack of papers in a folder with a picture of Matsuyama castle on the front.

'This is your tour pack. It has a full itinerary, a list of the hotels we'll be staying in, a participants list and a short guide to each of the places we'll be visiting. If you need anything, please don't hesitate to ask. I'll be travelling with you the whole way and I'll be only too happy to help with any problems.'

If only she could write my haiku for me, Josie thought. That would help with my biggest problem.

'Today and tomorrow we're in Matsuyama,' Hina went on. 'The bus takes us to Kochi on Wednesday. We have Thursday in Kochi and fly back to Tokyo in the evening. It's all in the pack. Please relax and enjoy the tour.'

'Thank you,' said Josie, trying to sound wide awake and interested. 'Have we got time to get a coffee before we board? I really need some caffeine.'

Hina checked her watch.

'We can't board until Mr and Mrs Ando get here,' she said, 'so I don't see why not.'

'How about you?' Josie said to Ken.

'I'd love a coffee, but let's just say hello to Eriko and Mr Mori first.'

'They're the Ando Investments people, right?'

'Yes. The woman standing next to the baggage counter is Eriko Ono. She's Mr Ando's assistant. The man is Mr Mori – I don't know him. I think he works in finance or something.'

Josie looked curiously at the pair, a young woman with a pile of papers and a distracted air, and an older man about a head shorter than her. Though they both worked for the same company and were about to go on the same tour, they seemed curiously unconnected, like two strangers who just happened to find themselves in the same check-in queue. They stood a little apart from each other; Eriko had an open folder in her hand and was ticking off some sort of list, while Mr Mori twitched and fiddled with his luggage tag as his eyes darted around, taking in everything that was going on.

Eriko looked up as though surprised when Ken approached, though Josie was sure she had been covertly studying them out of the corner of her eye. She smiled and bowed to Josie when Ken introduced them, but the smile quickly vanished. Josie got the impression she was worried about something. Maybe she didn't want to go on a haiku-writing tour any more than Josie did and had been dragooned into it by her boss just as Josie had by hers. Eriko didn't seem like the poetry-writing type, though Josie wasn't actually sure what the poetry-writing type looked liked – thin and ascetic maybe, whereas Eriko looked like she enjoyed her food.

Mr Mori didn't look the poetic type either. He was thin alright, but his restlessness was unsettling and his eagerness to be introduced was faintly repellent. He hung back with exaggerated humility at first, but when Eriko's eyes returned to her papers he stepped forward, bowed, and bared his teeth in an ingratiating smile.

'Pleased to meet you, Misss Clark,' he said, in the kind of old hissing Tokyo accent that was used in thirties movies by sinister oriental villains. You didn't hear it much nowadays, though the woman who ran Josie's local noodle restaurant had it too, making her hard for Josie to understand. 'It's a great privilege for me to be permitted to take part in this tour with ssuch interesting people. I hope that you will be able to sspare a little of your valuable time for me and permit me to ask you about Englissh life.'

'Of course,' said Josie, deciding to give Mr Mori a wide berth.

'We're just going to grab a coffee before check-in,' said Ken. 'Do you want to join us?'

'I'd love a coffee,' Eriko said. 'But I need to wait for Mr Ando. You go ahead.'

'Please, go and have your coffee. I wouldn't pressume to intrude,' said Mr Mori, twisting his body in a parody of humbleness.

'Thank goodness they didn't come with us,' said Josie as she and Ken settled in the far corner of Starbucks with a couple of caramel macchiatos. 'I don't think I could have coped with being sociable at this hour. Why on earth do you think they've come on the tour? Neither of them looks like a haiku fan to me.'

'It's not supposed to be for haiku fans,' said Ken. 'The idea is that, as Ando Investments are new clients, we should have a little getting-to-know-you trip. And as I've been transferred to Client Relations, I got stuck with organising it.'

'So was it your bright idea to have a haiku tour?'

'Of course not. Actually, it was Mr Ando's idea.'

'Mr Ando? It doesn't fit with my image of him at all.'

'You've never met him, have you?' said Ken. 'You wait. You're in for a surprise.'

Josie drank her coffee, grateful for the warmth and

the energising blast of caffeine hitting her veins. She felt blurry, as though she had jet lag, and she knew the dulling effect of lack of sleep would last all day. She hoped she wouldn't have to talk to the Ando Investments people on the trip down. She fancied just curling up and sleeping her way to Matsuyama.

'So why am I here?' she said. 'On the tour I mean. Was that Mr Ando's idea too?'

'As a matter of fact, it was. He heard we had an English girl on the staff and suggested to Mr Kimura that he bring you. I think his curiosity was piqued.'

'I've never heard of a haiku tour before,' said Josie. 'What exactly are we going to do? I won't really have to write haiku, will I?'

'Of course you will. That's the whole point. We all write haiku and then read them out to each other. Look at the itinerary.'

Josie opened the pack Hina had given her.

'You're right,' she said. 'There's a haiku reading slot scheduled every evening after dinner.'

'Exactly,' said Ken. 'I'm looking forward to it. I won a prize for haiku at school.'

'It's alright for you,' said Josie. 'I didn't write any haiku at school. I wasn't even any good at poetry – they called me the Catford McGonagall – and Japanese poetry is a closed book as far as I'm concerned.'

'Catford McGonagall?' said Ken, making McGonagall sound as though it had twice as many syllables. 'What's that?'

'McGonagall was the worst poet in the world,' said

Josie. 'Except for me. And Catford is in south London and is not exactly known as a hotbed of poetry. Couldn't you write a few extra haiku and let me read them out as though I'd written them?'

'You'll be fine,' said Ken.

'No really, I can't even remember whether it's five-seven-five or five-five-seven.'

'It's seventeen syllables in three lines split five-seven-five,' said Ken. 'And it's got to be about nature. That's why we're going on this trip, to get out into the countryside and commune with nature. Plus Matsuyama is the home of haiku.'

'What does Noriko think about your going off on this trip?' said Josie. Noriko was Ken's fiancée.

'She's fine with it,' said Ken. 'She and her mother spend all their time planning the wedding, so I think she'll be glad to have me out of the way so they can go and look at wedding dresses. And I'm quite glad to be out of it all too. All this fuss – I wish we could just go and sign the papers and get it over with.'

Josie looked at Ken thoughtfully. It could have been me, she thought. I went out with him before Noriko did. But then Dave turned up again, and Ken met Noriko. Otherwise... But things are better the way they are, even though Ken's got cheekbones like Keanu Reeves. Cheekbones aren't everything.

Back at the check-in counter they found Hina with some new arrivals, an older couple and a girl in her twenties, who seemed to be waiting for tickets. Then Mr Kimura hurriedly joined them and Josie realised this must be the Andos.

She'd had an image of Mr Ando firmly in her mind; one of those short, grim-faced businessmen who talk in gruff voices and ignore anyone of lower status to them. After all, he was head of a successful investment company with rocketing profits and a head office in fashionable Aoyama. But the real Mr Ando was nothing like that. He was average height, slim and stylish in a bespoke suit, with a mane of grey hair tumbling over his collar. Expressions chased each other across his face like clouds scudding across the sky and he moved like quicksilver, darting across to shake hands with Mr Kimura (who had been on the verge of bowing and seemed quite disconcerted) and giving Ken a friendly wave and nod. Then his eyes fell on Josie and a huge grin split his face.

'This must be your English assistant, Miss Clack,' he said, reaching out to grab Josie's hand and pump it up and down.

'Clark,' said Josie. 'Not Clack. Josie Clark.'

'Yes, of course,' said Mr Ando. 'I'm so glad you could come on this trip. I want to hear what you think of Matsuyama. Is this your first visit to Shikoku? I'm sure your haiku will be a revelation to us. That Western sensibility! Do you like T.S. Eliot? I so admire *The Waste Land*. Measured out my life with tea spoons, eh! Wonderful!'

'Coffee spoons,' said Josie. 'He measured out his life with coffee spoons. And it was *The Love Song of J Alfred Prufrock*.'

'Exactly! I can see you and I will have plenty to talk about. You must tell me all about English poetry on the plane.'

He turned to the woman with him, who Josie guessed must be his wife, though she seemed an unlikely partner for quicksilver Mr Ando. She was solidly built and stood firmly planted on two legs as though it would take an earthquake to shift her. Her hair had been fashionably cut and styled in a failed attempt to lighten her square, sensible face. She bowed to Josie, a deep bow that suggested she thought Josie was higher status than she was, which was odd given their true relative positions. Once again Josie was reminded of the woman who ran the local noodle restaurant, who always bowed in just that way even if you'd only had a bowl of plain noodles.

'Are the tickets sorted out?' said Mr Ando, twisting round to see where Hina was.

'Hina's doing it now,' said Mrs Ando. 'Not to worry – I'm sure she'll fix it.' Her voice was low and comfortable, as though nothing could worry her.

Hina came hurrying over from the ticket counter.

'No problem,' she said. 'I've arranged everything. I've got an extra plane ticket for your daughter and I've phoned ahead and warned the hotel to reserve an extra room.'

The girl with them held out her hand for the ticket. She had a spoiled, sulky face and didn't thank Hina for her efforts. She was expensively dressed in the latest Comme des Garçons jeans and a Chanel jacket, and carried a Prada bag over her arm, which she held so the logo was visible. She stood in a posed way with her hips thrust forward, which she obviously thought made her look like a catwalk model.

'Good,' she said. 'I'll see you on the plane. I've got some shopping to do.'

She flounced off, leaving Josie open mouthed. Mr Ando caught her expression.

'My daughter, Yuko,' he said. 'She decided to join us at the last minute. And why not eh? The more the merrier.' He gave an uneasy laugh which turned into a cough as he seized his bag and strode off, only to be waylaid by Eriko who immediately produced her folder of papers and started asking him questions about them, checking things off with a biro as she went, while Mr Ando fidgeted. Mrs Ando stood watching them, until Mr Mori sidled up to her and began to talk to her about autumn in Matsuyama in an unctuous voice and forced her to turn away.

How odd, thought Josie. I wonder why Mrs Ando is here when it's supposed to be a business trip. And what on earth prompted Yuko to turn up out of the blue like this?

She didn't have time to speculate any more as Hina gently herded them towards their departure gate, looking anxiously over her shoulder for Yuko, who appeared at the very last moment carrying a bag with the Haneda Airport logo, with the same sulky expression on her face that she'd had when she arrived.

*

Much to Josie's embarrassment, Mr Ando insisted

that she sit next to him on the plane and proceeded to interrogate her about her life in Catford and what she was doing working for AZT Insurance in Tokyo instead of marrying a nice English boy and settling down. Josie explained as best she could about working as a teaching assistant in Sapporo, learning Japanese and deciding to stay on when her teaching contract ended, but drew the line at telling Mr Ando about Dave, her English boyfriend, who now worked in Australia. She could feel Eriko, sitting in the row behind them, poised to waylay Mr Ando with another pile of papers, biro at the ready.

In Matsuyama, where they were met by a shiny blue and yellow minibus with *Haiku Country Tours Matsuyama* written on the side, it looked like she'd got her chance. Mr Ando got on the bus first and sat in the front seat. Eriko hurried on behind him and tried to claim the seat next to him, but Mrs Ando elbowed her out of the way and Eriko went and sat at the back, looking daggers at Mr Mori when he seemed inclined to join her. She waved to Josie when she got on and patted the seat next to her invitingly, forcing Mr Mori to look elsewhere, which was presumably the idea.

'Is this your first trip to Matsuyama?' Eriko said, and when Josie nodded said, 'Me too. I'm really looking forward to it. They say the yuzu ice cream is fantastic. Only I need to be careful how much I eat – I've only got to look at ice cream and I pile on the pounds.'

Eriko didn't look like she had much of a weight

problem – her body was firm and her arms well-muscled. She saw Josie looking and laughed.

'I'm a real gym-bunny,' she said. 'But if I stop for a moment, I'm in trouble. I like to eat, that's my problem. You're nice and slim, though. How do you do it?'

'Genetics,' said Josie. 'All my family are tall and thin.'

'Oh, I thought you must be a runner.'

'No way,' said Josie. 'Though I do a fair bit of walking.'

'There'll be plenty of walking in Matsuyama. We've timed it just right for the autumn leaves. Look.'

Josie looked out the window. They were driving along a winding country road through the mountains and the woods on either side were filled with maple trees, whose leaves ranged in colour from pale lemon yellow through gold and bronze to deep crimson. Although it was November, the weather was still as warm as an English summer and the sun glinted through the trees and turned the colours to fire. Josie didn't have much experience of the Japanese countryside – she was a big city girl, happy to exchange the crowds of London for the crowds of Tokyo – but now she began to wonder why she didn't get out of Tokyo more often. The occasional trip up to Hakone to visit the hot springs hardly counted.

The view outside the window gradually changed to a vista of ugly grey buildings, just like every other Japanese town Josie had ever seen. But then they turned a corner, slowed as the bus climbed a hill, and Ken, who was sitting in the seat in front, turned round and gestured out the window.

'Look,' he said. 'It's the Dogo hot spring.'

Josie looked where he was pointing to see a magical old building of dark wood with curved slate roofs piled on top of each other like turtles mating. At the corners were fantastical carved creatures and the apex of each roof was crowned with a heraldic carving. On either side of the entrance stood two ancient stone lanterns.

'It's amazing,' she said. 'But why do I have the feeling I've seen it before?'

'The film, of course,' said Ken. 'It was the model for the bath house of the gods in Studio Ghibli's *Spirited Away*.'

Something clicked in Josie's head and she looked at the building again. Now she saw it overlaid with the scenes from the film, as the little girl, Sen, raced around the complexities of the bath house's stairs and corridors trying to rescue her parents from a future as a pair of pigs.

There was a crowd of tourists standing in front of the building pointing and taking photos, then lining up to buy entry tickets from a little wooden hatch in the door.

'Can we go in?' she said to Ken.

'Of course. We'll go down after dinner and bathe in the hot spring. We've got some free time then.'

At the top of the hill the coach turned into the forecourt of a white-walled building with a glass portico swooping across the front. Above the portico were big silver letters spelling out *Dogo Resort Hotel*. Everyone stretched and lined up to get off the bus while uniformed porters unloaded their bags.

The hotel foyer was cool and quiet, with a mural of a traditional Japanese scene of court ladies and gentlemen on a bridge over a flowing stream painted on the one wall. In the centre of the room a little fountain tinkled pleasantly. There was an air of peace and calm, quite unlike the hustle and bustle of Tokyo.

'Please register at the desk,' said Hina, handing out registration cards. 'When you've checked in and found your rooms please assemble back here for our trip to the Ishite temple, which I hope will give you plenty of inspiration for our first day's haiku.'

*

Josie found the trip to the Ishite temple something of a trial. Partly because Hina insisted on telling them all about its history and status as an important cultural property and a stop on the pilgrimage road, but mainly because it was her turn to fall victim to Mr Mori's insatiable questions. Once again she found herself going through the Catford-Sapporo-Tokyo story until she was paralysed with boredom. She tried to turn the tables but Mr Mori was reluctant to talk about himself; she learned only that he was a Tokyo native, which she'd already guessed from his accent, and that he'd joined the haiku tour at the last minute as a substitute for the Chief Accountant who was ill.

'It'ss a privilege for me to be here,' he said. 'I would be grateful for your goodwill.' He bowed low as he spoke and for a odd moment Josie felt sorry for him. He really did seem to feel that he was too humble to be in such an august group. She wondered what he did at Ando Investments and how well he knew Mr Ando. Mr Ando had greeted him with a hearty handshake at the airport, but then Mr Ando seemed to get along with everybody.

But she had had enough of Mr Mori for one day, so when Hina said there was a wonderful view from further up the hill, she took the opportunity to hurry on ahead and leave him behind. As she climbed she saw a thrilling sight – a hawk soared high overhead, hunting its prey on long lazy wings. The whole party stopped to watch it until it flew out of sight.

As they started the climb, Yuko put a hand to her head as if in pain and turned Hina.

'I've got such a headache,' she said. 'I can't bear to walk around in the sun any longer. I'm going back to the hotel. Don't worry about me – I'll pick up a taxi back.'

She hurried away before Hina had a chance to say anything. The rest of the party were admiring the view and didn't notice, but Josie saw Eriko looking at Yuko's retreating back with dislike. Ooh, Josie thought. No love lost there. I wonder what Eriko's got against Yuko. And if the feeling is mutual.

*

When the group assembled after dinner for the haiku reading Josie could feel the butterflies in her stomach. The room was plain, just a wooden table surrounded by chairs and a side table with a green tea dispenser on it. The rest of the group were already assembled so Josie quickly helped herself to green tea to calm her nerves and sat down.

'Welcome to the first haiku-reading session of our tour,' said Hina. 'I'm sure we're all keen to hear what people have to share with us. Can I suggest that Mr Ando, as the moving force behind the tour, read the first haiku?'

Mr Ando looked pleased. He shuffled some papers in front of him, clearly deciding which of the many haiku he'd produced was worthy to launch the proceedings. Josie felt intimidated – it was all she could do to write one.

Mr Ando cleared his throat.

'*In the autumn haze, A starling's dry call startles, The distant pilgrims,*' he said. There was an appreciative pause and then a round of light clapping. He turned to Mr Kimura.

'Perhaps you would like to follow,' he said.

'I hesitate to follow such a masterly work,' said Mr Kimura, 'but if you insist.'

He opened the notebook that lay on the table in front of him and read, '*Temple bells ring out, Scent of incense fills the air, Golden autumn day.*'

Another polite patter of applause. Who would be next? Josie tried to shrink away out of sight, but since she was sitting next to Mr Mori, who was a good head shorter than she was, that was difficult.

'How about you, Eriko?' said Mr Kimura.

Eriko opened her notebook and, looking straight at Mr Ando, read, '*Hawk high in the sky, But when clear skies turn to storms, Harried by the wind.*'

Mr Ando's reaction to this struck Josie as extraordinary. He shifted in his seat, almost rising as if to leave, but then thought better of it and sank back down again. He smiled weakly and stared down at the bare table.

'Shall I go next?' said Ken, who had also noted Mr Ando's discomfiture.

'*Gold and russet leaves, Rustled by the passing breeze, Whispering of autumn,*' he read, and once again a polite smatter of applause went up.

Hina turned to Mrs Ando with an encouraging smile. Mrs Ando looked straight at Eriko and said, '*Hawk high in the sky, Soaring in the evening breeze, Fears no changing wind.*'

It sounded like a response, a rebuke even, to Eriko. Josie looked curiously from one to the other, but both were impassive. Only Mr Ando reacted, getting out his handkerchief and mopping his brow, though the room was on the chilly side. He looked down the table at Mr Mori, with something approaching pleading in his eyes. Mr Mori looked back at him and said softly: '*Hawk high in the sky, Fleeing doves see hidden clouds, Fear the coming storm.*'

Mr Ando got up and abruptly strode from the room.

TWO

'Thank you all very much,' said Hina after an awkward pause, 'I think that brings our haiku session to an end. Please enjoy the rest of your evening.'

'What was that all about?' Josie whispered to Ken, as the others stood up and began gathering up their papers. Mrs Ando swept out without a glance at anyone while Yuko almost skipped out of the room.

'Search me,' he said. 'Sorry you didn't get a chance to read your haiku. You'll have to go first at tomorrow's session to make up for it.'

'I'm not breaking my heart over it,' said Josie. 'Anyway, more time to spend at the hot spring. Give me five minutes to pick up my stuff then I'll meet you in the foyer.'

Josie hurried up to her room to get the cotton kimono and towel the hotel provided for guests visiting the hot spring. She felt ridiculously relieved to have been spared the haiku ordeal, just like the day at school when they were expecting an exam but a pipe burst and flooded the hall so the exam had to be put off. She was glad to get away from the rest of their tour party, too – there seemed to be constant undercurrents of tension and unspoken disagreements that made for an unpleasant atmosphere. Much nicer to go off with Ken and have fun. Though not too much fun, she reminded herself, thinking of Dave. He would be coming over to visit for Christmas. She didn't want to do anything to spoil that, not when they were getting on so well. And anyway, Ken was engaged.

The Dogo hot spring was a short walk down the hill from their hotel. They paid their four hundred yen at the entrance for the basic tour and entry to the baths and followed their guide and a considerable number of laughing, chattering Japanese tourists into a maze of passageways and stairs decorated with frequent paintings of the white stork that was the symbol of Dogo. The private room reserved for the Emperor produced a crescendo of oohs and ahs, though Josie was disappointed to find it was last used in 1952. She found it more amusing to peer into the special rest rooms for people who paid extra on their entrance fee. They were full of middle-aged Japanese gentlemen in cotton kimonos, their faces still red and sweaty from the baths, sitting comfortably on yellow straw mats drinking green tea and eating little round sweet *mochi* while huge fans blew cooling breezes across the room.

At the end of the tour they separated, Ken to the men's baths and Josie to the women's baths, with promises to meet up in front of the entrance in half an hour.

The changing rooms, with their wicker baskets for clothes and rows of little lockers for valuables, seemed to go on for miles. Josie quickly piled her jumper and jeans into a basket and put her watch and bag in one of the lockers. The locker key came with a rubber bracelet which she fixed round her wrist. Holding her little towel modestly in front of her she slid back the heavy frosted-glass door and stepped onto the stone floor of the bath house.

She had never been in such an imposing public bath; the stone pool was the size of a small swimming pool and there were at least twenty women lying in the steamy water or sitting washing themselves on three-legged wooden stools in one of the little bays with mirrors and shower sprays that ran along one wall.

The body wash in the shower bay where Josie soaped herself was made with charcoal and came out a disconcerting black colour but left her skin feeling silky smooth. Feeling clean and virtuous, she stepped into the steaming pool and slid gently into the water, which was hot enough to take her breath away.

She didn't spend long luxuriating in the pool. She tended to turn pink in the volcanic heat of a hot spring, so she soon got out and ran cool water over herself back in the shower bay before drying off and reclaiming her possessions.

As Josie left, someone familiar passed her on their way in and gave her a slight, almost imperceptible, nod of greeting. It was Mrs Ando. There was no sign of Yuko but Josie wasn't surprised – she was probably working her way round the fashion boutiques. Josie wondered if Mr Ando had come to the baths too, and whether he'd got over whatever it was that had spooked him at the haiku reading. Then she forgot about him and hurried outside to meet Ken.

Ken was waiting for her, dressed in the same patterned kimono and soft padded jacket as Josie, with his hair slicked down and damp from the pool. He had wooden sandals on his feet that made him walk with a slow, rolling gait like the actors in the samurai dramas on the television, which Josie found rather attractive; combined with his sharp cheekbones it gave him an air of Genghis Khan.

It was nearly nine-thirty, clearly peak time to visit the baths as a queue stretched from the entrance and a constant stream of kimono-clad people emerged from the exit looking clean and jolly, heading for the arched gate to the covered shopping arcade across the road. Josie and Ken did the same, Josie struggling to keep her balance on her stiff wooden sandals. Ken laughed and took hold of her arm to steady her.

They found themselves on a narrow path, just wide enough for a car (or a horse and cart when this place was built, thought Josie) lined with shops whose counters were piled high with boxes of sweets and cakes wrapped in decorated paper; traditional pottery, fans, purses and phone covers in gaily-coloured brocade; Hello Kitty key rings and all the other myriad souvenirs that any Japanese town worth its salt seemed to sell by the cartload. They dawdled by one brightly lit shop while Ken arranged for a giant box of *Tart*, a sort of swiss roll made of sponge cake and yuzu-flavoured sweet bean paste that was the Matsuyama speciality, to be sent to his parents back in Yokohama. Josie fingered a brocade handbag speculatively. Then she caught herself and put it back. She'd promised herself she wouldn't buy any tourist tat on this trip.

At the yuzu ice cream stall they waited their turn behind a group of girls buying three-scoop cones and screaming as the ice cream threatened to drip on their kimonos. Then they wandered on, licking their dripping cones and ignoring the efforts of the shopkeepers to lure them in with calls of *irasshaimase* and enticing descriptions of their goods.

'Do you want to go for a rickshaw ride?' said Ken, as they emerged from a ceramics shop to find they had to step aside to let a rickshaw pass.

'Well,' said Josie. 'It would be fun.'

'Come on then, I'll treat you,' said Ken, flagging down a rickshaw that had just deposited its passengers.

They scrambled in, feeling suddenly shy to be in such close proximity and self-consciously sitting with a six-inch space between them. Josie stared out at the passing scene with exaggerated concentration. But then she saw something that made her tug at Ken's arm.

'Look over there, she said. 'Isn't that Yuko?'
'Where?'
'Just down that side alley. Coming towards us,

look. She's with somebody but I can't see who it is.'

Their rickshaw driver paused to let a rickshaw coming the other way go first, and Josie got a clear view of Yuko and her companion. Yuko had a scarf over her head in an attempt to hide her face, but she was wearing the same blue Comme des Garçons dress with Jimmy Choos that she'd been wearing at the haiku session so Josie knew she hadn't made a mistake. Yuko was with a young man and they were deep in conversation, their heads bent, oblivious to what was going on around them. A secret boyfriend? Josie wondered but somehow their manner didn't feel like that. More like a co-conspirator, though Josie couldn't imagine what they could be conspiring about. She'd never seen the man before, but then she'd only met Yuko for the first time that morning, so that proved nothing. Only it was odd, that Yuko should have suddenly decided to join her parents on a trip to Matsuyama and then have run into someone who she obviously knew well. Or maybe not run into – maybe she'd arranged to meet him here. Maybe he was her boyfriend and her parents disapproved. If so, Josie hoped Mrs Ando had decided on an early night rather than a wander around the shopping arcade after her visit to the hot spring. Otherwise there was going to be an almighty bust-up.

*

Josie found it hard to get up for breakfast the next day. After the early start and the busy day she slept like a log. But she felt better when the enticing aroma of the hotel's breakfast buffet greeted her as she entered the sunny breakfast room. The buffet stretched down both sides of the room; western food in silver serving dishes on one side and Japanese on the other. Josie mixed the two sorts together, putting a plate of scrambled egg, fried tomatoes and bacon on her tray and adding a bowl of rice porridge and a little dish of boiled tofu, topping it all off with tinned fruit and yoghurt. She had a feeling she was going to need plenty of fuel for the day ahead.

Her boss, Mr Kimura, was sitting with Mr Mori at a big table that had a reservation label for Haiku Country Tours on it. Beside Mr Kimura's plate lay that morning's *Yomiuri* newspaper and from time to time he sneaked a glance at it, obviously itching to read it, but Mr Mori asked him an endless series of questions about what it was like to work for a big company like AZT and what the precise hierarchy was, which Mr Kimura answered with his customary politeness, though his face showed the strain. Mr Mori was just starting to draw a diagram to check his understanding when Josie joined them, to Mr Kimura's obvious relief. Ken arrived shortly after, his plate piled high with sausages, egg and bacon. He winked at Josie and she stifled a giggle. Clearly, he was stoking up for the day ahead too.

Hina flitted in and gave them all a big smile.

'Don't forget, we're assembling outside the hotel at nine thirty and walking down to the shopping arcade for a trip on the Botchan railway. Then it's on to Matsuyama castle and finally a bus tour of the countryside to see the autumn leaves before we move on to Kochi. I hope you've all got your notebooks ready – I have a feeling today will give us plenty of inspiration for our haiku.'

'Where's the rest of our party?' said Ken. 'Not sleeping in, surely.'

'Oh no,' said Hina. 'Mr and Mrs Ando went out for a walk before breakfast – they should be back soon. Eriko said she's skipping breakfast but she'll join us for a coffee. And here's Yuko now.'

Yuko appeared, helped herself to a bowl of miso soup and some tofu and sat down next to Ken. Josie looked at her, wondering if she realised Josie'd spotted her the night before, but she gave no sign of it.

'Did you enjoy yourself last night?' Josie asked her politely, and only a touch maliciously. 'Ken and I went to the Dogo hot spring. I saw your mother there. What did you do?'

'Nothing,' said Yuko. 'I had an early night.'

'What about you, Mr Mori?' said Ken.

'I, too, had an early night,' said Mr Mori. 'We had ssuch an early start yesterday, I was quite worn out. And it is a pleasure to be in the country and ssleep with the window open, and be woken by birdssong.'

Josie couldn't imagine Mr Mori staying quiet long enough to listen to birdsong. She turned to ask Mr Kimura what he had done, but he'd seized his chance to open up his newspaper and hide behind it.

There was a chorus of good mornings as Eriko

appeared, carrying a cup of black coffee.

'I ate too much yuzu ice cream last night,' she said. 'I knew I wouldn't be able to resist.'

'We had some too,' said Josie. 'Delicious.'

'I'm sorry we didn't hear your haiku last night,' said Mr Kimura to Josie, emerging from behind his paper. 'Maybe tonight we could have a little haiku game.'

'Haiku game?' said Josie.

'Yes, like they did in the old days. A thousand years ago, our ancestors would stand on a bridge over a stream and drop a camellia into the water. The challenge was to compose a haiku before it floated out the other side.'

'A sort of intellectual version of Pooh sticks,' said Josie, but Mr Kimura just looked blank.

'People would converse in haiku,' Mr Kimura went on. 'Lovers, especially, would write answering haiku, some of them very beautiful.'

'There are haiku card games too, that we play at New Year,' came a voice, and Josie turned to see Mr Ando, dressed in a smart polo shirt and slacks, with an expensive-looking brown leather messenger bag over his shoulder. 'There are two sets of cards, and when someone reads out the first half of the poem you have to find the card with the matching second half.'

'Sounds a bit beyond me,' said Josie.

'It's a lovely morning,' said Mr Ando, sitting down next to Mr Kimura. 'Perfect for our visit to the castle. *In Matsuyama, Higher than the autumn sky, Soars the castle keep* – eh Mr Kimura?'

'Indeed,' said Mr Kimura. 'Masaoka Shiki, I believe?'

'Correct,' said Mr Ando. 'My second favourite haiku poet, after Basho.'

Mrs Ando arrived with a tray piled high with food and took a seat at the end of the table, away from her husband who had naturally taken a place in the centre. The atmosphere had changed as he sat down, with a sense that now the senior member of the group had arrived a more formal attitude was required. Josie could almost see the lines of hierarchy radiating out from Mr Ando via Mr Kimura to Ken and herself, and via Eriko to Mr Mori and Yuko.

The trouble was, Mr Ando himself seemed determined to ignore all the protocol seething around him. He laughed and chatted with everyone without discrimination, drawing Ken out about his impending marriage and exchanging inaccurate snippets of haiku with Mr Kimura, whose agony in knowing how they should really go but not being able to correct them without being impolite was visible on his face. Mr Ando questioned Josie about London, but, as he seemed to think that it was a foggy place full of gentlemen in bowler hats, she found it hard to respond. She tried to suggest that east London was now better known for technology companies than dark alleys where killers lurked but she could see nothing would shake Mr Ando's conviction that Jack the Ripper was alive and well and still on the loose.

At quarter past nine they all stood up with a great scraping back of chairs and headed off to get ready for the bus's departure. A holiday mood seemed to overcome them all as they boarded the bus, which was reinforced by the Botchan railway, a replica steam train that ran through the centre of town, pulling a replica carriage, wood panelled inside with red velvet seats. It wasn't quite a full size train, and its smallness gave it the feeling of a toy train set.

'*Dinky like a matchbox and only three sen,*' said Mr Ando with a knowing nod to Mr Kimura, who explained to Josie, 'The Botchan railway is named after the novel by Natsume Soseki, which is set in Matsuyama. Mr Ando is quoting what Botchan himself said about the railway. Sen were the currency at the time.'

There isn't a man in the world who can resist a steam train, thought Josie, watching Mr Kimura's normally solemn face soften into a pleased grin, as Mr Ando leapt from side to side pointing out the sights. Only Mr Mori seemed immune, but Josie had the impression that under the surface he was watching everything closely, particularly Mr Ando. She wondered about the haiku session the day before; it was after Mr Mori's contribution that Mr Ando had walked out. And there was an odd atmosphere between Mr Ando and Mr Mori. They seemed to be keeping well away from each other, but once Josie caught Mr Ando looking at Mr Mori with a knowing twinkle in his eye, and receiving a knowing look back.

Eriko was the only one who didn't seem to enjoy the train ride. She seemed to sink into a state of gloom as they went along, as though something was weighing on her mind.

That's what happens when you skip breakfast, Josie thought. It always catches you out. I bet she's desperate for it to be lunchtime.

The train chugged into the main square and stopped. They all got out, stretching their legs theatrically, and Hina lined them up in front of the engine and took a photograph.

'I'll email it to you all,' she said. 'It will be a lovely souvenir of your trip.'

*

Matsuyama castle was perched on a hill overlooking the town. Josie had already seen it in the distance a number of times but wasn't prepared for how high up it was when you stood at the bottom looking up.

'How do we get up there?' she said to Ken.

'Are you afraid you'll have to climb?' he said. 'Not to worry. Theres a chairlift, like the ones you get at ski resorts. We'll go up on that.'

Josie imagined the chairlift would be rather high tech and was disconcerted when she found herself thrust onto an ancient metal chair that immediately swung up and out into the fresh air. She felt a momentary stab of fear, imagining herself swooping up high with nothing to keep her on the chair but her own grip on the cold metal pole that held it up. But then she looked around her and laughed at her own foolishness. The chair, which proceeded at a stately pace, was suspended a mere couple of metres above a grassy bank, and between her and the bank was a stout net to catch anyone silly enough to let go of the pole and fall off. She relaxed, enjoying the view of russet autumn leaves that spread out before her, gradually getting more and more extensive as she rose up higher. At the top a uniformed attendant grabbed her chair and helped her off.

She watched as the rest of the party negotiated the drop-off without incident, though Mr Mori seemed uncomfortable on his metal seat and glad to be free of it, while Eriko disdained the helping hand the attendant offered and leapt off by herself. Mrs Ando had to be heaved off the chairlift bodily.

They set off into the castle, where Josie was dismayed to find that they still had higher to climb, and that the way up was by a kind of ladder with ambitions to be a staircase that failed to provide the advantages of either. It was too steep to walk up normally, but didn't provide any kind of rail that you could hang onto for security. The rest of the party seemed to take it in their stride, but Josie made a mental note to steer clear of castles in future.

Finally they reached the last staircase, which led to the castle keep, surrounded on all four sides by verandas from which you could look out across the mountainous landscape. The view from the top almost made the perilous stairs worth it; it felt like there was nothing between the veranda and the horizon. Below them Matsuyama basked in the autumn sunshine, and on the distant mountains the shimmering golden-bronze leaves looked like a Van Gogh painting. The air was clear and everything had a glow about it.

Josie took out her phone and took a photo of the view. She turned to Ken, who had joined her on the veranda.

'This is amazing,' she said. 'This is what I love about Japan – moments like this, places like this.'

'Your eyes are shining,' said Ken. 'It makes your face look completely different.'

Josie laughed. 'I don't have much chance to get out in the country,' she said. 'Maybe it does me good.'

They worked their way around the four verandas, each with a different view of town and country. There were surprisingly few tourists, apart from their little party. But then, it was a normal working day for most people, and, with twelve o'clock approaching, most visitors would already be making their way to one of the local restaurants for lunch. If there was one thing you could rely on in Japan, it was the inevitability of the twelve o'clock lunch.

Mr and Mrs Ando were on the south veranda, standing together gazing out at the mountains in what seemed like companionable silence. Eriko stood a little further along, filming a panoramic view on her mobile phone. Mr Mori hovered in the background, looking for someone to talk to. Ken and Josie quickly ducked back into the keep before he could latch onto them.

It took a moment for Josie's eyes to adjust to the darkness inside the keep after the brightness outside. Then she made out Mr Kimura, scribbling in his notebook with an expression of contentment on his face, and Hina, looking a little anxious and checking her watch, obviously worried that they were running late for lunch. Yuko was sitting on a bench in the corner looking bored and sulky while a young couple pored over the glass display case in the centre of the room. The couple read their way studiously through all the explanatory text and then stepped out onto the veranda and started taking pictures, just as a group of elderly women came back in, discussing where to have lunch. They disappeared down the steep staircase with more confidence than Josie could muster.

Hina came over to Josie and Ken.

'You can start back down if you like,' she said. 'I'll get everyone together and join you on the lower level. Then we'll go and have lunch.'

'Lunch sounds good,' said Ken. 'All that fresh air has given me an appetite.'

Ken and Josie started back down the stairs, Josie throwing all dignity to the winds and going down backwards as if it was a ladder while Ken walked down as though it was a normal staircase.

At the bottom they stopped to wait for the others to catch up. A few more visitors heading off to lunch passed them and Josie began to wonder what the rest of their party could be doing. Then a scream came from above.

'What's that?' said Josie. 'What's going on?'

'I'll go and see,' said Ken, starting to climb the staircase again. But before he had got half way up a face appeared in the lightwell above. It was Hina.

'Go back,' she said, fighting to keep her voice level. 'Go back down and find an attendant. There's been an accident. Mr Ando has fallen from the veranda.'

THREE

For a moment they both stood there paralysed, then Josie started to climb back up the stairs.

'What are you doing?' said Ken. 'Hina said to stay down here.'

'You stay,' said Josie over her shoulder. 'I'm going to see what's happened.'

She went up the stairs a good deal faster than she had the first time and reached the top to find the rest of their party huddled in the keep. Mr Kimura had his hand over his face; Eriko looked stricken while Mrs Ando looked stunned. Hina was attempting to comfort Yuko who had burst into noisy tears. Josie ran out onto the veranda. Mr Mori was there, peering down at a small crowd that had gathered far below them. The sides of the castle were steep at that point, only a couple of levels of grey-slated curly-edged roof before the sheer drop of the castle walls.

'Did you see what happened?' said Josie.

'No, I was on the veranda round the other side. I just heard a strange ssound – a sort of sscuffling.'

'So who raised the alarm?'

'A young couple who'd been on the next veranda to Mr Ando. They came round to this sside and when they looked over they saw the body down below.'

They stood in silence for a moment.

'Nobody could ssurvive a fall like that,' said Mr Mori.

Josie turned away from the railing, wondering how Mr Ando had managed to fall over it. Granted, it wasn't that high – only about waist height – but even so it was hard to see how a grown man in possession of his faculties could have tipped over it. Unless he did it on purpose, thought Josie. But that didn't seem very likely. She couldn't think of anyone who looked less likely to kill himself than Mr Ando. Maybe he had been leaping about in that energetic way of his, leaned over to point something out and toppled over before he could grab on to anything.

Mr Mori turned and went back into the keep. Josie followed him, just as a castle attendant appeared at the top of the staircase.

'Is everyone up here all right?' he said. 'We've called an ambulance and the police, but I'm afraid you should probably prepare yourselves for the worst.'

There was a low moan from Yuko and Hina put her arm round her.

'We need to go back down,' she said gently. 'Come with me, and watch your step. We don't want any more accidents.'

They started down the stairs. Eriko followed, then

Mrs Ando. Josie hung back while the castle attendant checked the other verandas, but there were no other visitors left. The young couple who had raised the alarm clung to each other as they waited their turn to descend. Mr Mori and Mr Kimura followed them and the castle attendant motioned to Josie to go next. He stayed in the keep, no doubt to make sure that no stragglers found their way in there before the police arrived.

Ken was waiting at the next level. Together they made their way down to the bottom of the main castle building and out into the sunshine. Mercifully, the exit from the castle was on the opposite side to the side on which Mr Ando had fallen.

Everyone milled about, unsure of what to do, apart from Yuko who sobbed hysterically and demanded to be allowed to see the body.

'That's not a good idea,' said Hina gently. 'Wait here while I go and see what's happening.'

'I'll come with you,' said Josie.

They walked around the outside of the castle, passing groups of tourists happily taking photos with no inkling of the tragedy just around the next corner. When Hina and Josie reached the spot where Mr Ando's body lay they saw an ambulance had arrived, and the paramedics were preparing to lift Mr Ando's body onto a stretcher. Josie took one look and looked away. The paramedic covered the body with a blanket but not before an odd, irrelevant thought popped into Josie's head. Where was Mr Ando's expensive leather messenger bag? She hadn't seen it on the body, and it was nowhere to be seen in the area round about. Maybe it slipped from his hand as he fell and ended up some way away.

'I think I ought to talk to the police,' said Hina. 'To tell them who Mr Ando is and give them our details.'

'Of course,' said Josie. 'By the way, ask them to look out for his bag, will you? I can't see it anywhere.'

'I will. Can you go back to the rest of the group and get them to board the bus and wait for me? Then I think we'd better go straight back to the hotel.'

Josie nodded and turned back. Just then Mrs Ando came panting up.

'I want to go with him,' she said. 'To the hospital. Let me go.'

Hina and Josie exchanged glances, then Hina said gently,

'Yes, of course. We'll speak to the paramedics. I'm sure it will be alright.'

Mrs Ando's creased face relaxed.

'I'll go with him,' she said. 'I always go with him.'

Josie walked slowly back to the castle entrance. The bus had arrived and the group were standing hesitantly beside it, not sure whether to board or not.

'Hina says to get on the bus and wait for her,' Josie said. 'She won't be long.'

'Where's my mother?' said Yuko.

'She's with Hina. They're just sorting everything out now. By the way, has anybody seen Mr Ando's bag? The brown leather one he was carrying?'

Nobody said anything, and nobody met Josie's eyes. After a few moments Mr Kimura boarded the bus and Mr Mori followed him, but sat down on the opposite side to Mr Kimura. For once, it seemed, the little man had run out of conversation.

'I'm going to see what my mother's doing,' said Yuko suddenly, running off before Josie could stop her.

'I'm going too,' said Eriko.

Josie hesitated and then followed them back around the castle wall. As she turned the corner a man passed her going the other way, back towards the castle entrance, with his head averted. She noticed him because he was not wearing the kind of smart casual outfit most tourists adopted; he was in a business suit and carried a large briefcase. She stared at his retreating back, wondering what he was doing. Visiting the castle in his lunch hour? It seemed possible, but then why the briefcase?

She forgot about him as she saw Hina and Yuko coming towards her, walking either side of Mrs Ando. So they hadn't let her go with the body after all. Eriko emerged suddenly from a little side entrance to the castle Josie hadn't noticed before and the little group made their way slowly back to the tour bus.

The ride back to the hotel took place in silence. When they arrived Hina stood up and said, 'After the terrible thing that has happened I'm sure you'll all want to get back to Tokyo as quickly as possible. I'll get my office to cancel the arrangements for the rest of the tour and I'll rebook you all onto flights back to

Tokyo today. Your bags are already packed and loaded on the bus, and we've checked out of the hotel, so I'll ask at reception to see whether we can wait in the room we used for our haiku reading last night. I'll get them to send in something to eat.'

They filed off the bus, followed Hina into reception and waited while she conferred with the girl behind the desk. Finally a key was handed across and Hina unlocked the door of the meeting room.

The room seemed dry and dusty in the afternoon sun. Mr Kimura went over to the green tea dispenser and poured out cups of tea which people passed along the table to each other. After a brief interlude there was a knock at the door and one of the hotel staff came in with a tray of sandwiches which everyone picked at listlessly. Time seemed to pass incredibly slowly. Josie couldn't keep herself from thinking about how Mr Ando had been at breakfast, so full of life. And now it was all over. She didn't know who to feel more sorry for, Mrs Ando or Yuko. She shuddered and thought of her own father, back home in Catford. She hadn't seen him for nearly a year. She resolved to ring home as soon as she got back to Tokyo, just to hear the reassuring sound of his voice.

'I'd better let the office know what's happened,' said Ken. 'And Noriko too.'

He picked up his phone and started texting. The others all got out their phones and followed his example, except for Josie. She lived by herself in a little company flat in Ichikawa, and would disturb nobody by her early return.

The door opened, and they all jumped. It was Hina with a sheaf of papers in her hand.

'I've rebooked all the flights,' she said. 'I couldn't get you all on the same flight back, but you're all on flights some time today. Mr Kimura and Mr Mori are on the five-thirty flight, Josie and Ken on the six-thirty and Eriko on the seven-thirty. Mrs Ando, Yuko and I are on the last flight at eight-thirty.'

'We've got some time to spare, then,' said Ken. 'I don't fancy spending it in this stuffy room. I know it sounds a bit callous, but why don't we go out somewhere?'

'I'm up for that,' said Josie. 'We can just walk around town and get a bit of fresh air.'

She looked doubtfully at Mr Kimura.

'I shall stay here and contact people back at the office,' he said.

'I'll do the same for Ando Investments,' said Eriko. 'There's a lot of people to tell and a lot of arrangements to be made. The funeral, for instance.'

The funeral — Josie hadn't thought of that. It seemed indecently early to be mentioning it at all, but she knew that in Japan people were cremated very soon after they died — within twenty-four hours if possible.

'I'll stay here with Mrs Ando, of course,' said Hina.

'I'm going out on my own,' said Yuko. 'I can't bear to be with anybody else.'

Mr Mori said nothing, just took his new plane ticket from Hina, bowed and left the room.

*

It felt awful, wandering around Matsuyama after what had happened. The town was full of happy tourists snapping pictures of each other at every turn. There was even a smattering of foreigners, Josie noticed, no doubt drawn there by the association of the Dogo hot spring with an Oscar-winning film. She watched an American family, dressed in shorts and open-necked shirts, posing for a photo in front of the Botchan train. She couldn't believe that only a few hours before she had been doing the same thing. Though not wearing shorts. Not on a tour with her boss.

'Look,' said Ken. 'There's a cafe where you can sit outside with your feet in the water from the hot spring. Let's give it a go.'

They sat down at a wooden table with wooden benches either side of it, set into a little trough where hot volcanic water bubbled. Josie peeled off her shoes and socks, rolled up the bottom of her slacks and let her feet dangle in the water.

'I'll get us some coffee,' said Ken. 'Cappuccino?'

Josie nodded.

The warm autumn sunshine beat down on the back of her head. She tried not to let her mind drift back to the castle and what she had seen from the veranda.

The glass door of the cafe slid back and Ken came out carrying a tray with two cups of cappuccino and a plate of red-bean-paste-filled dorayaki pancakes.

'I thought we needed some sustenance,' he said,

handing her a dorayaki. 'Those sandwiches at the hotel didn't have much to them, and anyway we were all too shocked to eat much. We need something to keep us going until we get to the airport.'

Josie peeled the cellophane off her dorayaki. Normally she loved the sweet pancakes but right now they tasted like sawdust.

'What an awful thing to happen,' said Ken, putting his rolled-up socks inside his shoes and easing his feet into the near-boiling volcanic water. 'Though how he could have fallen off that veranda beats me. Do you think he could have been drinking?'

'I don't think so,' said Josie. 'He was with us all morning – he didn't have the chance to drink.'

'Well it must have been a heart attack, or a seizure or something.'

'Maybe,' said Josie. Mr Ando hadn't looked like the heart attack type. 'I wonder—' she said and stopped.

'Go on,' said Ken.

'Well, it's just that this whole haiku tour has been so odd.'

'Odd?' said Ken. 'What's odd about it?'

'I don't know. Yes, I do. It's what happened last night at the haiku reading.'

'You mean Mr Ando walking out like that?'

'Not just that. I'm no haiku expert, but didn't you think the haiku that Eriko and Mrs Ando and Mr Mori wrote were a bit, well, unusual?'

'Because they were about the hawk we saw? Why shouldn't they write about that?'

'It's not the hawk. It's the things they said. You know, about storms and winds and stuff.'

'I think you're getting this a bit out of proportion.'

'I hope I am. Tell me, what do you know about Ando Investments?'

'Mr Ando set it up about six or seven years ago. It's done very well but people say that's mainly because of Mr Wada, their investment strategist. Word is that Mr Ando lured him away from one of the big derivative firms by promising him a free hand to pursue his own ideas, and it paid off big time. Mr Ando just looks after the business administration end of things.'

'Where did Mr Ando get the money to start the company?'

'No idea. I've only come across him since the company became an AZT client earlier this year. I don't know anything about his history.'

'Why didn't Mr Wada come on the haiku tour?'

'I expect he had more important things to do. Come on, Josie, be sensible.'

'Okay. You're right. I'm just speculating in a vacuum. All the same though...'

'What?'

'Well, Mr Ando fell off a veranda that no reasonable person could fall off. Doesn't that suggest something to you – like, that maybe he was pushed?'

Ken stared at her.

'I know it's far-fetched,' said Josie. 'But let's just think about it for a minute. Where was everybody when the accident happened?'

'You and I were on the next level down from the keep, waiting for the rest of them to catch up,' said Ken. 'Not exactly well-placed for spotting where everybody was.'

'Mr Mori was in the keep when we went downstairs,' said Josie. 'And when I went back up he was out on the veranda that Mr Ando fell from. The north veranda. He said he'd been on the one of the other verandas when it happened, and the couple who raised the alarm were on the next veranda to Mr Ando. That must had been either the east or the west veranda. He didn't mention anyone else being there.'

'Yuko was in the keep when we went down,' said Ken, getting into the swing of it.

'And she was still there when I went back up. Same with Mr Kimura and Hina. Though I suppose that doesn't mean they all stayed in the keep the whole time. They could have gone out onto one of the verandas and come back in again.'

'Mr and Mrs Ando and Eriko were all on the south veranda when I last saw them,' said Ken.

'Mrs Ando and Eriko were in the keep when I went back up. But they could have walked round the outside to one of other verandas, or come back into the keep and gone out onto one of the verandas again. If only we'd stayed in the keep instead of going back down. We'd have seen what everybody did.'

'Mr Kimura might know. Or Hina.'

'Yes, that's right – we could ask them. Though at the moment I can't think of a tactful way to do it.'

'There's never going to be a tactful way to do it,'

said Ken, piling their empty cups back on the tray. 'And I suggest you don't try. It's all very well the two of us speculating like this, but you don't want anybody else getting the idea you think there might be something funny about Mr Ando's accident. Especially not Mrs Ando or Yuko. It's bad enough for them as it is without you raising suspicions.'

He dried his feet on his handkerchief, put his shoes and socks back on and took the tray back into the cafe.

Josie got her hand towel out and dried her feet too, feeling a bit resentful about the way Ken had dismissed her ideas. But he was right about one thing; she didn't want to do anything to upset Mrs Ando and Yuko, and if that meant keeping her mouth shut, then that was what she would do. Even though she was becoming more and more convinced that there was something very odd indeed about Mr Ando's supposed accident.

FOUR

Black dress, thought Josie, staring hopelessly into the murky depths of her wardrobe. I don't have a black dress. Or jacket. Or skirt. Or cardigan. Or anything. I never wear black. It drains all the colour from my face and makes me look like a – she stopped herself before the next word. Like a corpse. Not a good thought when you're planning on going to a funeral.

Her mum always kept a black suit carefully put away in the wardrobe in case of funerals. The old folk at the day care centre where she helped out two days a week popped off on a regular basis and Josie's mum never liked to be caught unprepared. Not like Josie, who hadn't given a thought to the need for a black dress until now.

She scrabbled about some more and came up with a navy coat.

'What do you think?' she said to Keiko, who was sitting on the sofa ready to pass judgement, her round face unusually serious. Keiko was Josie's best friend and had come to help Josie pick out the right clothes to wear to Mr Ando's funeral. 'It's navy blue, not black but I could wear it with black tights and a dark jumper and skirt.'

'Navy blue is fine. You're not family, just a business associate, so navy blue is actually more correct,' said Keiko. 'Have you got some black shoes?'

'No, but I've got black boots. And it is nearly the end of November.'

Keiko nodded. Josie scrabbled around in the bottom of the wardrobe and pulled out some boots. They could do with a polish, but she'd got time to do that.

'Maybe I could wear some plain jewellery too?' she said. 'I've got a nice gold chain.'

'No, no jewellery, unless it's pearls.'

'I don't have any pearls.'

'Then no jewellery.'

'Then I think we're done,' said Josie.

'Not quite. Don't forget the envelope for your gift.'

'Gift? I have to give something?'

'Everyone who goes to a funeral gives money. It's to help with the funeral costs. You need to put it in a special envelope – black and white with ribbons. They sell them in Ito-ya. I had some spares so I brought one with me – I knew you wouldn't have any.'

'Thanks, you're a star. How much should I give?'

'You're not very closely connected with the family so I think 5,000 yen should do it. Make sure you get a brand-new 5,000 yen note, not creased or anything like that.'

'Right,' said Josie, scribbling furiously on her memo pad.

'Have you heard anything more about the accident?' said Keiko, getting up and dusting off the boots with a paper handkerchief.

'They still don't know how it happened, The postmortem didn't show up anything unusual. They think it was just a terrible fluke, though the authorities in Matsuyama are talking about putting a higher barrier round the veranda.'

'A bit late now.'

'Yes, locking the stable door after the horse has bolted,' said Josie to herself in English, but when Keiko said 'What?' she just replied, 'Nothing.' Some sayings were untranslatable.

'It's funny, you being there when it happened,' said Keiko.

'Why is it funny?'

'Well, you know, after Mai-chan and everything. It's like it's all happening again.'

Josie knew what she meant. The two girls had stumbled on Mai-chan's body after a party back in the spring, and Josie had tracked down the murderer.

'But this time it's an accident,' said Josie. 'Or at least, that's what they say.'

'Well then, you should leave it at that. You don't want to get involved.'

'No, I'm not going to get involved. I'm just going to the funeral, that's all. I'm not going to have anything to do with it after that.'

'Good,' said Keiko.

*

The day of the funeral dawned damp and chilly. Josie was glad of her navy coat, to which she added a thick navy scarf, which she wrapped several times round her neck before shivering her way to the station.

Ken was waiting for her when she got to Setagaya. He was dressed in a navy blue suit and overcoat and looked like he went to funerals all the time, making Josie uncomfortably aware that she looked like she had thrown her outfit together at the last minute from whatever she could find. Which she had, of course, but all the same she would have preferred not to look like that.

Ken looked at her appraisingly and retied the scarf in a more elegant shape.

'There, you'll do,' he said, as Josie wondered why Dave never did that kind of thing for her. It was a red letter day if he even noticed what she was wearing, let alone worried about whether she looked her best. But then, Dave had other advantages. She suddenly felt a wave of excitement at the thought of seeing him again. He'd be arriving in a couple of weeks.

She followed Ken as he set off down the street.

'I've got an envelope like I'm supposed to,' she said. 'Do I give it to Mrs Ando?'

'Certainly not. There'll be someone to take it when we get there. You'll see.'

The funeral parlour wasn't far away. It was a large

anonymous concrete building with net-curtained windows. The sign over the entrance said *Setagaya Institute* with no mention of its function. Josie was glad she'd arranged to meet Ken at the station; by herself she'd just have walked past this place, mistaking it for an office block.

They found Mr Kimura waiting for them in a little anteroom panelled in pale polished wood with an arrangement of chrysanthemums on a coffee table in the centre. He wore a black suit and his long face looked suitably mournful.

'I can't get over the fact that this terrible thing happened on a company-sponsored tour,' he said. 'It reflects on AZT, of course it does. I feel responsible. I'm sure the Director of Corporate Support holds me responsible too. What a thing to happen.'

'I'm sure the director realises there was nothing you could have done,' said Ken. 'Client Services put in a full report on the tour and the accident, and our director said he was quite satisfied that we were not to blame.'

'Blame?' said Mr Kimura. 'It's not a question of blame. It's a question of responsibility. I will always feel that I did not carry out my responsibilities properly, and I'm sure AZT will feel like that too.'

Josie wished there was something she could say to cheer him up, but she knew how seriously he took anything to do with his work. It was a Japanese trait, and she had long since resigned herself to his worship of the company and all it stood for.

They went back out into the entrance hall, where a

solemn-faced man in a black suit stood behind a cloth-covered table piled with envelopes like the one Keiko had given Josie. They handed him their envelopes and he solemnly recorded their names and the amounts of their gifts in a big ledger that lay open in front of him.

Ahead of them was a long room filled with lines of the kind of upright upholstered chairs they had in hotel conference rooms, all with their backs to the door and all occupied by a mass of black and navy. There must have been a couple of hundred people there, with more women than Josie had expected, some of whom wore black kimonos. Just like my mum, thought Josie – I bet they've always got a black kimono to hand in case of funerals.

The kimono-clad women reminded her of her mum in other ways. They were generally comfortably built with broad, kind faces. Not at all the kind of people Josie had expected to see at the funeral of a financier like Mr Ando. Surely the room should have been full of businessmen in sharp suits, surreptitiously checking their Rolexes to see how long before they could decently return to their offices? But there didn't seem to be anyone like that in the room. Just ordinary people, who seemed genuinely upset at the loss of a friend. Josie felt a new respect for Mr Ando. He had been a man of the people, and the people had come to mourn him.

Down at the front Josie could just make out Mrs Ando and Yuko sitting together, both wearing kimonos. In front of them were long tables covered with incense and candles, and beyond that a huge bank of white chrysanthemums in long rows. Each pot was placed a precise distance from its neighbour and the rows were graded in height so the effect was of white-haired soldiers standing guard. At the precise centre of the rows was the coffin, with the lid mercifully shut, covered with an embroidered cloth and with a picture of Mr Ando looking stern and businesslike on top.

'Normally the coffin would be open,' whispered Ken. 'But in the circumstances… '

Mr Kimura led the way to a row not far from the back, where there were three empty seats at the far end. They squeezed their way past the other occupants of the row and sat down, Josie feeling grateful that her view of the coffin was obscured by the head of the man in front of her. She didn't want to spend the whole service staring at it.

As they waited for the service to begin, Josie looked around at the display of memorial wreaths that lined the walls, so many of them that they jostled for space. They were enormous and a surprising number were decorated with bunches of fruit, sometimes arranged in elaborate flower patterns. Each wreath bore a white paper with the name of the donor's company on it. Josie spotted AZT's wreath – it was hard to miss it as it was one of the biggest, with a good position close to the front of the room. The director will be pleased, she thought. Maybe he won't be so down on poor Mr Kimura once the funeral's out of the way.

They had been sitting there for around ten minutes when the solemn music coming from speakers set round the walls stopped and a chiming sound began at the back of the room. Three priests in glittering kimonos processed down the aisle and sat in elaborate gilded chairs at the front. They began a mellifluous chanting, helpfully relayed by the hidden PA system. Josie couldn't understand what they were chanting but the sound of it was soothing. She sat back and let it wash over her.

It was all very different from the only other funeral she had been to, her grandfather's, back in Catford. There the family had met up in the sunshine under the trees at Lewisham crematorium. Very few of them had worn black, apart from Josie's mum, of course. Josie had a feeling that might have been the first appearance of the funeral suit. Inside, the crematorium was like a church, and the coffin was piled high with great bunches of flowers so you could hardly see it. Their local vicar had conducted the service and talked about her grandfather's life, how he had been loved and valued and died with his family around him. They'd sung his favourite hymns, though the organist had pitched *Rock of Ages* too high so nobody could reach the top notes. (Auntie Marge had tried valiantly, much to the suppressed amusement of Josie and her sister.) Afterwards they'd gone back to her mum's flat and had tea and cake and a bit of whisky, and her mum and Auntie Marge had put their arms around each other and had a little weep, while her Gran had kept a ramrod-straight back and a resolutely dry eye.

That was what a funeral should be like, thought Josie, missing the warmth of the family singing half-remembered hymns together. It didn't look like the congregation here would be doing any singing. The priests' monotonous chanting was still going on. Josie sneaked a surreptitious look at her watch and discovered they'd been singing for over half an hour. Everyone else was sitting still and rapt, but Josie found herself wriggling in her too-low seat, unable to find a comfortable position for her long legs that didn't risk inadvertently rubbing knees with Ken. She glanced at him out of the corner of her eye. He gave her a serious look and she tried to concentrate on the priests' singing again.

Finally the singing stopped and the priests left the room. The man who had collected their envelopes came to a rostrum in front of the coffin. Josie perked up, thinking that at last they would hear something about Mr Ando and his life, but instead the man began reading from a pile of telegrams, each of which seemed to be trying to outdo the last in the number of platitudes it could include in its formal condolences. Josie's stomach gave an embarrassing rumble and she thought longingly of the steaming bowl of ramen she hoped to have when all this was over.

At last the final telegram was read, the man who read them bowed and returned to his place and Mrs Ando and Yuko got up to pay their respects at the coffin, followed in a slow procession by everyone else. Josie looked over the heads of the line of people in front (easy to do given she was several inches taller than anyone else there) and spotted Eriko, also dressed in a black kimono, her face set in firm lines, as though she was taking part in an assault course rather than filing past a coffin. Mr Mori was just ahead of her, his eyes darting around the room as usual. He spotted Josie and gave her the vestige of a bow. Josie nodded back, feeling grateful that on a day like this even Mr Mori's talent for questions would have to be suppressed.

Yuko looked far more mature than she had down in Matsuyama. Her hair had been twisted into an elegant chignon and for a moment Josie caught a resemblance to her mother in her grave expression. Mrs Ando looked more than grave; she looked like she was fighting back the tears and it was only the formality of the occasion that kept her from shedding them. Josie wondered what she would do now. What would happen to Ando Investments now that Mr Ando wasn't there to run it? Could Mrs Ando or Yuko carry it on themselves? I wouldn't put it past them, Josie thought, or not Yuko at least. Never underestimate Japanese women, even if they act like spoilt teenagers. Inside they're steel and rock.

When everyone had filed past the coffin the funeral parlour staff placed long nails in the top of it and gave Yuko and her mother a square grey rock each, which they used to hit the coffin nails. Everyone else took it in turns to do the same and then the staff finished the nailing down.

'What happens now?' Josie whispered to Ken.

'Now we go to the crematorium,' he whispered back. 'There'll be cars to take us there.'

They filed outside where everyone milled around a little uncertainly. The coffin was loaded onto a spectacularly decorated hearse, covered in gold and decorated with painted dragons, like something out of a kabuki show.

Josie, Mr Kimura and Ken ended up sharing a car with Eriko and a man Josie hadn't met before, though she felt an odd sense of déja vu when she looked at him, as though she'd seen him somewhere before but couldn't remember where. He had a very round face and flat cheeks, and his eyes seemed to pop out of his head like a pug dog. Maybe that was what was familiar about him – he looked so like a pug that Josie was confusing him with her neighbour's pet. She wondered if he had an annoying bark too.

Nobody said very much on the journey. Mr Kimura and Eriko exchanged a few platitudes about the weather and the funeral wreaths; Mr Kimura seemed pleased when Eriko praised the AZT wreath, which he had been responsible for choosing.

Josie wondered how Eriko was taking Mr Ando's death. They must have been quite close, as Eriko had been his assistant, but Josie had never got the impression in the short time she'd seen them together that they were friends. They didn't laugh and joke together, though Mr Ando was normally such a lively conversationalist. But when he talked to Eriko it was all strictly business. Now Eriko's face was a mask. Was she holding in her emotions or did she actually not care very much?

At the crematorium there was a long line of ovens, all roaring away trying to keep up with the number of deaths a city the size of Tokyo produced every day. Josie counted twenty of them, though she suspected there were more that she couldn't see. Each had a number above it. Mr Ando's coffin was slid into machine number eleven and the doors closed behind it.

That must be it, thought Josie. Funeral over. I wonder how fast we can get out of here and into that ramen bar by the station. She tried to find Ken but they'd got separated in the crowd behind the coffin. It didn't matter; Josie found she had no choice as to where she went next. The whole party was ushered down the street to a large hotel and through a pair of double doors into a big sunny room where long tables were set out with square lacquer boxes and chopsticks at each place. Lunch, thought Josie. We get lunch. Thank goodness.

She looked around for Ken and saw him waving to her from the other end of the room. She hurried to join him and Mr Kimura, who was waiting patiently to open his bento box.

Josie took the lid off her bento box and laid it to one side. The top layer was prettily laid out with glistening raw fish, vegetables and cold egg roll; on the lower layer was cold beef, sushi, and pink and white sweet *mochi*. Waiters brought round trays of beer and soft drinks.

It wasn't the ramen Josie had hoped for, but it was

a perfectly adequate substitute. She tucked in and for a while the room was quiet as everybody else did the same. Once hunger was satisfied Josie paused and looked around.

'You see that man down at the end of the next table,' she said to Ken. 'The one who came in the car with us. Do you know who he is?'

'Yes,' said Ken. 'That's Mr Wada. Haven't you seen him before? He's visited AZT a couple of times.'

'No,' said Josie, 'I've never seen him at AZT. But I'm pretty sure I've seen him before. I just can't remember when.'

'He isn't the most memorable person,' said Ken. 'He's quite bland. I don't think I've ever heard him say anything interesting. In fact, he hardly says anything at all. But they say he's the one who's made Ando Investments a success.'

'Why's it called Ando Investments then?' said Josie. 'Why not Wada Investments?'

'It was Mr Ando's money that financed the company to start with. As it's a private company Mr Ando held all the shares; Mr Wada doesn't have any. He's just an employee like everybody else.'

'Who inherits Mr Ando's shares?'

'That I don't know,' said Ken. 'It could be Mrs Ando or Yuko, or even someone we don't know about. It could be Mr Wada, though I think that's unlikely.'

Josie looked across at Mr Wada again. Black hair cut short, round face, pop eyes. Where had she seen him before? She just couldn't think.

She noticed that everyone around her had finished their bento and put the lacquer lid tidily back on their boxes, so she did the same. She wondered how much longer the funeral was going to go on. For all she knew they'd be expected to stay all evening and into the night.

There was a flurry of activity at the far end of the room near the door. Ken pushed back his chair and stood up.

'Come on,' he said. 'It's time to go back.'

Josie didn't have time to ask him what he meant as everyone started moving towards the doors again. She followed and found herself in a room that had a hushed and reverential air. At one end was a white table like an altar, covered with a random-looking collection of bones, bits of wood and charcoal, coins and even a melted pair of glasses. The funeral parlour staff picked over the pile, separating out the bones which one of them arranged into sets – bits of head in one place, ribs in another and legs in another. With horror Josie realised that this was what was left of Mr Ando after the furnace had done its work.

Yuko and Mrs Ando stepped forward, holding long chopsticks, and Mrs Ando began to pick out the larger bones and pass them across to Yuko, who put them into an ornately decorated urn. The rest of the people, who had been enjoying their bento just a few minutes before, formed an orderly queue and took their turn to pick up pieces of bone and put them in the urn.

'Upper body first, lower body next,' whispered Ken as the unwinding of the queue led them inexorably to the urn and the pile of bones. Josie gulped and nodded, and when her turn came managed to put her piece of bone in the urn without dropping it or committing any other sort of faux pas.

I wish Ken had warned me this was going to happen, Josie thought. But then, if it's what always happens at funerals I suppose he didn't see any need to mention it. He expected me to just know, like everyone else.

When everyone had had their turn the funeral parlour staff got out a big pestle and ground the contents of the urn to dust, making a horrible cracking, grating noise that Josie knew she would remember for a long time to come. Then they wrapped the urn in velvet and presented it to Mrs Ando.

Josie had a sudden, unwelcome vision of herself, her mum and her sister picking up granddad's bones with a pair of chopsticks. She shuddered, feeling grateful to be English and not Japanese.

'Is there any more?' she said to Ken.

'Well, the family and friends will go back to the funeral parlour now with the urn and there'll be more ceremonies, but not everybody stays for that.'

'I shall stay, of course,' said Mr Kimura. 'To represent the company. But you two can go back to work if you like.'

'Thank you,' said Ken. 'I do have rather a lot on my desk at the moment.'

'I just want to say something to Mrs Ando or Yuko before we go,' said Josie. She spotted Yuko nearby and hurried across to her.

'I'm sorry about your father,' she said. 'I pray for his soul in the next life.'

She knew that was the right thing to say – she'd looked it up in her online dictionary on the train.

'Thank you,' said Yuko.

'It's awful to lose someone in an accident like that. I can imagine how you must be feeling,' said Josie.

'Can you?' said Yuko. 'I don't think you can. You see, my father didn't die in an accident. He was murdered.'

FIVE

Josie fought her way out through the crowds at Shibuya station, turned left under the railway bridge and headed up the hill towards Aoyama, not without a regretful backward look at the fashion and technology maelstrom that was Shibuya on a Saturday afternoon. She'd spent many a happy hour shopping for quirky clothes there and then stopping for a cappuccino at the big Starbucks that overlooked the Scramble Crossing, the beating heart of Japanese street style.

But today she turned her back on its temptations and walked steadily upwards until the bustle faded behind her, to be replaced by wide pavements lined with architect-designed buildings of shining glass or polished brick. The cheap and cheerful fashion shops gave way to designer boutiques and lifestyle shops full of pale wood furniture and expensive glass vases. Even the passers-by were different, with the smooth appearance that comes from designer clothes and expensive makeup.

The closer she got to Omotesando the more

exclusive the shops became; Max Mara on one corner, Japanese handbag designer Samantha Thavassa on the next, and a shiny new Daylesford Organic cafe across the road. Beyond the big stone lanterns that marked the entrance to Omotesando, the old pilgrim's way to the Meiji Shrine, came the full force of designer luxury; Chanel, Gucci, Vuitton. Tokyo's equivalent of Knightsbridge, with only Harrods missing.

I wonder what it's like living in Aoyama, Josie thought. Especially when you're only young like Yuko. I'd find this air of wealth quite intimidating, but I suppose she's used to it. When you're privileged you don't know how strange your life is – it just seems normal.

Yuko's invitation had taken Josie by surprise. It turned up in her work inbox the day after the funeral – Yuko must have got her email address from the list Hina handed out on the tour. It was short and left Josie baffled as to why Yuko had contacted her, but curious to find out. *I'd like to talk to you about what happened to my father. I don't want to meet up anywhere – I want to talk in private. Can you come to our house on Saturday at 3 o'clock?* It gave an address in Aoyama and directions how to get there – turn right at the second street after Omotesando station and look for a house with an art deco ironwork balcony.

Josie was never one to resist a mystery, and besides, she was curious to see where the Andos lived. She dressed carefully, not in her usual weekend uniform of jeans and sweatshirt but in a skirt and jumper that she hoped made her look mature and a bit stylish.

She reached Omotesando station and turned down the second turning as instructed, into a narrow road hardly wide enough for a car; she had to press herself against the wall to let one of the ubiquitous little box-shaped vans, that had looked incongruously dinky on the broad street she had just left but fitted this narrow road to perfection, pass by. Before she'd walked more than fifty yards the roar of the traffic on the Aoyama Dori had faded behind her and the tall glass buildings had been replaced by narrow two- and three-storey houses which snuggled close together, though each one was individually constructed in its own unique style. She passed one that had a frontage of Grecian columns topped with gold leaf and another that had a tiny waterfall incorporated into its smooth wall. Then came a tiny wooden wayside temple, overhung with evergreen branches and alive with chattering sparrows.

Beyond that was the house she was looking for. It wasn't large – there was no such thing as a large house in Tokyo, space was too scarce for that – and its frontage was about as wide as a cheap terrace house back in Catford, but that was where the resemblance ended. It was built of cream brick that looked clean and cool, and the elaborate ironwork balcony had a curved front, giving the building a wavy frontage like a billowing curtain. There was a garage on the ground floor; the door had been left up to expose a parking mechanism that enabled two cars to be parked, one above the other. It was very new and very expensive.

Josie rang the bell and gave her name. Immediately the door buzzer sounded and the latch clicked open.

Yuko was waiting for her at the top of a narrow flight of stairs leading to the first floor. She stood back as Josie reached the top and waved her into a long sunny living area with a pair of french windows at the end that led onto the balcony Josie had seen from the street below. It was furnished in exquisite but impersonal taste – pale sofas flanked a fireplace that held an engraved glass panel behind which realistically lifelike flames flickered; along one wall shiny black lacquer shelving displayed a collection of little ivory netsuke, while on the other side a glass and chrome console table bore a collection of single-malt whisky bottles. The floor was polished wood scattered with thick cream rugs that looked to Josie like a trap for unwary feet. It wasn't a room for cuddling up in front of the television – in fact, there wasn't a television at all, which struck Josie as odd until she realised that if you were this rich you probably had a separate room to put the television in.

It was not what she had expected. Neither of the Andos had struck her as the kind of people who would live in this impersonal opulence. It must be like living inside one of the lifestyle shops she had passed on her way up the hill from Shibuya. But then, maybe her impression of them had been all wrong. She'd only seen them for a brief time, out of their usual habitat. Or maybe, if she'd seen Mr Ando in this sterile room he would have brought it to life with his energy and enthusiasm. She wished she'd had the chance to find out.

She turned to Yuko.

'I've brought you this,' she said, handing over a box of carefully wrapped Harrods biscuits she'd bought specially that morning in a Ginza department store. 'It's just a trifle but I hope you will accept it.'

'How kind,' said Yuko. 'I'm sorry to put you to so much trouble.'

The exchange of formalities seemed to relax them both.

'Sit down,' said Yuko. 'I'll get a plate for these.'

She vanished through a swing door into a kitchen which, from the glimpse Josie got of it, seemed to have every kind of cooking device imaginable, all polished to a dazzling shine. Josie sat rather gingerly on one of the pale sofas. It was hard and unyielding.

Yuko came back carrying a tray with the biscuits on a Wedgwood china plate, a little glass teapot and two china teacups.

She sat on the sofa opposite Josie and poured them both some green tea and offered Josie the plate of biscuits. Josie took one; they'd been ridiculously expensive and she hoped to eat several while she was there.

'Thanks for inviting me over,' said Josie. 'What a lovely house. Is it new?'

'It was built a couple of years ago,' said Yuko. 'Before that we had a very old-fashioned place. It really had to go. A friend of mine found the architect who designed it. If it had been left to my mother we'd still be living in the old place.'

That makes sense, thought Josie. This place has Yuko's fingerprints all over it.

'Have you always lived in Aoyama?' she said.

'No, we used to live out in the sticks – Saitama City, and not even in the middle of town. It was such a pain travelling into Tokyo from there. Aoyama is much more convenient.'

'It must be wonderful to live in Aoyama,' said Josie. 'You're right in the middle of everything. I'd love that. I live in a company flat in the suburbs and it takes me ages to get into work in the morning, on a crowded train where I never manage to get a seat. And then I have to trail back out again at the end of the day.'

'At least you've got your own place,' said Yuko. 'I don't want to go on living with my mother, but I don't have any choice at the moment. Especially not after what happened to my father.'

'I'm really sorry about the accident,' said Josie.

'Thanks,' said Yuko. 'It doesn't seem real somehow. I keep expecting him to walk back through the door.'

'You said in your email that you wanted to talk to me about what happened to him,' said Josie.

Yuko hesitated, sweeping the biscuit crumbs that had fallen on the table into a little pile as if to buy herself time before replying.

'Yes,' she said slowly. 'But I wonder if I can trust you?'

'Trust me with what?' said Josie briskly. She had no patience with self-dramatising. Yuko seemed slightly taken aback at her tone, but went on, 'You remember what I said to you at the funeral – that my father was murdered?'

Josie nodded.

'Nobody believes me when I say that, but I'm sure of it.'

'If you think there's anything wrong about your father's death you should talk to the police. Or your mother.'

'I can't talk to her about anything. And the police have already decided it was an accident. But I know it wasn't. And now I'm frightened.'

'Frightened? Why?'

Yuko stood up and walked over to the window where she stared out at the quiet street.

Josie waited.

'What did you think about that haiku trip?' Yuko said, turning away from the window and coming to sit down opposite Josie again. 'I mean, didn't you think it was a bit strange?'

'I'm not sure. It seemed like an odd collection of people. What made you decide to come along?'

'It was a last minute thing,' said Yuko. 'I would never normally do anything like that. But I had a sort of… premonition, yes, that's it, a premonition, that something awful was going to happen.'

'And you felt you could do something about it if you were there?'

'Maybe. I don't know. I just felt I had to follow my

instincts.'

Hm, thought Josie. This all sounds highly unlikely. But let's see what else she has to say about it.

'And then, when my father died,' Yuko went on, more confidently now. 'I knew I was right. It couldn't have just been an accident. My father would never have done anything so stupid.'

Fair point, thought Josie.

'I think someone was after his money,' said Yuko.

'How does that work? Don't you and your mother inherit?'

'Yes, of course. But I mean... well, I mean, there's the company for instance. There's already a row about who's going to run it now.'

That's not what's really bothering you, thought Josie. But you're not going to tell me what's really on your mind, so let's go with this one.

'I heard your father was a good businessman,' said Josie, 'but someone said that Mr Wada was the real brains behind Ando Investments.'

'Mr Wada!' said Yuko. 'He's not got a business brain. He can do sums, that's what he can do. Algorithms, flow charts, spreadsheets, yes. But business strategy, spotting an opportunity, striking at the right moment – he can't do that. My father was the one who did all that.'

'But you think Mr Wada is trying to get control of Ando Investments?'

'I'm not afraid of Mr Wada,' said Yuko. 'Eriko is the one to watch out for. And Mr Mori too. He knows more than anyone about what goes on at the company.'

Josie was surprised.

'I thought Mr Mori was just someone from the accounts department,' she said.

'He likes people to think that. He likes people to think he's just someone unimportant who doesn't know anything. But all the time he's asking questions, ferreting things out. He had some sort of hold over my father, I'm sure of it. They'd go off somewhere together in the evenings and my father would never talk about it when he got back. But he always looked really worried when he went out and when he came back he was relaxed and smiling.'

'Did they go out drinking?'

'No, I think they had the odd drink but he didn't come back drunk. That's not what it was about. There was something more to it.'

Yuko stopped, as though she felt she'd gone too far.

'So you decided to keep an eye on them all down in Matsuyama,' said Josie. 'What did you find out?'

'Well, there was that business with the haiku for a start,' said Yuko.

'Yes, what did you make of that?'

'She was threatening him. Eriko I mean. And then Mr Mori joined in. The two of them were up to something.'

'What about you, Yuko?' said Josie. 'Are you sure you weren't up to something too?'

'What do you mean?' said Yuko, standing up and walking to the window again. 'How could I be up to anything? I only joined the tour on a whim.'

'Then who was the guy I saw you talking to in the evening after the haiku session? Just a casual acquaintance? Only it didn't look like it.'

'You saw us?' said Yuko. 'You don't miss much.'

'So who was he? Someone you knew in Matsuyama?'

'No, actually, if you must know, it was my boyfriend, Jiro. When I decided to go down to Matsuyama I told him and he said he'd take a couple of days off and join me there. So we could have some time together.'

'But you were on the haiku tour. You didn't exactly have a lot of free time.'

'No, well, he said he didn't mind. I ducked out of the Ishite temple visit to see him. And then I met him again that evening, after the haiku session.'

'And that's all it was?'

'Yes, that's all it was.'

'Yuko,' said Josie. 'Why did you really ask me to come here today?'

'I told you, I'm frightened. I need someone to find out what really happened. I can't do it myself – it wouldn't be appropriate. But you're a foreigner. Everybody knows that foreigners behave differently to us. If you go around asking questions, people will just put it down to your foreign ways.'

Oh, thanks, thought Josie. I get to be the one who puts their foot in it just because I'm a foreigner. All the same, she felt a prickle of interest. It was odd, the way Mr Ando had died. And everyone had behaved strangely down in Matsuyama. And there was clearly a lot more that Yuko knew and wasn't telling.

'Suppose I do help you,' she said. 'What do you expect me to do? I don't really know any of the people involved. I only met your mother and Eriko and Mr Mori in Matsuyama. I don't know Mr Wada at all.'

'I can introduce you to him. We can say we got to know each other on the haiku trip. And as you work at AZT, you can talk to the other people on the trip any time you want and just pretend it's to do with work. That's why you're the perfect person.'

'Well,' said Josie. 'Maybe I could just ask around a bit.'

'Oh, thank you! It's such a relief.'

'I can start with you, then,' said Josie. 'No time like the present.'

Yuko looked startled.

'Me?' she said.

'Yes, you were there when it happened. Tell me everything you remember. Take your time.'

Josie couldn't help feeling a little twinge of satisfaction at Yuko's disconcerted expression. It's all very well her summoning me here and telling me what she wants, Josie thought, but there's consequences to what she wants to do and this is the first of them. It's only a little bit unpleasant, but there'll be worse to come if I really do find out something. I wonder if Yuko will be strong enough to handle it?

'I was in the top room, the keep, when it happened.

I was looking at the information board that told you about the castle. Someone came in from the veranda shouting that a person had fallen over the edge. I didn't realise it was Dad at first. When I did—' Yuko stopped, tears welling up in her eyes. She got up and went into the kitchen and Josie could hear her blowing her nose.

When she came back she looked calm and composed, as though she'd made up her mind to get through it. She sat down again and continued in a sing-song voice, as though she was trying to distance herself from the events she was describing.

'Once I realised who it was that had fallen,' she said. 'I just couldn't think straight. I don't have a very clear memory of what happened next. I just remember getting on the bus and going back to the hotel. Everything else is a blur.'

'Who else was in the keep with you when the accident happened?'

'I'm not sure. Hina was, and your boss, Mr Kimura. And maybe another tour group, though I think they went back downstairs before it happened. That's about it. Sorry I can't remember any more.'

'That's okay,' said Josie. 'It gives me somewhere to start. Now, I need to talk to Jiro. Can you arrange something?'

'Jiro? Why do you need to talk to him? It was nothing to do with him. he wasn't even there.'

'He was in Matsuyama. And he can corroborate what you say about what you were doing the night before.'

Yuko's eyes filled with tears.

'You think I had something to do with it,' she said. 'Why would I get you to come here and ask you to help me if I was up to something?'

'I have no idea,' said Josie. 'But I can't assume anything. So I need to talk to everyone and form my own opinion. And that includes Jiro.'

'Alright, I'll text him and ask him to get in touch. Is it okay to give him your number?'

'Go ahead.'

Yuko picked up their empty cups and took them through to the kitchen, from which Josie inferred that her visit was over. She took a last look round the room. What struck her most about it was how impersonal it was – it had no feeling that family life went on there at all. It was like a stage set. Maybe other rooms in the house were more welcoming. Maybe they were full of things that would give a clue to Mr Ando's personality and help explain why someone would want to push him off a veranda to his death. She wondered if she dared ask Yuko to show her around but decided it would be pushing her luck. Maybe when she'd found out more about Matsuyama and Yuko decided to trust her, then she could come back and take a good look around. Maybe.

Yuko came back from the kitchen and held out her hand to Josie.

'Thank you for coming,' she said.

'I'll be in touch,' said Josie, starting back down the stairs. But then she turned around and said, 'By the way, has Mr Ando's messenger bag been found?'

'His messenger bag?'

'Yes, he had it with him when he fell. It wasn't there when they took him to hospital, so I wondered if it had been found anywhere and returned.'

'No,' said Yuko. 'That is, I don't know. Maybe it will turn up. Yes, I'm sure it will turn up. I don't think you need to worry about it. It's sure to turn up.'

SIX

Josie sat down in front of her computer and angled the screen so the self-facing camera gave a flattering view of her face. She'd learned her lesson the first time she'd skyped Dave, sitting on her low sofa peering down into the camera lens, so all you could see was her neck and chin, which looked grotesquely large, as though she'd been bingeing on doughnuts for a week. Dave hadn't said anything, but when she caught sight of herself in the little thumbnail screen she vowed never to skype on the sofa again. Now she sat on a proper chair with her laptop balanced on a couple of books on the table in front of her so it was exactly at eye level. Satisfied, she clicked the connection.

Dave's flat in Sydney sprang into view. He was sitting directly facing his laptop too, but that was because he had a huge apartment with room for a proper desk and table while Josie just had a six tatami sized room which had to serve her for eating, sleeping, TV-watching and everything else. A tatami mat was the size of a single bed, making her room about nine metres square. It didn't actually have any tatami mats, but that was how you measured rooms in Japan.

Dave's bulky shoulders filled most of the screen and Josie knew that his long legs would be stretched out under the desk and that, just out of sight of the camera, there'd be a giant mug of coffee and an untidy pile of computer magazines. She was surprised at the feeling of warmth that filled her at the sight of his familiar face and tousled brown hair, so different from the smooth black hair of Japanese men, and somehow comforting in its English ordinariness. When Dave smiled at her from the screen with his usual easy familiarity she felt her heart lift.

'Hi there,' he said. 'I've missed you. How was Matsuyama?'

'I've missed you too,' said Josie. 'Matsuyama was, well, good and bad, I suppose. On the up side, the weather was glorious, warm and sunny and we saw lots of autumn leaves and visited all the sights. On the down side... one of the people in our party had an accident so we had to cut the whole trip short and come home.'

'That's terrible. I hope they're alright,' said Dave.

'Well no, actually, he isn't. He fell off the top of the castle and— ' she stopped, overcome by the memory.

'I'm sorry. That must have been awful for you.'

'Yes, it was. His wife and daughter were there at the time so you can imagine...'

'Yes, not good at all.'

They were both silent for a moment and Josie found herself wishing that Dave was in the room with her and could put his arms around her and hold her tight to make the memory of Mr Ando's body lying at the foot of the castle wall go away. But then she pushed the thought away. She was strong enough to stand on her own two feet, not dependent on Dave for emotional support. She'd been living on her own in Japan for three years now – she wasn't a novice any longer.

'I went to the funeral this week,' she said. 'It was a strange experience. Nothing like a funeral at home.'

She described the funeral, making it into an interesting story so as to distract them both from the fact of Mr Ando's death. She shied away from telling him about that. It was partly that she didn't want to have to remember it, but also because she didn't want to tell him she thought it was murder. She didn't want him worrying about what she might be getting herself into.

So, when she'd finished telling him about the funeral and its oddities, she moved straight on to talking about his visit to Tokyo, which was only a couple of weeks away.

'It'll be so good to see you,' she said. 'And to spend Christmas together. We haven't done that since we were at university.'

'It's not just Christmas,' said Dave. 'I expect you to show me all the sights of Tokyo. You know, all the ones you've seen a million times before and are sick of the sight of. I'm going to be a proper tourist and I expect you to take care of me.'

'I'll do my best,' said Josie. 'But you know I'll have to work a lot of the time. I used up all my leave visiting you in Australia in September.'

'Then you'll have to give me detailed instructions every morning.'

'That I can do. Oh, don't forget to bring some warm clothes. It may be spring where you are but it's autumn turning to winter over here and the nights are getting chilly. It could be snowy in December. We might even get a white Christmas.'

'Well, if we get snowed in we'll just have to huddle under the duvet in your little flat and find something to do to entertain ourselves,' said Dave. 'I expect we'll manage.'

'Yes, I expect we will,' said Josie with a smile that answered his. 'Though I hope you won't be disappointed when you see my flat. It really is terribly small. It's quite a tight fit even for one person. It's meant for small, deft Japanese people not two lanky foreigners like us.'

'It'll be fine,' said Dave. 'We'll be out most of the time. And when we're not out we'll be in bed. I'm looking forward to long lazy nights in bed with you.'

'Me too,' Josie said. 'It's a shame we can't see each other more often.'

'Whose fault is that?' said Dave. 'It wasn't me that went off to live in Japan.'

'No, I know. It's just, it would be good if we could work something out.'

'We will,' said Dave. 'I've got some ideas – I'll tell

you when I see you. I've got to go, I've got a rugby match this afternoon. Love you.'

'Love you,' echoed Josie, feeling lonely as Dave's picture disappeared from her screen. To distract herself she dropped her phone into the speaker dock, but then on an impulse searched through the song list for an old mix tape Dave had made for her just before she left for Japan. It was a mad collection of old standards, punk rock and disco divas, a far cry from the J-pops that were her usual listening nowadays, but it reminded her of Sunday nights in her and Dave's old flat in Camberwell, when they'd get in an Indian takeaway, open a bottle of cheap wine and curl up on the sofa together and just talk. Why was the lure of Japan strong enough to make her leave all that behind? She'd almost lost Dave because of it, and even now their relationship balanced on a knife edge, threatening to break apart under the strain of being so far apart. It worked when they were together, but Josie wondered if they'd ever be together longterm again. And what would happen to them if they weren't.

*

Josie hadn't been to the Marunouchi Orbis in months. The last time had been her date with Ken, when they'd had dinner in a ramen restaurant in the basement. It was a bit embarrassing to think about it now she was back with Dave again, but at the time it had seemed really promising, like a new start and a commitment to her new Japanese life. After all, what could be more Japanese than a Japanese boyfriend? But it hadn't worked out; Ken had hooked up with Noriko just as Dave came back into Josie's life and they'd terminated the relationship amicably. Which was just as well, given they both worked for the same company.

She looked around as she entered the foyer of the building, expecting it to be filled with pots of orchids as it had been before, but it was bare and a bit forlorn. Not surprising really; the last time she'd been there it had only just opened and all of Tokyo was beating a path to its door. But since then newer buildings had opened and the fashion lemmings had moved on, fighting to get tables at newly opened restaurants whose one attraction was their novelty. Josie ruefully recalled having to eat spaghetti and meatballs at eleven in the morning in one new Italian restaurant because Keiko wanted to try it and that was the only time it was possible to get in without standing in a queue for two hours.

She wondered briefly how she would recognise Jiro, and then laughed at herself. There was no need. All he had to do was look out for the only tall foreign girl in the place and it would be her.

Sure enough, as soon as she walked into the foyer a young man came hurrying up to her. He was dressed in the unvarying uniform of the *salaryman*; worn black suit, white shirt a little too loose around the neck, conservative tie and shiny black shoes. He was quite short, so Josie had to look down at him, but she was used to that – most of the men she met in Japan were shorter than her. Jiro had carefully combed black hair and a shiny black briefcase. He moved awkwardly and his clothes looked cheap. Not at all the sort of boyfriend Josie would have expected Yuko to choose. Surely she was more into the Shibuya fashion plate kind of guy? Or, at the very least, someone rich who could take her to the sort of posh places she was used to. A struggling bank clerk didn't seem like her kind of thing at all.

'Er… Ms Clark?' said the young man hesitantly, and when she nodded, bowed low and said in English 'I am Jiro Kazama. Pleased to meet you. I am sorry my English is not good.'

'That's okay,' said Josie, in Japanese. 'My Japanese is fine.'

Jiro fumbled in his pocket and took out a business card which he presented to her formally, using both hands. Josie took it and studied it seriously for a moment to be polite, then put it carefully in her bag and gave him her AZT card, which he received with reverence.

They hesitated for a moment and then Josie said, 'Shall we go down to the basement and find somewhere to have a cup of tea or something? Then we can talk.'

Jiro bowed again and hesitated, so Josie led the way to the escalator. From her previous visit she remembered the underground street of restaurants as humming with people. Not this time. There were a few groups of workers heading to what had clearly become their favourite haunts, but even though it was a little after five, when the great city of skyscrapers that was Otemachi began to spew forth its populace, there was nothing resembling a crowd. But then, thought Josie, since the Fukushima disaster hit the economy so hard, everyone works late, intent on putting things to rights by hard work and long hours.

They found a branch of Veloce, which had become Josie's favourite coffee chain because of the cheapness of its coffee and the addictive quality of its coffee jelly with a blob of artificial cream on top. Jiro ordered an egg mayonnaise sandwich, the runny egg oozing out from between two thick slices of white bread. Josie had a cappuccino with her coffee jelly.

They sat down at one of the tables that lined the back wall, on hard wooden chairs that were a Veloce speciality. In the middle of the room lone diners sat at intervals around a big wooden table, their phones in their hands and an expression of intense concentration on their faces as they texted or watched videos or the news on live streaming.

'So, Jiro,' said Josie. 'Tell me a bit about yourself.'

Jiro, who had been picking ineffectually at the thick cellophane wrapping on his sandwich, jumped to attention.

'Don't be nervous,' said Josie. She felt like saying *this isn't the Spanish Inquisition*, but there was no chance that Jiro would get the joke. And anyway, she didn't know the Japanese for Spanish Inquisition.

'It's just... I haven't met many foreigners before. This is the first time I've had an actual conversation with one.'

'I'm not really any different to you. I work in a big company in Otemachi doing boring admin stuff, like thousands of other people.'

'I'm training as a bank teller. I've not being doing it long. You spend the first year watching what the trained tellers do and helping out with the routine stuff. That suits me. I like to be sure I understand what I'm doing. I joined the bank because their training programme is so thorough.'

'I'm trained in IT – that's what I really want to do. I've been trying to get into the IT department ever since I started at AZT, but no luck so far.'

'I don't know a lot about IT but I like playing computer games. Do you ever play?'

'I've tried a few, but they took up too much of my time so I've given it up.'

'I know what you mean. I spend a lot of time playing. It's what I mainly do when I'm not with Yuko.'

'How long have you two been going out?'

'Not very long. A couple of months.'

'Do you live in Aoyama too?'

Jiro laughed.

'Me? No chance. I live in a one-room flat in a company block in Meguro.'

'So how did you and Yuko meet?'

'At a party. It wasn't the sort of party I usually go to, but one of the guys from work took me. I was amazed Yuko was interested in me. She's so pretty and well dressed. I don't understand what she sees in me.'

Josie could see what he meant. She couldn't see what Yuko saw in him either. His name, Jiro, meant 'second son' and that fitted him perfectly. The boy who always came second; second to a pampered, successful older brother and no doubt to a petted younger brother too. The one in the middle that no one gave much thought to, that was Jiro. An ordinary young man like thousands of others walking the Tokyo streets and sitting in cafes drinking coffee and staring at their mobile phones. Josie was pretty sure that if you asked the occupants of the tables either side of her and Jiro's – a couple of girls whose mobile phones were weighed down with glittering phone charms on one side and a big group of women who'd pushed two tables together on the other – to describe him afterwards, they wouldn't be able to do it. The lanky foreign girl yes, but her companion? No idea.

'So tell me about Matsuyama,' Josie said. 'What made you go down there?'

'It was Yuko's idea. She texted me the night before to tell me she was going and asked me to go too. I called in sick at work and got the plane after hers with a return the next evening. The ticket was quite expensive, but I thought we'd have some time together. I thought it would be fun. I didn't think it would turn out the way it did.'

'Where did you stay?'

'I've got an aunt in Matsuyama. She put me up for the night.'

'And you met up with Yuko on Monday evening?'

'Yes, we went round town a bit together. Then she went back to her hotel and I got the bus to my aunt's place.'

'I saw you together, you know. You looked like you were deep in conversation. Were you making plans for the next day?'

Jiro shifted uneasily in his seat.

'No, well, not anything special. Yuko was on the tour so we couldn't get much time together. It was a bit of a waste of time my going, to be honest.'

'Why do you think she asked you then?'

'She wanted me to help her out with something, I think. I don't know what it was. Anyway, it didn't come to anything because of what happened to her father.'

Jiro finished his sandwich and put the cellophane wrapper neatly back on the tray, folded into precise quarters. Josie added her empty glass dish and cup, ready to be returned to the crockery collection point when they left.

'Did you go to Matsuyama castle?' she said.

Jiro looked embarrassed.

'Well, yes, I did, as a matter of fact. Yuko said she might have some free time to have a coffee or something.'

'So you were going meet her there?'

'Yes, no, well, maybe. It wasn't like we'd fixed anything up. She said she'd let me know.'

'So what happened?'

'I saw you all going up on the chairlift so I thought I'd wait until you came back down again.'

'Did anyone see you?'

Jiro glanced around and licked his lips.

'That sneaky little bloke. Yuko doesn't like him. He spotted me hanging around. I could tell because he gave me this funny look and then he looked at Yuko like he was putting two and two together.'

'You mean Mr Mori?'

'Yes, him.'

'So what did you do after that?'

'Nothing much. When the accident happened, I didn't know what to do. I hung around a bit and then went off and got some lunch in cafe. I texted Yuko and she...' he paused and reached out to refold the cellophane wrapper of his sandwiches. 'She just said to go back to Tokyo. So that's what I did.'

'On the evening flight.'

'Yes, the six thirty.'

'What did you do between lunchtime and getting your flight?'

'Nothing. I just... I just hung around.'

'Did you meet Yuko?'

'No, of course not. I mean... She was busy.'

'She had some free time in the afternoon. Her flight wasn't until seven-thirty.'

'Yes, well, er, maybe she did. I don't know. I don't know anything. I just came back on my own, that's all.'

He shuffled his feet and looked at his watch.

'Did you want to know anything else?' he said. 'Only I need to get to Yokohama. I forgot, I'm supposed to meet somebody there. I don't want to be late.'

He half stood and picked up the tray.

'Well, just a couple of things. I won't keep you long, I promise.'

Jiro looked as though he'd rather be anywhere but there, but he sat down again and put the tray back on the table.

'So you're saying you didn't meet up with Yuko that day. Not even when you got back to Tokyo?'

Jiro looked startled.

'Why do you ask?'

'Well, her flight got in not long after yours. I just thought you might have waited to see her.'

Jiro stood up again.

'I have to go now,' he said. 'I'm really sorry, it's this… appointment that I forgot about. I'm really in a rush.'

He stumbled away, leaving the tray on the table behind him.

Josie waited until he was out of sight and then took the tray to the pick-up point and got herself another cappuccino. She understood now what Yuko saw in Jiro. He might think he was Yuko's boyfriend, but from Yuko's point of view he was a convenient acolyte, someone who would do her fetching and carrying and come at her bidding, even if it meant spending his hard-earned salary on a plane ticket to Matsuyama. And if Yuko had any secrets she wanted keeping, Jiro would keep them. Or at least he would to the best of his ability, which wasn't saying much.

Josie drank her second cappuccino quickly,

listening idly to the group of women at the next table discussing their husbands and how lucky they were that their husbands worked such long hours, giving their wives time to go out with their women friends and enjoy themselves. None of the women had jobs – their generation was one that stayed at home and brought up the children. Josie wondered when things would change so that Japanese women could have careers like women in the west. Maybe they never would.

The thought depressed her. She left Veloce, hearing the laughing voices of the women fade behind her, and walked along the rows of restaurants, passing the ramen house where she and Ken had eaten dinner. She was pleased to see it was still popular, with a queue of five people sitting on seats outside waiting for table. Not as many as the night she and Ken had gone there, but still a good total.

She wondered if Jiro had gone off to phone Yuko and tell her how things had gone. She was pretty sure he had. What would Yuko say when she heard? She wouldn't be very pleased. Josie had never met such an unconvincing liar as Jiro. Yuko had clearly told him what he should and shouldn't say and he'd done his best, but every time he opened his mouth the look of panic on his face gave him away. There was more to Jiro's trip to Matsuyama than he'd been prepared to admit. And Yuko was at the bottom of it. The question was, what was she up to and why had she asked Josie to find out about her father's death when she was hiding secrets of her own?

SEVEN

Josie looked up from the presentation she was working on and checked the clock, hoping it would say it was twelve o'clock and time to go for lunch. It didn't. It said eleven twenty-three, which meant she had to go on writing long convoluted sentences about how the changing structure of AZT was making it a truly global twenty-first century company, for another thirty seven minutes. Then she would be released to join the race to the canteen for a plate of *ten-don,* which she knew from experience would not be the light-as-air creation of her favourite tempura restaurant but a couple of slightly soggy prawns in sad batter.

She looked around the big room where she and the other clerks in the Corporate Support section at AZT worked. Every head was bent over a laptop, every brow furrowed in earnest concentration. Except for one of the office ladies, whose computer was being worked on by a techie from IT. Josie eyed him enviously. I could do that, she thought. I bet I know way more about how to fix a software glitch than he does. Maybe next time one of our laptops packs up I should just fix it myself, then they'd know how good I was. But she knew there was no chance of that. Mr Kimura played everything strictly by the rules and wouldn't let her near any machine but her own.

She glanced down the long room to where Mr Kimura sat, at a desk that was slightly larger than the others and strategically placed by the window – one of the very few perks of office. He had his head bent too, but he was staring blankly at his screen, with a glum expression on his long face. He was clearly miles away, and Josie didn't need any clues to help her guess what was on his mind; the haiku tour and its disastrous ending.

Mr Kimura clearly felt a personal sense of responsibility for what had happened, but the trouble was, everyone else in the section seemed to hold him responsible too. No one openly criticised him, they just avoided talking to him. It was as though he had become a bad luck symbol; no one wanted to be seen with him. Josie thought back to the spring and the office cherry blossom viewing party in Ueno Park. Then Mr Kimura had accepted a glass or two of sake and been encouraged by his colleagues to sing melancholy songs of love and loss with that curious ululating sound that traditional Japanese songs demanded. Everyone had clapped and congratulated him on his skill, and he had beamed, modestly denying any vestige of talent. Now he looked as though he'd never sing again.

Josie felt sorry for him. What had happened wasn't his fault, but somehow he had ended up with the blame as far as Corporate Support was concerned.

She buried herself in her presentation again and even managed to make some progress without checking the clock every five minutes. So it took her by surprise when everyone suddenly shut their computers and headed for the door. She looked at the clock, which said twelve o'clock precisely, and cursed inwardly. Now she'd missed her chance to be at the head of the queue and would have to gobble down her lunch in order to be back at her desk by one o'clock.

The only other person left was Mr Kimura, who looked as though the thought of mixing with the crowds in the canteen was too much for him. Josie stood up, planning to leave by the door at the end of the room away from his desk so as not to embarrass him by walking past him on her way out, but then she heard a familiar voice call her name. It was Mr Tanaka. He'd been her mentor ever since she'd got involved in investigating Mai-chan's murder and her regular visits to his little house in East Azabu, where his wife made lunch and their little dog Toto leaped around her feet barking enthusiastically, had become a regular highlight of her weekends.

'Mr Tanaka,' she said, smiling as she looked at his thin frame and his threadbare suit, which he had worn as long as she could remember. 'This is good timing. I was just going to go down to lunch.'

'I thought you might be. I came to see if you wanted to have lunch together.'

'Absolutely,' said Josie. 'It feels like ages since I've seen you, and I've got something I want to ask your advice about.'

At the other end of the room Mr Kimura, who had looked up a the sound of Mr Tanaka's voice, hurriedly buried his head in his papers again. Mr Tanaka walked over to his desk.

'Mr Kimura,' he said. 'I know how busy you are, but I wonder if you can make the time to join us for lunch. We'd really value your company, wouldn't we, Miss Clark?'

Josie nodded vigorously.

Mr Kimura seemed half inclined to refuse. But Josie smiled her best smile and Mr Tanaka put his hand on Mr Kimura's shoulder encouragingly. After a moment's hesitation he stood up.

'Thank you,' he said. 'If you're sure it's alright...'

'Of course,' said Mr Tanaka.

'Then I think I will.'

They took the lift down to the first floor in nervous silence but Mr Kimura visibly relaxed as they stood in the canteen queue and it became clear that no one was taking any notice of him. They found some seats together on a wooden bench at a trestle table in the corner of the huge room.

'I was sorry to hear about what happened to Mr Ando,' said Mr Tanaka. 'But I heard the funeral went well and his company appreciated the AZT presence.'

'Yes, the funeral was very well done,' said Mr Kimura. 'I'm glad we were able to attend. He was a remarkable man, you know. I wish I'd had the chance to get to know him better.'

'Me too,' said Josie. 'Did you know him, Mr Tanaka?'

'Yes, I did. He was an interesting man, with a vast range of knowledge, but he could never stick to one subject long enough to become really expert in it.'

'I know what you mean,' said Josie. 'He had a bit of a grasshopper mind.'

'I find it hard to see how he could have fallen as he apparently did,' said Mr Tanaka. 'One can't help wondering... but I'm sure the police explored every possibility.'

'I'm sure they did,' said Mr Kimura. 'But all the same, I wonder how Mr Ando could have been so foolish. He wasn't a foolish man.'

'Actually,' said Josie. 'That's what I wanted to talk to Mr Tanaka about.'

Mr Tanaka nodded and put down his chopsticks to give her his full attention.

'I was talking to Yuko the other day,' Josie said, putting her chopsticks neatly across the top of her rice bowl too. 'She seemed to think that it maybe wasn't an accident.'

'Not an accident?' said Mr Kimura. 'What do you mean?'

'Well, maybe, I don't know, he didn't just fall by himself.'

'You mean someone might have pushed him? I can't believe it. Please don't let anyone at AZT hear you say that.' Mr Kimura looked around the room, as though afraid it was full of eavesdroppers ready to report them for heresy.

'Did Yuko say why she thought that?' said Mr Tanaka.

'Not really. I got the impression there was more behind it than she was telling me though.'

'And what do you think?' said Mr Tanaka.

'I think she might be right. There was something very odd about what happened.'

'Tell me about the tour,' said Mr Tanaka. 'Who was on it?'

Josie thought back to the morning at Haneda airport when she'd met everyone and did her best to describe them to Mr Tanaka. When she finished, he looked thoughtful for a moment and then said, 'Where was everyone when the accident happened?'

'Well,' said Josie. 'Ken and I had gone back down to the next level. But Mr Kimura was still in the keep.'

They both turned to Mr Kimura, who looked startled.

'Oh, ah, well, I'm not sure I can remember exactly who else was there,' he said. 'I was in the keep, I remember that, and so was Hina. Mr Mori was out on one of the verandas. I saw the Andos go out onto the north veranda together a bit before. I don't remember seeing Yuko.'

'She said she was in the keep too.'

'Well, she could have been. It was quite large and not very well lit.'

'What about Eriko?'

'Eriko? I don't remember seeing her either. But I'm

fairly sure she went out onto one of the verandas earlier.'

'And when it happened?'

'Everyone rushed out onto the north veranda after the alarm was given. Mrs Ando was distraught, poor woman.'

'I was a bit surprised that Mrs Ando came on the tour,' Josie said. 'You know, because it was a work tour really and I didn't think people were bringing their partners along.'

'That's right,' said Mr Kimura. 'But Mr Ando told me it was their wedding anniversary on the Wednesday, and it seemed like a nice way to celebrate it. He had a special dinner planned for us all in Kochi that night.'

'But we never got there,' said Josie.

'No, we never got there.'

'Do you know why Mr Ando wanted to go on a haiku tour?' said Mr Tanaka.

'He said it was because of Matsuyama. He was very fond of it, apparently. And of course it's the home of haiku.' Mr Kimura sighed heavily. 'So many great poets; Shiki, Chodo, Santoka. And such inspirational countryside. I was looking forward to visiting the Shiki Memorial Museum. What a poet! *A willow, And two or three cows, Waiting for the boat.* Beautiful. Ah well.'

'Matsuyama,' said Mr Tanaka thoughtfully. 'Did Mr Ando have business connections there?'

'No, I don't believe so. Though I think his family did originally come from there.'

'Did you notice Mr Ando's messenger bag anywhere after the accident happened?' said Josie.

'Not after the accident, no. But I did see it before that – he'd left on that bench in the corner of the keep. He must have sat down there and forgotten it. I meant to remind him when he came back in.'

'Why do you ask about the messenger bag?' said Mr Tanaka.

'It went missing the day he died. They can't seem to find it.'

'I expect someone picked it up,' said Mr Kimura. 'Probably they'll send it on to Mrs Ando before too long.'

'I expect so,' said Josie, though she didn't think so and she could see that Mr Tanaka didn't either.

Mr Kimura stood up and picked up his tray. Mr Tanaka and Josie followed, dropping their disposable wooden chopsticks into an overflowing tub and stacking their empty trays as they left the canteen.

As they waited for the lift Mr Tanaka turned to Josie.

'I came by Mr Ueda's office on my way down to see you,' he said. 'He told me he was going to visit Haiku Country Tours this afternoon to close up the account on your Matsuyama tour. I believe he's meeting Hina there.'

'Oh, really?' said Josie, thinking furiously. 'Actually, I've got some expense details to sort out with him. I'd better get it done before he goes, hadn't I?'

'You certainly should,' said Mr Tanaka.

'Mr Kimura, is it okay if I go up and see Client Services this afternoon?' said Josie.

'If you've still got outstanding expenses, you'd better sort it out right away,' said Mr Kimura. 'Off you go.'

Josie hurried off before he changed his mind. She found Ken just closing down his laptop.

'I'm glad I caught you,' she said. 'Mr Tanaka said you were going over to Haiku Country Tours this afternoon to settle up about the Matsuyama trip. Well, can I come too?'

'I don't suppose anyone will mind. It means a trip out to Shinjuku, though.'

'No problem,' said Josie. 'Will anyone from Ando Investments be there?'

'Yes, Eriko's coming.'

'Good, I'd like to see her again. And Hina too.'

*

They walked together to the entrance to the Marunouchi line just outside Tokyo station. Ken walked with long easy paces. Josie found it relaxing, for once to walk with someone whose stride matched hers.

'Did you tell Noriko about what happened to Mr Ando?' she said.

'Sort of,' said Ken. 'I played it down a bit. What did you say to Dave?'

'I played it down a bit too. It's hard to talk about it properly with him being so far away.'

'But he's coming over soon.'

'Yes, he'll be here next week. I'm really looking forward to seeing him.'

'I bet you two are great together. Do you think you'll get married?'

Josie was so shocked she stopped in her tracks.

'Married? No, I don't think so.'

'Why not? You love each other, don't you?'

'Well yes, but marriage... that's a big step.'

'Not really. It's what Noriko and I are doing and we haven't known each other nearly as long as you and Dave. It's the natural thing to do if you want to be with someone, isn't it?'

'I don't know. I mean, it hasn't come up. I mean, I don't know if he even wants to... Anyway, he's in Australia and I'm in Japan.'

'I know it's none of my business, but I think you should make up your mind what you want. If you want to be with Dave, maybe you should find a way to make it work. Even if it means leaving Japan.'

Josie couldn't think how to reply. She didn't want to give up Japan. But then, she didn't want to give up Dave either. It was unkind of Ken to try and force her to choose between them.

Ken saw her reaction.

'I'm just trying to help, Josie,' he said. 'I want to see you happy and I get the impression that being apart from Dave so much is making you unhappy, that's all.'

Josie forced a smile.

'Thanks, Ken,' she said. 'You're a good friend and

I appreciate what you're trying to do. But it's not that easy.'

Ken didn't pursue it; on the train to Shinjuku they chatted amicably of other things. But Josie couldn't help remembering how sad she'd felt when she'd had to leave Sydney and leave Dave behind. Maybe Ken was right – maybe Dave was more important to her than Japan. But what could she do about it?

The offices of Haiku Country Tours were down a scruffy back street. Josie nearly walked straight past the battered sign over the door, but Ken led the way up a narrow flight of stairs to a big room crowded with old wooden desks covered in piles of papers. Clearly the computer age had not yet arrived as far as Haiku Country Tours was concerned.

An office lady led them into a small meeting room and provided them with cups of green tea. Eriko was already there, her green tea already drunk and a laptop on the table in front of her. She looked up when they came in but didn't smile. She looked bitter and angry, not at all like the friendly woman Josie remembered from the tour. Eriko tapped nervously at her keyboard as though she needed to keep herself occupied. Shutting out unwelcome memories? Josie wondered. I didn't think she and Mr Ando were that close.

'Josie offered to give me a hand with the spreadsheets,' said Ken. 'She's good at that sort of thing.'

Eriko nodded and turned back to her screen.

Hina came hurrying in, a folder full of papers in her hands.

'I'm so sorry, my boss has been called away. He sends his apologies. Is it alright to go ahead without him?' she said, sitting down across the table from Eriko.

'Of course,' said Ken, taking his laptop out of his bag and switching it on. 'I've got all the expense records here. We just need go through and agree them.'

The process turned out to be longer and more tedious than Josie had bargained for. About as much fun as writing presentations back at the office.

'So that's it, then,' said Ken at last. 'We'll get the final payment made on Monday and it's all settled.'

'I hope what happened to Mr Ando hasn't affected your business,' said Josie to Hina, spotting her opportunity.

'It is a bit worrying,' said Hina. 'But hopefully people will understand that it wasn't our fault.'

'It must have been a terrible shock. You were in the keep when it happened, weren't you?'

'Yes, but I didn't see anything. You can't see much of the verandas from inside the keep and he must have fallen from the corner, away from the door.'

'I feel sorry for the young couple who found him,' said Josie.

'Yes, what a thing to happen on your holiday,' said Hina. 'I talked to them afterwards and they were so upset.'

'Do you know how to get in touch with them?' said Josie.

'Why would you want to do that?' said Eriko. 'They were nothing to do with us. They didn't see anything.'

'No, I know,' said Josie. 'I was just curious that's all. I'm interested in anyone who was around that day. I suppose I feel they might be able to help us understand how an accident like that could happen.'

'I don't know how to contact them,' said Hina. 'But the police did talk to them at length so I'm sure if there were lessons to be learned they will have passed the information on.'

'What do you think, Eriko?' said Josie. 'Do you have any theories about how it could have happened?'

Eriko licked her lips.

'It's dangerous, that veranda,' she said. 'I thought so as soon as I saw it. Much too low. And you know how Mr Ando was, always leaping about. He could be a bit... uncontrolled.'

'Where were you when it happened?' said Josie.

'I was on another veranda,' said Eriko.

'It must be hard for you, losing Mr Ando like that,' said Hina.

'Yes,' said Eriko. 'It's probably harder for me than for his wife. We were very close, you know, Mr Ando and me. Closer than anyone knew.'

Josie wondered what that meant. She hadn't seen any sign of them being close on the tour. If anything, Mr Ando had tried to stay away from Eriko. But maybe that was a pretence. Maybe they were closer than they should have been and trying to cover it up. The thought opened up all sorts of interesting possibilities, and it also might explain why Eriko and Yuko so obviously hated each other. Josie resolved to do some asking around about Eriko and Mr Ando.

Eriko was shutting down her computer and getting ready to leave. As she stood up, Josie asked casually, 'By the way, did you see what happened to Mr Ando's messenger bag?'

'Why are you asking about that?' said Eriko. 'The bag wasn't important. Nobody cares what happened to it.'

'Well, it's just that it seems to have gone missing so I wondered if you'd seen it.'

'It's nothing to do with me,' said Eriko.

'Josie didn't mean anything,' said Ken. 'She's always asking questions. It's because she's a foreigner. Please forgive her.'

'Yes,' said Josie, grateful that Ken had rescued her from an awkward situation but vowing to give him piece of her mind afterwards for making her sound like an ignorant foreigner. 'That's right. Sorry if I've given the wrong impression.'

Eriko relaxed slightly, but Josie could see that she was still annoyed.

'Have you spoken to Mrs Ando since it happened?' Josie said to Hina.

'No. I thought I'd leave her alone for a bit. She was so upset down in Matsuyama. They were a lovely couple, and it was their wedding anniversary too. I do need to get in touch with her about something but it's not urgent. I'll leave it a week or two.'

Eriko put her laptop in her bag and stood up.

'Thank you so much for your help,' said Ken hastily. 'I'm sorry we took up so much of your time.'

'Not at all,' said Eriko. 'I expect we'll see each other again. Mr Ando may not be with us any longer but the company goes on.'

'Yes indeed, a valued client,' said Ken. He and Hina both bowed formally.

When Eriko had gone the atmosphere lightened considerably.

'I'm sorry the tour turned out so badly,' said Hina.

'It's a pity,' said Ken. 'The whole idea was for us to get to know some of the people from Ando Investments and for them to get to know us. It makes it much easier to do business when you've broken the ice with each other. Now we'll have to start again, and it will be doubly difficult because of what happened to Mr Ando. And it's not clear who will be taking over.'

'Mr Mori seems to think there'll be a battle over it,' said Hina. 'Apparently Mr Wada will make a bid for control.'

'Have you spoken to Mr Mori recently then?' said Josie.

'Yes, he dropped in to the office a few days ago. Funny, he mentioned Mr Ando's messenger bag too. If I'd know it was important I'd have tried harder to find it at the time. But everything was so chaotic... '

'You did everything you could,' said Ken. 'I'm surprised Mr Mori has been to see you, though. I thought he was just someone from the finance side.'

'There's more to Mr Mori than you think,' said

Hina. 'He and Mr Ando were very close, you know. They planned the tour together.'

'Really?' said Josie. 'He told us he only joined the tour at the last minute.'

'No, that's not right. I wonder why he said that.'

'I must have misunderstood,' said Josie. 'I'm sorry.'

'Well, you'll get a chance to ask him why yourself,' said Hina. When Josie looked blank she went on, 'At the unveiling of the plaque to Mr Ando at Ando Investments. I thought we'd all been invited.'

Ken looked sheepish.

'The AZT invitation arrived a few days ago. But it's for me and Mr Kimura. it doesn't mention you.'

'I'm sure they wouldn't mind if you came along,' said Hina. 'You were on the tour as well, so I think it would be only polite if you were to attend.'

'We'll sort it out,' said Ken. 'I'm sure there won't be a problem if you really want to come.'

'Yes, I do,' said Josie. 'Apart from wanting to pay my respects, I'd like the chance to talk to Mr Wada. There's something about him that's familiar but I can't put my finger on it. Maybe it will come back to me if I see him again.'

'Fine,' said Ken. 'I'll get you an invitation.'

EIGHT

Josie looked at her watch. Ken was late, but there was no way she was going to venture into Ando Investments without him so she dawdled around in front of the Aoyama Theatre some more, squinting up at the modern sculpture in the forecourt, a metal tree with coloured faces at the ends of the branches. She wondered whether to text him again or just hang on. Just as she walked round to look at the back of the sculpture for the third time, she heard running feet behind her.

'I'm really sorry,' said Ken. 'My meeting overran and I couldn't get away. I tried to text you but my battery was flat. I've pretty much run all the way from Shibuya and I'm knackered. Give me a minute to get my breath back before we go in.'

'I'm just glad you got here,' said Josie. 'I'm already nervous about this dedication; there was no way I was going to go in there on my own.'

She waited as Ken leaned against the low wall outside the theatre, panting. Gradually his breathing returned to normal.

'Maybe you need to shape up a bit,' she said.

'Hey, I go to the gym regularly and I swim every Saturday. You try running up that hill and see what it does to you.'

'Fair enough. You don't look out of condition, I must say.' Josie eyed his muscles and then realised what she was doing and stopped.

'How many people do you think are going to be there?' she said.

'Don't know, but I don't think it will be that many. Around twenty or thirty, maybe. The invitation said it would be a small ceremony to unveil a plaque in Mr Ando's honour.'

'That's not many,' said Josie. 'I thought Ando Investments would have invited lots of people.'

'Well, they didn't. Don't ask me why.'

'Were they okay about it when you said I wanted to come?'

'Fine. It's no problem.'

The Ando Investments offices turned out to be not as big as Josie had imagined. She'd expected it to have a whole skyscraper to itself but the board behind the polished wood reception desk listed a number of companies and they were directed to take the lift to the eleventh floor where Eriko met them.

'Thanks for coming,' she said. 'The unveiling and dedication of the plaque will take place at six o'clock in the boardroom. Before that we're serving refreshments in the main meeting room.'

They followed her down a short corridor lined with

doors to a pair of double doors at the end. As Eriko opened them a low hum of conversation greeted them. Josie's heart sank. The room was filled with businessmen in black suits, standing together in groups, chatting, with serious faces. No wonder they didn't invite me, she thought. I'm going to stick out like a sore thumb in this lot.

The meeting room was larger than the meeting rooms at AZT and was obviously meant to be impressive. It had been panelled in dark wood with a parquet floor. The windows were flanked by thick green velvet curtains held back by twisted gold ropes and there was a bookcase along one wall filled with books in old bindings whose gold-lettered spines glittered dully. But somehow, rather than giving the impression of old-fashioned probity that Josie assumed it was aiming for, it seemed stagey, like a film set. Josie had the odd feeling that, once they had left, it would all be whisked away into a van leaving bare lino and scruffy painted walls behind.

Why did she feel like this? she wondered. Ando Investments was a valued AZT client, or at least that was what everyone kept telling her. And AZT itself was a pillar of respectability. Surely it wouldn't take on a company that was at all dodgy or fly-by-night. And yet, the uneasy feeling persisted. It was like Mr Ando himself; not at all what you expected it to be.

The refreshments were less than impressive too. They amounted to a table by the door with a small selection drinks – red and white wine, orange juice and Oolong tea. Josie took a tea and looked round for

Ken, but he already had a drink and Eriko was introducing him to one of the groups of businessmen. Josie spotted Mr Kimura in a far corner and made her way through the room, pausing from time to time as snatches of conversation reached her: '...went for twice the expected price at the Tokyo Book Fair...', 'share price fell three points...', 'binders made a terrible job of it...'

A tap on the shoulder made her jump.

'Hey,' said a familiar voice. 'I didn't expect to see you here.'

'Oh, Yuko,' said Josie. 'I didn't expect to see you either.'

'I'm here to represent the family,' said Yuko, draining the last of her glass of wine and looking round in vain for somewhere to put it. 'My mother didn't feel up to it.'

She surveyed the room critically.

'It's all people Mr Wada wants to impress,' she said. 'But the clients all loved my father. They didn't want anything to do with Mr Wada. He just did the investing, the nuts and bolts of it. It was my father who made the company work and everyone here knows it.'

'Why does Mr Wada want to impress them?'

'Because he wants to take over the company,' said Yuko with unexpected viciousness. 'And he thinks that if he gets enough people on side they'll let him do it. Look at him now, trying to work the room. Trouble is, he's got no idea how to do it.'

They both looked over to where Mr Wada, his pug-like face sweaty with effort, was trying to insinuate himself into a group of businessmen who looked less than happy to see him. Josie stared, and then caught herself and looked away. She'd definitely seen him before, but where could it have been?

'Do you think you could introduce me to him?'

'If you want me to. But I warn you, you won't find him very interesting.'

Yuko dived across the room to where Mr Wada had given up on the businessmen and was looking around with an expression close to panic in his eyes. Josie followed her at a more sedate pace.

'Mr Wada,' Yuko said. 'I want to introduce Josie Clark from AZT. She does a lot of their liaison work and I hear she's rather influential at board level.'

Mr Wada turned to Josie with an ingratiating smile on his face.

'I'm so glad you were able to come,' he said. 'Are we looking after you all right?'

'I'll just go and get another drink,' said Yuko. 'I'm sure you two will have lots to talk about.'

'So where do you fit in at AZT?' said Mr Wada, his little pop eyes fixing themselves on Josie.

'I work with Mr Kimura in Corporate Support,' said Josie. 'I went on the haiku tour with him. That's where I met Mr Ando.'

'A sad loss.'

'I'm so sorry about the accident. What a shame it had to happen in a lovely place like Matsuyama. Have you ever been there?'

'Why, er, er, yes, I have been there. A very

attractive town with a great deal of history. Not just the home of haiku, but of *Botchan* too. Do you know *Botchan*, Miss Clark?'

'I heard about it in Matsuyama.'

'I think *Botchan* is my favourite book. Soseki is such an elegant writer – there's no one to touch him for the beauty of his prose. And his humour, of course, is unique. I often re-read *Botchan* when I need something to cheer me up. His adventures never fail to lift my spirits.'

Josie found herself thinking better of Mr Wada. Anyone who cared about a book as deeply as he did, especially a book like *Botchan,* which was about a young man who defied convention and did what he wanted, must have some good in him.

'I plan to read it soon if I can get a good translation.'

'Yes, the right translation is very important, but I'm afraid even the best translator won't be able to convey Soseki's remarkable facility with words.'

'Are the books in the bookcase yours?' Josie indicated the bookcase along one wall of the room.

'No. They, ah, they mainly belonged to Mr Ando.'

'Oh. I didn't realise he was a book lover.'

'No, he didn't talk about it much. Did you go on the Botchan railway when you were in Matsuyama?'

'Oh yes, and visited the Dogo hot spring.'

'If you go up to the private rooms on the top floor at the Dogo hot spring they have pictures of the schoolteachers who were the originals of the characters in *Botchan*. And there's a wonderful view of Matsuyama castle from the terrace.'

As he said the words Matsuyama castle the light in Mr Wada's eyes died and the animation left his face. His eyes flickered as he looked around the room, searching for an excuse to talk to someone else, but as Josie was several inches taller than he was, it was difficult for him to see past her and spot an opportunity.

'What will happen to the company now Mr Ando's gone?' Josie said.

'The company will go on, of course,' said Mr Wada. 'That's what he would have wanted.'

'Who will take his place?'

'It's far too early to say.'

'What about you?'

'I will serve the company in whatever capacity is appropriate.' Mr Wada started to edge away, tapping his empty glass as a sign he needed to get a refill.

Eriko's voice behind her came to his rescue.

'I'm sorry to interrupt, but we need Mr Wada in the boardroom now to prepare for the ceremony.'

'Of course,' said Mr Wada, extricating himself with an obvious sense of relief. 'I've enjoyed our little chat. Good luck with your search for a translation of *Botchan*.'

Eriko didn't go off with Mr Wada as Josie had expected. Instead she lingered, as though she had something she wanted to say to Josie but didn't know how to start.

'I hadn't met Mr Wada before,' said Josie, to fill the awkward silence. 'Have you know him long?'

'Yes, quite a long time. From before he started working for Ando Investments.'

'Do you think he'll take over now Mr Ando's gone?'

'It's up to Mr Ando's heirs to decide that.'

'You mean Mrs Ando and Yuko?'

'Yes, I suppose so. It's not been determined yet who the heirs will be.'

'You mean there's some doubt about it?'

Eriko hesitated and Josie got the feeling that she had something she wanted to say.

'Yes,' she said. 'There could be a doubt about who inherits. I can tell you more about it, but not here. It's all a bit sensitive. Maybe, if you've got the time, we could meet up somewhere outside of work and have a chat about… some things.'

'Absolutely,' said Josie. 'You know my email address and phone number. Get in touch any time. I'll be happy to meet up.'

'Thanks,' said Eriko, looking across the room at Yuko who was chatting to Mr Kimura. 'Please don't mention this to anyone.'

'No, of course I won't,' said Josie.

Ken came up to join Josie and Eriko hurried off after Mr Wada.

'Been having a good time?' said Ken.

'You could say that,' said Josie.

'I've just been talking to someone really boring and not at all useful from an obscure securities management company. But I saw you talking to Mr Wada. Did you put in a good word for AZT?'

'Oh no, I forgot.'

'I don't know why I bothered bringing you,' said Ken, with a twinkle in his eye.

'Ken, what does Ando Investments actually do? I mean, I know they invest, but where does the money come from?'

'Well, they've been very successful on the investment market, so some it comes from their investment profits. But the rest comes from their investors. They've got a very select list of people they're prepared to take on. I know some quite substantial investors who've been turned down.'

Josie looked around the room with new eyes.

'So that's who these people are? Investors?'

'A lot of them, yes.'

Josie stared at the people around her, as though she could determine what qualified them to be Ando Investments clients just by looking at them.

'But where did the money to set up the company in the first place come from?' she said.

'The original stake came from Mr Ando.'

'Where did he get it from?'

'I don't know. I just assumed he was rich. He probably comes from a rich family, something like that.'

'So he wasn't in business before he started Ando Investments?'

'I don't think so, but I don't honestly know. Does it matter?'

'I'm not sure. But I'd like to find out a bit more about Ando Investments.'

Eriko had reached the door. She turned to face into the room and clapped her hands for silence. When it was quiet she said, 'Would you all be so kind as to move into the boardroom for the dedication ceremony?' and stood to one side as people began filing obediently out of the door. Josie and Ken hung back and waited while those in front made their way out.

'What iss it you'd like to know about Ando Invesstments?' said a familiar voice at her elbow.

She looked round to see Mr Mori, who had quietly appeared in that disconcerting way he had.

'I couldn't help overhearing your converssation with Mr Wada,' he said. I bet you couldn't, Josie thought. I expect there are a lot of conversations you can't help overhearing.

'Nothing in particular,' said Josie. 'I'm just naturally curious, that's all.'

'But you were asking some interessting questions. Like, who will take over the company now. That must have embarrasssed Mr Wada considerably.'

'Why should he be embarrassed?'

'Because everybody at Ando Investments knows that he has been trying to oust Mr Ando and get the company for himself. There have been terrible rows between them. Nobody listens on purpose, of course, but ssometimes one cannot help overhearing. I must say, when Mr Ando had his unfortunate accident, I did at first wonder whether Mr Wada might not have had a hand in it. But of course, that can't be the case. It was just an accident.'

Josie felt distinctly uncomfortable. It was an effect Mr Mori always had on her, but it seemed particularly pronounced today. What exactly was he insinuating? That Mr Wada had had Mr Ando bumped off so he could get his hands on the company? Josie felt quite indignant until she remembered that she had been thinking the same thing. And she was the one who was convinced that Mr Ando had been murdered. So she was no better than Mr Mori and his insinuations.

She suddenly felt quite grimy, as though she had been doing something grubby, like when she was a little girl and had brought home a dead rat she had found in the street, thinking it was sweet and furry until her mother took it from her and threw it in the bin with an expression of disgust on her face.

But then she pulled herself together. It was not Mr Ando's death that was the dead rat; it was Mr Mori and his ability to make everything he touched seem slimy and morally dubious.

'Mr Mori,' she said. 'Why did you tell us you'd only joined the tour at the last minute when actually you'd been booked on it all along?'

Mr Mori laughed.

'Oh, so now it's me you ssuspect,' he said. 'But I'm afraid the ansswer won't help you very much. Mr Ando liked to pretend that he didn't need me as much as he actually did. He liked to suggest when I turned up with him that it was just accidental, just last minute, just anything except a deliberate plan.'

'Oh,' said Josie. The explanation sounded plausible but odd. Like most things to do with Ando

Investments.

'And why were you on the tour, if you don't mind me asssking?'

'I was there because my boss asked me to come,' said Josie.

'And so was I,' said Mr Mori. 'So shall we stop ssuspecting each other of things? Come, let's make up and be friendss.'

'Alright. But tell me something. Was there anything going on between Mr Ando and Eriko?'

'Who has been saying that?' said Mr Mori sharply. 'Did she tell you that?'

'No, nobody told me. I just wondered, that's all.'

'You should be very careful of Eriko,' said Mr Mori. 'She is not what she sseems.'

'I get the impression that nobody at Ando Investments is what they seem,' said Josie.

Mr Mori laughed.

'Is anybody ever what they sseem?' he said. 'Are you what you sseem, Miss Clark? Am I?'

Josie didn't reply. That was the trouble with Mr Mori; he always made you feel that the world was full of sinister possibilities, when, in fact, everyone was just going about their normal business and not plotting anything.

They had reached the door and Josie followed the line of people down the corridor to the boardroom while Mr Mori melted back into the crowd. The boardroom was panelled like the meeting room, but it was smaller and a large mahogany table filled the centre so that everyone had to squeeze themselves in round the edges. It was uncomfortably hot.

Mr Wada was standing next to a pair of red velvet curtains mounted on the wall, with a gold rope attached to them. He took a folded sheet of paper out of his pocket and started making a speech about Mr Ando but his voice was so quiet that Josie, who was at the back, could hardly hear a word. Then he pulled the gold rope to open the curtains and reveal a modest plaque. Everyone clapped and began moving towards the exit.

Josie struggled through them towards the plaque to read what was written on it. *In Memory of our Beloved Founder, Hiroshi Ando*, it said. Then there was a relief carving of an open book with a haiku written on it: *On a journey, ill, My dream goes wandering round, Over withered fields.*'

'Basho's last haiku,' said Ken, appearing beside her. 'Appropriate, don't you think?'

Mr Wada stood at the door, formally bowing to the guests as they left. Josie stared at him and suddenly it came back to her where she'd seen him before. At Matsuyama castle the day Mr Ando died. The businessman with the over-large briefcase who had seemed so out of place. She kicked herself for not recognising him before – that pug-like face was unmistakeable – but somehow seeing him in such a different context had thrown her off the scent. He had been in Matsuyama the day Mr Ando died. He'd even been at the castle when it happened. So why had he sneaked away like he had something to hide?

NINE

Josie cut and pasted the final piece of text into the presentation she'd been working on all morning and hit the save button. She attached the presentation to an email, sent it through to Mr Kimura and relaxed. Time for a bit of light relief and a chance to find out a bit more about the set up at Ando Investments.

She googled the company name and got a hit on the company website. She'd been prepared for it to be in Japanese, which would present a challenge as her ability to read financial terminology in Japanese was limited; what she hadn't expected was for it to be quite so uninformative. She was used to company websites that had been given serious attention by professional web designers, with branding and colour coding and mood pictures. Ando Investments didn't have any of that. What they had barely qualified as a website at all in Josie's view.

It was all text, in a very small font and gave the impression that it had been put together by the office junior working with a *how to build your first website* manual in one hand. At the top was a statement from the company chairman – Josie recognised Mr Ando's name at the end of it – which consisted entirely of bland platitudes and was totally lacking in any informative content. And also meant that they updated their website so rarely that the fact that their company chairman had died still hadn't registered.

There was a link marked *financial highlights*. Josie clicked on it and was rewarded with a page of bar charts in fetching shades of grey. The figures meant nothing to her. How well should a company like Ando Investments be doing? And anyway, what exactly did it do?

She clicked back to the home page where there was a list of the annual reports for the last three years, each one attached in PDF format. Josie clicked on the most recent one. This was all in grey as well, but scrolling down at least took her to the consolidated balance sheet and statement of income. They showed that over the previous six years Ando Investments' income and assets had both shown an upward trend. It was doing well, and the fiscal projections for the coming year suggested they expected to do even better in the future.

So far so good, thought Josie, going back to Google. But I wonder what the real story behind the figures is?

She tried googling Ando Investments in English but all she found were listings for defunct companies of that name that had once been registered in New Zealand or South Africa or Hong Kong, or for companies called D and O Investments or variations of the 'and O' theme. There was nothing about an Ando Investments in Japan.

She clicked through to the second and third pages of results without finding anything meaningful. On the fourth page a snippet from the *Japan Times* caught her eye. It was from a couple of years before and was a footnote to an article about new financial regulations in Japan. Companies which had commented on the proposals included Ando Investments.

She closed down her browser. It was no good doing research on the internet if you didn't know what you were looking for, or what the information meant when you found it. She'd have to try another route.

She picked up her phone and called Mr Tanaka. When he answered she said, 'Have you got any spare time to talk to me about Ando Investments?'

There was a pause at the other end. Then Mr Tanaka said, 'I'm pretty tied up on a big case right now and I'll be working late all week. But if you don't mind the lateness of the hour, I'd be happy to talk to you at home this evening – shall we say ten o'clock?'

*

That evening Josie stayed in town after work and had dinner in a tonkatsu restaurant in the basement of Hibiya Chanter. She and Keiko had eaten there a lot in the days when they were fans of the Takarazuka Revue and belonged to Tammy Izumo's fan club. It was just across the road from the Tokyo Takarazuka Theatre and a good place for a quick meal before the show. But Tammy had left Takarazuka now. She was married, and Josie had heard there was a baby on the way. That part of Josie's life was over.

At nine thirty she got the Hibiya line to Hiro and walked down the quiet back street to Mr Tanaka's house. The trees that overhung the road had lost most of their leaves and the stone figure in the wayside shrine looked chilly, as though it would be as glad as anyone when spring came again. Only the crows seemed unaffected by the changing season, cawing overheard with their usual persistence.

At Mr Tanaka's house Josie rang the bell and was rewarded with enthusiastic yapping from Toto. Mrs Tanaka opened the door and smiled as she offered a pair of heelless slippers for Josie to step into.

'He's in the tatami room,' said Mrs Tanaka. 'Go in – I'll bring you some tea.'

Josie did as she was told. Mr Tanaka was standing at the window looking out at the little garden, where the leaves of a maple tree that overhung the tiny pond shone crimson in the reflected light.

'Autumn is turning to winter,' said Mr Tanaka, turning away from the window to greet Josie with a smile. 'Perhaps we'll have snow this year. I love the quiet that snow brings.'

Mrs Tanaka slid open the door and put two rough pottery cups of steaming brown *hoji* tea on the low table. They sat down on the tatami-mat floor either side of it, Josie, as always, failing to match the grace with which Mr Tanaka moved.

'So, what do you want to know about Ando Investments?' said Mr Tanaka, sipping his tea.

'Anything really. Starting with, what do they actually do?'

'They're an investment company. They invest in stocks and shares and make their profit that way.'

'And they're good at it?'

'So it would seem from their results. They've grown fast since they were set up.'

'People say that's because of Mr Wada.'

'I've heard that too. But I'm surprised. I knew him before he joined Ando Investments and he didn't seem like a star then. Quite the contrary – rather plodding, I'd say.'

'Did Mr Ando know a lot about stock and shares?'

'No, and he'd have been the first to admit it. He had a wide range of interests, but I never heard that investment strategy was one of them.'

'But he started the company, didn't he? That's why it's called after him. So where did the money come from in the first place?'

'The initial capital all came from Mr Ando. It was never very clear where he got it from. It's possible there were other investors in the background.'

'How do they attract investors? I looked at their website and it didn't seem very accessible.'

'They're a bit old-fashioned. It's all done by Mr Ando through his contacts. But that's not unusual;

plenty of Japanese companies still operate in the traditional ways. Older people like me don't use the internet, and as older folk tend to be the ones with money to invest, it's actually more effective to work that way. I get the impression there's a small group of investors who are closely linked to Mr Ando personally so they invest through his company. And it seems to work – they're able to move fast when an opportunity comes up because so few people are involved. They seem to have access to some substantial reserves and they trust Mr Ando implicitly.'

'But that's not going to work now that Mr Ando's gone, surely? The company must have a problem, without him to bring the investors in.'

'We'll see. It's time for Mr Wada to show he really does have the talent people say he has.'

Mr Tanaka glanced at the window and Josie realised he was hoping to be alone to commune with his garden again. She put her teacup down on the table and stood up.

'It's been really good of you to talk to me when you're so busy,' she said. 'There's just one more thing. At the ceremony the other day, Mr Mori said that there might be a problem over the inheritance. That maybe Yuko and her mother wouldn't get it.'

'I hadn't heard that,' said Mr Tanaka. 'That would certainly affect the company's ability to keep going. Did he say who he thought might inherit instead?'

'No, he didn't. Have you any idea who it might be?'

'Ah,' said Mr Tanaka, his forehead creasing into worry lines. 'There have been rumours.'

'What kind of rumours?'

'Of a liaison.'

'With Eriko?'

'Yes, with Eriko. But there are odd stories around about her. She's not a straightforward person.'

'But she might be in line for something now Mr Ando's dead?'

'She might. It depends on what Mr Ando's wishes were.'

'And what about Mrs Ando?'

'There's more to Mrs Ando than you might think. A strong woman. An admirable woman in many ways.'

'But if Mr Ando was having an affair?'

'Then I don't know what she would do.'

Josie nodded.

'That's what I thought too,' she said. 'Thank you so much for helping me. I'll let myself out.

She tiptoed back to the entrance hall so as not to wake Mrs Tanaka and put her outdoor shoes back on. All the way back to the metro station she thought about what Mr Tanaka had said. A liaison; a complication with the inheritance. Was Mr Ando planning to leave his wife? And did Mrs Ando and Yuko know? Josie needed to find out but she couldn't see how to do it. She just knew the best place to start was with Mrs Ando.

*

Josie woke early on Saturday morning, determined to make a start on the end-of-year cleaning marathon. Once December arrived, every woman in Japan began the great cleanup so that their homes would be shiny and pristine for the start of the new year. And, as Josie had learned, cleaning meant proper cleaning. Not a quick whisk round with a duster and the vacuum cleaner, but a systematic turning out of cupboards, washing of little-used crockery, searching out of grime in obscure corners and polishing everything to a shine. The previous year she'd left it all to the last minute and had even skimped on one or two of the finer points, but with Dave due to arrive from Australia the following week, time was getting short. And soon the end-of-year parties would start and she would be out all the time 'forgetting the old year' in sake and whisky with colleagues from AZT.

At least she didn't have to get hundreds of new year cards printed and delivered to the Post Office in time for guaranteed delivery on New Year's Day, or spend hours in a department store ordering *osechi ryori* – complex boxes filled with countless different kinds of New Year's Day food.

She'd sent off her Christmas presents weeks ago; a pashmina for her mum, a football shirt for her dad and a polo-neck cashmere jumper from Uniqlo for her sister. Plus some little trinkets, a few Japanese things that would remind them of her. A brocade purse, a Hello Kitty cushion cover. She'd sent them Japanese Christmas cards with pictures of cherry blossom thickly coated in tinsel, like something from the 1950's.

She emptied the kitchen cabinets and rinsed everything thoroughly before drying it and putting it back tidily on the newly scrubbed shelves. Feeling virtuous, she headed for her wardrobe but the thought of what she might find if she delved around in the back of it made her heart quail. Tomorrow, she thought. Or maybe next week.

She decided instead on a shopping trip to Shibuya to look for a present for Dave, followed by a walk up to Aoyama for tea at the Aoyama Flower Market Tea House. Yuko had said her mother always went there on Saturday afternoons, so it seemed liked the perfect place for a casual encounter. She checked the tea house's website; it was on a street just off the Aoyama Dori, close to Omotesando station. It shouldn't be hard to find.

She got dressed carefully, trying to look like the kind of person who might naturally drop into a fashionable tea house in Aoyama. She was uncomfortably aware that anyone who knew anything about fashion would know that her jumper and jeans came from Uniqlo, but she didn't think Mrs Ando would be likely to spot that.

Shibuya was in its usual Saturday afternoon state of hubbub as the youth of Tokyo peacocked through the streets and packed into the stores and boutiques. Josie dodged her way between them and headed over the Scramble Crossing to Loft.

Loft was a lifestyle shop. It sold all the things you

didn't know you needed until you went to Loft and realised how pale and inadequate your life had been up until then. It ran to seven floors of what Josie's mum would call frippery. Cosmetics, kitchen accessories, bedding, travel essentials (and not so essentials) and, above all, stationery. Japan's obsession with mobile phones had not dented its parallel obsession with pretty stationery.

She headed for the leather accessories counter, where she chose a new wallet for Dave, red with an interesting grain in it, and a matching case for a suica card, the Japanese equivalent of an oyster card in London. She'd already got him a suica card to use while he was in Tokyo. She lingered among the rolls of patterned adhesive tape, rack after rack of them, covered with abstract designs, cute animals, Hello Kitty, flowers, even skeletons, before settling on a roll of cabbage roses and another of hamsters. Then she headed upstairs to the household department where she spent a long time choosing new sheets. She tried to tell herself it was part of the great end of year clean-up to buy new sheets, but really she knew it was because Dave was coming. Hm, what is it about Dave that makes you think of sheets? said a mocking voice in her head.

Shopping for Christmas made her homesick for London and the way the whole city seemed to build up towards Christmas with the lights on Regent St, Christmas decorations in all the offices, jingles and glitter in the shops and tinsel on the computers at work. Japanese shops did jingles and glitter too – in fact did way too much of it in Josie's opinion, going completely over the top so that it seemed more of a parody than a genuine celebration. And then, as she had discovered to her shock on her first Christmas in Japan, on Boxing Day (not that they called it that) it was all gone, vanished overnight to make way for New Year's decorations.

She took her purchases to the payment counter and said no when the assistant asked her if the wallet was a gift. She didn't want it carefully wrapped with the paper folded just so and tied up in ribbon. She wanted to wrap it herself in her own messy style and stick it down with too much Sellotape so it took hours of wrenching to get it undone. That was what a proper Christmas was like. Like a proper Christmas dinner was turkey and roast potatoes cooked in the fat and brussel sprouts. Not Kentucky Fried Chicken and strawberry cream cake which was what people had in Japan. How on earth had Colonel Sanders convinced an entire nation that chicken nuggets were what Christmas was all about? She'd once tried to explain to Keiko about brussel sprouts, but Keiko had never seen such things. Apparently they didn't have them in Japan.

She took her yellow Loft bag and headed back out into the crowded street and up the road towards Omotesando. She wasn't sure what time Mrs Ando would get to the tea shop so she planned to get there early. And anyway, she was hungry. She could get something to eat, and then linger over coffee and surf the net on her phone while she waited.

She made her way back to Hachiko Square, which was now a solid mass of people, and dodged round the edge and under the railway bridge to the other side of the train tracks, where the crowds gradually thinned and the rarefied atmosphere of Aoyama asserted itself. She'd put on a coat as it could be chilly in the shade, but where the sun shone it was still as warm as an English autumn. She undid the buttons of her coat as she walked and loosened the chiffon scarf round her neck, quite looking forward to lunch in a flower shop.

The Aoyama Flower Market Tea Shop didn't disappoint. The entrance was through the flower shop, so the heavy scent of chrysanthemums and peonies hung around you as you slid open the glass door to the tea house, hidden away at the back. Inside it was green with plants, growing in long tubs that ran underneath glass tables, with stalks trained up though little holes in the glass so that the flowers bloomed at the table. A tall curved metal structure provided support for long strands of greenery to grow up and across the ceiling to trail over the diners heads. The room smelt of flowers and wet earth. It was like having lunch in a greenhouse.

One of the servers, a girl in a beige T-shirt and khaki trousers, which seemed to be the uniform of the place, came to greet Josie. There was already a queue of people waiting for tables, sitting on a row of chairs at the side of the room by the door, but when Josie said she was on her own the girl showed her to a seat at the wooden counter that looked out over the tiny garden. It was next to the kitchen where the servers went in and out, but Josie took it gratefully. At least she could get something to eat right away, though she was pretty sure she was soon going to get tired of sitting on a hard wooden bench with no backrest. She looked enviously at people sitting at the glass tables, who had proper chairs with wire backs and cushions on the seats. It was inconvenient, too, when you were looking out for someone, to end up with a seat with its back to the rest of the room. But Mrs Ando wouldn't arrive for an hour at least, so Josie resigned herself to a long wait on her hard bench, ordered a tartine and salad and got out her phone.

There was an email from Dave, quite a long one, which she spent some time reading and re-reading. She couldn't wait for him to arrive for Christmas. It would be fun showing him Tokyo – it was his first proper visit to the city. She hoped he liked it. It meant so much to her, she would be crushed if he didn't.

Reluctantly she closed the email and moved on to her workaday emails; from her bank, the shops whose lists she was on, Rakuten Travel telling her how many points she had in her account. She went onto the JR website to check the times of the Narita Express for the next week when Dave would arrive and then let her fingers wander across travel websites, wondering whether she could get enough leave to take a holiday with Dave in the spring. They could go in Golden Week, when there were three bank holidays all in a row, but the trouble was that everyone went away in Golden Week so the flights were crowded and the fares sky high. And Josie had hoped to go back to England and see her mum and dad in the spring. She hadn't been home for so long, and neither of her parents were much good at emailing.

Her tartine arrived. She ate it slowly, looking out at the peaceful garden and letting her mind drift, forgetting that she was supposed to be keeping a look out for Mrs Ando. But some sixth sense made her turn just as Mrs Ando walked past, following the girl in the beige T-shirt to an empty table for two in the corner. She was neatly dressed and her hair had just been styled, but her square face was etched with deep lines. She seemed to have aged ten years since Josie had last seen her.

'Oh,' said Josie, in genuine surprise. 'Mrs Ando, hello. It's Josie Clark. You know, from the Matsuyama tour. How are you?'

Mrs Ando looked down at Josie doubtfully.

'Josie Clark?' she said. Then her face cleared. 'Oh, from AZT. Yes of course. I'm very well, thank you.' She turned to walk on as the girl in the beige T-shirt waited. Josie thought fast.

'Are you meeting anyone?' she said. 'Only, if you're on your own, would you mind if I joined you? I got put here when it was crowded but this bench is so hard I can't bear to sit here. I was just going to ask to be moved when you walked past.'

The tea house wasn't so crowded now, but even so there were no empty tables apart from the one waiting for Mrs Ando. As Josie had calculated, Mrs Ando found it hard to say no to a direct request. She nodded, and Josie jumped to her feet before she could change her mind.

They sat down, Mrs Ando with her back to the wall, facing into the room, and Josie opposite her.

'Have you already eaten?' said Mrs Ando.

'Well yes, I have, but I wouldn't mind having a dessert,' said Josie.

'Then try the rose parfait. It's a speciality here.'

'Sounds wonderful,' said Josie. 'Is that what you're having?'

'Yes, it is. Two, then, please.'

Josie put her coat and scarf over the back of her chair and her haversack in the big leather bucket under her seat. Mrs Ando put her handbag in the bucket under her seat too. The bag was worn and looked as though it had seen a lot of use. It was the handbag of someone who didn't take fashion seriously, though it had a Samantha Thavassa label. Josie tried to imagine Mrs Ando living in the perfect architect-designed house that she'd visited but failed utterly. Mrs Ando was far too sensible and down to earth to fit in there.

'I'm so sorry about what happened to Mr Ando,' said Josie.

Mrs Ando gave a little bow but didn't reply.

'I went to the dedication of the plaque at Ando Investments this week,' Josie said. 'It was very moving. Yuko was there too. She kindly invited me round to your house the other week, did she tell you? It's a beautiful house. When was it built?'

'Two years ago,' said Mrs Ando. 'It was time to

rebuild but I'm sorry we couldn't keep the old house. It was more homely than this one.'

'Yuko said you moved to Aoyama quite recently.'

'Yes, we used to live in Saitama. We had a house out in the suburbs. Our street had cherry trees all along it, and people used to come from miles around to see the blossom in the spring. Then in the summer it was green and shady. We had a little garden, not much but I could grow azaleas and cosmos daisies. We used to sit on the veranda in summer and watch the bees going from flower to flower. It was so peaceful. you'd think you were in the countryside.'

'It sounds wonderful. Why on earth did you move?'

The smile left Mrs Ando's face.

'It wasn't my idea. Yuko wanted to live closer in and it meant my husband could be close to the business. It seemed like a good idea, particularly as the business was doing well and we needed to invest some of the profits. We kept the old house though – it's let at the moment.'

'Was Mr Ando always in finance?'

Mrs Ando laughed.

'Finance? No. We ran a bookshop back in Saitama. He always loved books, especially books for kids. He was never happier than when he was in the bookshop and the kids came in after school. They all loved him.'

'So what made him change?'

'You can't stay as you are. If opportunities come you have to take them. And an opportunity came.'

The waitress arrived with their rose parfaits. They were the prettiest dessert Josie had ever seen, served in round glass blows filled with yoghurt and berries, topped with rose jelly, a scoop of ice cream and a scattering of dried rose petals. Josie tried hers; it tasted faintly of roses and had something crunchy, rice flakes maybe, hidden in the smooth yoghurt.

'This is great,' she said. 'Do you mind if I take a photo?'

'Go ahead,' said Mrs Ando. 'Yuko does it all the time.'

Josie got out her phone and took a photo of her dessert, with the peony that grew through the hole in the glass table in the background. She could post it on her Facebook page later – her English friends were fascinated by her Tokyo life.

'My husband took a liking to you, you know,' said Mrs Ando. 'When we were down in Matsuyama. He was always interested in London. We were planning to go there in the summer.'

'You could still go,' said Josie.

'Not without him,' said Mrs Ando. 'It wouldn't be any good without him.'

She suddenly looked much older and very sad.

'Tell me about Saitama,' said Josie, hoping to cheer her up. 'You said you ran a bookshop.'

'That's right. I used to do the ordering, manage the stock, that kind of thing.'

'But you don't do anything like that at Ando Investments?'

'No, I don't. All that is nothing to do with me.'

All what? Josie wondered. Did she mean the investing or something else?

'So what made Mr Ando give up the bookshop? You said an opportunity came?'

'In a way. My husband came into some money – quite a lot, actually. But managing it was complicated. Setting up the company made it easier.'

'And then Mr Wada joined?'

'Yes. That was Mr Mori's idea.'

'Mr Mori?' said Josie. 'I thought—'

'You thought Mr Mori was just a nobody,' Mrs Ando finished for her. 'He likes people to think that. It puts them off guard.'

The tea house was starting to thin out a bit now; there was no one sitting on the chairs lined up along the side of the room waiting for a free table, and when the couple at the table next to them left nobody took their place. It was very quiet and their being in the corner gave a feeling of privacy. Josie decided to risk raising the subject that had been on her mind.

'Eriko seems very upset by Mr Ando's death,' she said, watching Mrs Ando's reaction closely. She wasn't disappointed. Mrs Ando's lips tightened into a thin line. When she spoke, her voice was unnaturally controlled.

'Eriko was a good assistant,' she said. 'But that was all. She wasn't as close to my husband as she liked people to think.'

'Oh,' said Josie. 'I didn't realise…'

'That business with the haiku,' said Mrs Ando. 'That was typical of her.'

'You mean the haiku she wrote down in Matsuyama?'

'Yes. My husband was very upset, as you probably saw.'

'What do you think Eriko's haiku meant?'

'Meant? It meant nothing. How could it? It was just a silly trick. But my husband was very susceptible to things like that. Superstitious about them. She should have know better.'

'And Mr Mori's haiku?'

'Mr Mori does what he does. It's nothing to do with me, not any more. And nor is the company.'

'Yuko seems very concerned about what will happen to the company. About who will inherit.'

'Yuko worries too much about such things,' said Mrs Ando. She finished her rose parfait and stared out of the window at the sun-dappled garden. Josie hurriedly finished her parfait too.

'By the way,' she said. 'Did you ever get Mr Ando's messenger bag back? Only I noticed it didn't seem to be anywhere around in Matsuyama.'

'No,' said Mrs Ando. 'It never turned up. Let it go. It doesn't matter any more now he's gone. Whoever's got it, I wish them well of it.'

TEN

Dave strode across the threshold, crossing Josie's tiny kitchen in one giant pace, and dropped his bag with a thud that rattled the glass doors of the kitchen cabinets.

'God, it's great to be here,' he said. 'Just point me at the bed and leave me alone for a few hours. I promise I'll wake up full of beans and ready to show you how pleased I am to see you.'

He put his arms around Josie and hugged her like a six-foot grizzly bear.

'On second thoughts, why don't I show you how pleased I am to see you first, and then we can both have a little nap?' he said, kissing her neck and refusing to let her go even though she struggled (not too vigorously) to get away.

'First you need to bring your case in from the landing before someone falls over it. And then I need to make the bed.'

'Hey, no need to stand on ceremony. I don't mind an unmade bed.'

'No, I mean really make it. I pack it away during the day and get it out at night. The room's not big enough to leave it there in the daytime. It's what everyone in Japan does.'

'You mean, this is all there is?' said Dave looking around the room. 'There isn't any more?'

'I told you it was small,' said Josie. 'It's a company flat and the rules are that anything with a bedroom is reserved for couples. Now stand back while I get the futon out.'

She moved the table and chairs to one side of the room, unpacked the stack of bedding in the corner and laid it out on the floor while Dave did his best to squash his large frame into the small amount of floorspace left. As soon as Josie had the futon in place he grabbed her again and pulled her down onto it. She made a pretence of resistance but both of them knew she wasn't being serious. They hadn't seen each other for three months and they had a lot of absence to make up for. Finally Dave rolled over with a sigh and fell asleep while Josie extricated herself from under his heavy arm and slid her laptop out from its corner.

*

It was well into the afternoon before Dave stirred and looked up at her through sleepy half-shut eyes.

'Food,' he said. 'I need food. You can't imagine what the food on the plane was like, and there wasn't enough of it to keep a cat alive. Take me out and feed me.'

'What do you want?' said Josie. 'I know a good *tonkatsu* place, or we could have *shabu shabu* or *sukiyaki* or noodles or—'

'Sushi. I'm in Japan, I want to eat sushi.'

'There's lots of other things to eat in Japan besides sushi, you know,' said Josie. 'You don't want me to think you're boringly predictable do you?'

'I've got other ways of showing you how interestingly unpredictable I can be. For now, I want sushi. I've been looking forward to it all the way over. If you don't let me have sushi I'll make you take me to McDonalds.'

'Okay, okay, point taken. Sushi it is then. I know a place in Ginza where they do a happy hour – all you can eat for three thousand yen.'

'Sounds good to me.'

Dave reached for his suitcase and pulled out some clean clothes.

'Can I get a shower before we go?'

'Of course. It's in the bathroom. I'll show you.'

Josie led the way into her broom cupboard of a bathroom. Dave looked over her shoulder and reeled back in mock astonishment.

'Call that a bath? It's more like a Roman sarcophagus.'

'Welcome to Japan. Everybody has a bath like that. They're tall and narrow so you can fill them to the top and sit there with the water up to your neck.'

'So how do I have a shower?'

'The shower's outside the bath. Look, here on the wall. It's like that time we went to the hot spring. You have a shower first and then you can sit in a hot bath when you're nice and clean. Or you can just have a shower. It's up to you.'

'I'll just go for the shower, thanks. See you in a minute.'

Josie could hear him singing to himself as he washed. She hoped she was the only one who could hear him; she wasn't sure what her neighbours would make of *Jumping Jack Flash* echoing through the walls. She hoped nobody would make a fuss about her having a man to stay in her apartment. She didn't think they would, but sometimes Japanese attitudes could be remarkably old-fashioned.

They walked to the station with Dave exclaiming at everything he saw. Josie enjoyed seeing her neighbourhood through his eyes. She'd lived there long enough for it all to seem natural to her, and it was fun to see it freshly again. The neat, pavementless streets where cyclists weaved slowly along and cars hardly ever came, the tiny shops selling flowers and groceries, the old ladies with their full bags of shopping – it was what she loved about Japan but had forgotten to notice. Dave made her see its charm all over again.

It was funny to see Dave through Japanese eyes too. He was like a giant thudding down the street on his big trainer-clad feet. The quiet deft people who passed by turned to look at him, and two little girls looked up at him with amazed eyes and ran giggling away. In a way Josie regretted the loss of her hard-won ability to blend in, but everyone was so fascinated by Dave, and he by them, that she soon started to enjoy it. Sometimes not fitting in was okay too.

They got the train into Tokyo station. Josie gave Dave his suica card and explained to him how to top it up, just like an oyster card. She tried to show him how to get around by himself, but he was more interested in whispering silly jokes in her ear so she gave up on the lesson and just enjoyed having him with her again.

The sushi restaurant was in the basement of Ginza Core, a big complex of shops and restaurants close to the Waco department store. By the time they got there it was five in the afternoon. As it was Sunday, Ginza was closed to traffic and pedestrians wandered where they liked in the broad street while cafes served drinks at tables placed where normally traffic roared. Dave seemed mesmerised by it all.

The sushi bar was beginning to fill up. The small counter, where the sushi aficionados sat so they could chat to the sushi chefs and point out their next fish in the glass display case, already had most of its seats taken so Dave and Josie sat at one of the tiny tables. Dave looked at the menu, which had colour pictures of all the different sushi.

'I'm baffled,' he said. 'You choose for us.'

'Okay,' said Josie. 'We'll have tuna and salmon and shrimp because that's what you like, then we'll have *hamachi*, *hotate*, *uni*, *ikura*, *unagi* and *saba*. That should keep you on your toes.'

The waiter who came to take their order hesitated

at the sight of a pair of foreigners but broke into a smile when he recognised Josie, who was a regular. Josie ordered their sushi with a couple of Kirin beers.

When the beers came they clinked glasses in a toast (Josie just stopped herself saying *kanpai* and said *cheers* instead) and beamed at each other.

'I'm sorry I'll have to work while you're here,' said Josie. 'But you can go and do the tourist sights in the daytime – the Imperial Palace, the Sky Tower and so on. Then in the evening we can go out to eat and go to Shibuya and Roppongi, places where there's a bit of nightlife.'

'Great. Are we going to see Keiko and Yoshi?' Dave had met Josie's friends on his previous, all too brief, visit to Tokyo.

'Yes, and Yoshi's offered to take you to an *izakaya* with his mates one evening. That's a sort of Japanese pub.'

'Great. And I want to go to that place where they have all the computers and games and things. What's it called? Electric Town?'

'Oh yes, Akihabara. You could go there tomorrow if you like. There's plenty there to keep you busy while I'm at the office.'

'I'm cool with eating out a lot, but let's skip the nightlife. I'm planning on a lot of early nights now we're back together.'

He grinned at her across the table and she grinned back. She hadn't felt this happy since – well, since she'd got back from seeing him in Australia.

'It's up to you. The only time we have to go out is

Christmas Eve. I've booked us into this really romantic restaurant for dinner. You may not realise it, but not having a date on Christmas Eve has been a real downer these past few years. It's the most romantic night of the year here.'

'You mean like Valentine's Day?'

'Exactly like Valentine's Day. All my mates feel sorry for me on Christmas Eve, but this year it's going to be different.'

'Suits me. Romance is what I'm here for.'

Dave paused then said in a changed tone, 'You didn't ever go out with anyone else? When we split up?'

Josie hesitated.

'No, well, not really. Not on Christmas Eve, anyway.'

'But you did go out with someone?'

'There was this one guy but it really didn't amount to anything.'

Dave visibly bristled.

'You don't need to worry, it was only the odd date and he's getting married soon.'

'What's his name?'

'Ken. I met him at work.'

'Not the Ken you went down to Matsuyama with?'

Josie bit her lip. She'd forgotten she'd mentioned to Dave that Ken was going to Matsuyama too.

'Well, yes, but that was just work.'

'So you didn't hang out with him in Matsuyama or anything.'

'No, not really. We weren't there long enough,

given what happened.'

'Oh. So you would've hung out with him if you'd stayed longer?'

'No. There was nothing in it. You don't have to worry.'

She poured them both some more beer. Luckily the waiter arrived with their first plate of sushi.

'I worry about you,' Dave said. 'I worry about you all the time. What you're doing, how you're getting on. Whether you're with someone else. We need to sort ourselves out, Josie. We can't go on living in different countries like this.'

Josie didn't reply. Dave knew how much living in Japan meant to her.

Dave looked at her set face.

'I can see it's up to me to do something about it,' he said. 'I've been talking to my company about getting a posting over here. They're starting to come round to the idea.'

'That'd be great,' said Josie.

'So you can stop hanging out with this Ken, alright?'

'Alright. Though I'm not hanging out with him, I told you.'

'Is there any more news on the guy who fell off the castle in Matsuyama?'

'Well, not exactly news. But there's been some... developments.'

Dave stopped with a piece of sushi halfway to his mouth and looked at Josie.

'Don't tell me you're starting this again,' he said.

'Starting what?'

'You know. Getting involved. Investigating things. Deciding it wasn't an accident. That's what "developments" means, isn't it?'

'Not necessarily. It's just that there was something odd about what happened.'

'Josie, don't pretend. I can read you like a book. You're on the trail again, just like last time.'

'This is different. Yuko – that's his daughter – asked me to help her. So I asked a few questions and it all looks very suspicious. Even Ken had to admit—'

'Ken again, eh?'

'No, I told you, there's nothing going on. But we were both on the trip so naturally I've talked to him about what I've found out. And he's been really helpful. He took me along to the dedication ceremony and I found out there that—'

She stopped. Dave's face was like thunder.

'So you have been going out with him?'

'Only to this ceremony thing at Ando Investments. It was really useful. There's something fishy about the company and I'm sure it's got something to do with Mr Ando's death.'

'Josie,' said Dave. 'Don't do this. Don't get yourself involved in another of these obsessive quests of yours. You know it nearly did for us last time I came over. It's got trouble written all over it. Don't do it, please.'

Josie put down her chopsticks and took a drink of her beer. Why was nothing ever simple? Dave had been in Japan less than twenty-four hours and already they were disagreeing. They'd been looking forward to seeing each other so much, and they couldn't even get through the first day without quarrelling. Anyway, why should Dave stop her from asking about Mr Ando's death? It didn't make any difference to him. They could still have a perfectly good time together.

She could feel her face settling into an expression of rigid defiance and, looking across at Dave, she saw the smile fade from his face.

'Just do this one thing for me, Josie,' he said quietly.

'I don't see why it's so important. And anyway, I can't stop now. I promised Yuko.'

'That's not it. It's not about Yuko. It's about us.'

Josie tried again.

'There's this bag,' she said, trying to sound persuasive and rational. 'Mr Ando was carrying it the day he died but nobody knows what happened to it. I'm sure that's the key to the whole thing. If I can just find out about the bag, it'll all be clear.'

'So it's just about the bag?'

'Yes.'

'Nothing else?'

'Yes.'

'Promise?'

'What's there for me to promise? I'll just find out about the bag and then... and then I'm sure everything else will fall into place.'

Dave glared at her and absent-mindedly ate another piece of sushi. It was *hamachi*, which was Josie's favourite. She hastily grabbed the last remaining piece before he ate that too. The waiter brought a plate of *uni* and *ikura*, both of which she'd deliberately ordered to give Dave a surprise. *Uni* was sea urchin – it was beige and squishy-looking and sat on top of a roll of rice wrapped in seaweed daring you to eat it. The flavour was mild and delicate, as Josie knew from experience, but it took a leap of faith to try it. *Ikura* was fish roe, little orange gelatinous balls that burst in your mouth with a sudden sharp taste of the sea.

'Try this,' she said to Dave, passing him the plate. 'This is what sushi is really about.'

She sat back and watched as he tried first a piece of *uni* then one of *ikura*. The expression on his face made her laugh. He laughed too, and everything was all right again.

They had some sake to go with the last of their sushi, then went to an *izakaya* and had some more beer. Dave put his arm round Josie as they walked back to Tokyo station through the brightly lit streets, taking a short cut through the big open square outside the new entrance to Yurakucho station. The Oi City department store was just closing and the shop assistants were heading for the steps down to the metro to get their trains home.

Josie thought back to their conversation in the sushi bar. There wasn't really any reason why she should go on trying to find out what really happened down in Matsuyama. Like Dave said, it wasn't anything to do with her and she didn't owe Yuko anything. What if it had been murder? There was no way to prove it, even if she was sure that it was. It was just the messenger bag that nagged at her. She couldn't get away from the feeling that, if she could find out what happened to the bag and why, she'd know why Mr Ando had been murdered. But nothing she found out seemed to give her any clue about it. She looked up at Dave who smiled at her.

'You're right,' she said. 'I'm going to stop worrying about Matsuyama and have some fun while you're here. It would be mad not to.'

'That's my girl,' said Dave, holding her close.

Josie's phone rang.

'It'll be Keiko,' she said to Dave. 'She'll want to know if you've arrived safely and what we've been doing. I'd better answer it.'

She stopped and ducked into one of the arches under the Yurakucho platforms, where the railway ran overhead. Dave wandered on down the street to look at the windows of a Chinese restaurant that had a *show window* display of plastic replicas of food.

It wasn't Keiko on the phone, it was Yuko. Josie nearly hit the *don't answer* button, but curiosity got the better of her. It couldn't hurt just to find out what Yuko wanted, and maybe tell her that Josie wasn't going to go on helping her. She put the phone to her ear.

'I need to talk to you,' said Yuko without any preamble. 'Can you come over right away?'

'No, I can't,' said Josie, resenting Yuko's assumption that Josie was at her beck and call and feeling a little smug that she was about to tell Yuko to solve her own problems.

'Tomorrow, then, after work. Can I meet you then?'

'Not really. I'm going to Akihabara with my boyfriend. He's visiting from Australia for Christmas.'

'Akihabara, perfect,' said Yuko. 'You know the AKB48 cafe?'

Josie glanced at Dave. He had got bored with looking in the restaurant window and was strolling back towards her.

'I can't talk now,' she said. 'I'm with someone.'

'But you do know it?'

'Yes, I know it but—'

'I'll meet you there at six tomorrow – by the entrance.'

'Look, Yuko, what is this? I can't just drop everything I'm doing to help you.'

'You've got to help me over this. Jiro's been attacked and his flat's been ransacked.'

'Ransacked? Why?' said Josie. 'What were they looking for?'

'For my father's bag, of course.'

ELEVEN

Josie took the Electric Town exit from Akihabara JR station into a broad square flanked by the railway track, with the flat brick frontage of the AKB48 cafe below it. For a moment she feared that Yuko would have got there first, but there was no sign of her; just the usual scattering of geeky men studying the rows of pictures of the AKB48 girls on big wooden boards in front of the entrance. She looked around for Dave; he was already there, sitting on a seat made from thick aluminium pipe that encircled one of the trees that dotted the square. He smiled and waved when he saw her.

'There you are,' he said. 'I've been wondering what I'd do if you didn't show up. Akihabara is mad and the further in you go, the madder it gets. One place I went to, the guy tried to sell me a three foot model dragon, with a remote control you could press to make it breathe fire. I went in a maid cafe but all the girls did when they saw me was giggle, then they went and got the manager, who looked about seventeen and nearly died when he saw me. I stayed in Yodobashi Camera for hours, it's gigantic. They have every kind of technology known to man, including 3-D printers which is what I'd like for Christmas, please. I had lunch in this sort of Korean fast food place. Have you ever had bibimbap? It's awesome. We should go to Korea, I bet the food there is terrific.'

'It is if you like your food spicy. And don't mind eating pickled cabbage for breakfast, lunch and dinner.'

'I could get used to that. Are we going to eat here tonight?'

'In Akihabara? Sure, if you want to. But not at the AKB48 cafe. It's strictly for the fans.'

'What is AKB48?'

Josie laughed.

'It's a sort of girl group,' she said. 'Only there's hundreds of them. They're on the television all the time. You must have seen the pictures.'

'Those girls with all the eye make up and short skirts who all look about fifteen?'

'Yes, that's the way they like them over here,' said Josie. 'By the way, a friend is coming to meet us in a minute. I just need to talk to her about something. It won't take long.'

'A friend?' said Dave.

'Well, actually, it's Yuko – you know, I told you about her. She's the girl I went to Matsuyama with. It seems that, well, something's happened to Jiro and she wants to talk to me about it so I said I'd meet her here.'

'What do you mean, something's happened to Jiro? Who's Jiro? What kind of something?'

'Jiro's her boyfriend. She wasn't too specific on the phone but she said someone searched his flat.'

'Josie, this isn't about that Matsuyama business again, is it? You said it was just about the bag, nothing else.'

'Yes it is just about the bag. Jiro's got into a bit of trouble about it and we're going to sort it out, that's all.'

'Why do I get the feeling this is the tip of the iceberg?' said Dave.

'It'll be okay,' said Josie. 'It's no big deal.'

She looked at her watch. It was five to six. She saw Yuko walking towards them, wearing a short skirt and knee boots. She'd tied her long hair up in two bunches that made her look young and cute and like she hung out in Akihabara all the time.

'Hi, Yuko,' said Josie. 'This is my boyfriend, Dave. He doesn't speak Japanese.'

Yuko nodded to Dave, who said, '*Hajimemashite*,' in a passable Japanese pronunciation. Josie knew he only spoke six words of Japanese but Yuko was impressed.

'He's so tall,' she said, 'That must be great for you, seeing you're so much taller than normal people yourself.'

Thanks for pointing that out, thought Josie. But she just said, 'Where shall we go?'

'I don't have much time,' said Yuko. 'Let's just go

somewhere nearby.'

'There's an Excelsior Caffé on the other side of the square,' said Josie, linking her arm through Dave's.

'That'll do,' said Yuko.

The Excelsior was relatively quiet, considering they were in Akihabara. Josie ordered cappuccinos for her and Dave and an orange juice for Yuko, who made a beeline for a table in the non-smoking section.

'I hate the smell of cigarette smoke,' she said, tossing her head so her bunches swished. 'It gets in my hair.'

'Are you going to be okay for a bit?' said Josie to Dave. 'Only I need to talk to Yuko and we can't do it in English.'

'You go ahead, I'll be fine. I'm going to play with my new toy.' He reached into his bag and fished out a brand new Sony SmartBand fitness-tracking bracelet, still in its bubble pack. Josie turned back to Yuko.

'Right,' she said. 'Now what's all this about Jiro? Is he hurt?'

'No, he's not hurt, at least not badly. Someone came up behind him in the street and hit him. He fell over and they took his wallet and mobile phone and his keys. He had to go to the police and report it which took ages, and then, when he got back to his flat, he found they'd let themselves in and ransacked the place.'

'Did he get a look at the person who attacked him?'

'No, they were behind him and they were dressed all in black with their face muffled. He couldn't even tell if it was a man or a woman.'

'What makes you think it wasn't just a mugger?'

'Muggers don't take your keys and search your flat.'

'And you think they were looking for your father's bag?'

Yuko shifted in her seat and took a long drink of her orange juice before replying.

'Yes,' she said, with a sly sideways glance at Josie. 'Someone must think he has it. But he hasn't.'

Josie resisted a strong desire to take Yuko by the shoulders and shake her. What was the point of asking Josie to help her and then telling lies?

'So why would anyone think that he did?' Josie said, trying to keep the exasperation out of her voice, and when Yuko shrugged and looked blank she added, 'Come on, Yuko, you'll have to do better than that.'

Yuko took another straw out of the box on the table and bent it between her fingers. Dave glanced up but then went back to changing the settings on his fitness band.

'It's Mr Mori's fault,' said Yuko, dropping the mangled straw on the table and picking out another one. 'He must have told someone that Jiro had it.'

'Why would he do that?'

'To distract them. Maybe they thought Mr Mori had it and he told them Jiro had it to get rid of them.'

'Has Mr Mori got it?'

'How would I know?' Yuko tossed her head again, as though she thought that Josie was treating her unfairly. 'Maybe it's not him. Maybe it's Eriko. I wouldn't put it past her.'

'Why should Eriko have it? And how would she have got it?'

'I don't know. But she's always making trouble one way or another.'

'Don't you think you're getting things a bit out of proportion?' said Josie, tiring of the histrionics that seemed to accompany Yoko's every utterance.

'No, I'm not. You don't understand how frightened I am. And so's Jiro.'

'Okay,' said Josie. 'I'll see what I can find out and I'll let you know.'

'What will you do?' said Yuko, giving Josie that odd sidelong glance again.

'I'll talk to Mr Mori and to Eriko and see what they have to say about the bag.'

'Great. Thank you so much for helping me. I really do appreciate it. And I've got you something to show how grateful I am. Here.'

She pushed an envelope across the table. Josie opened it and pulled out the contents.

'Two tickets to the AKB48 show tonight. How on earth did you get hold of them? They're like gold dust.'

'Oh, you know, people can get hold of things for you if you know who to ask. Enjoy the show.' Yuko jumped up and practically ran to the door, her high heeled boots clacking on the parquet floor. Dave put his fitness band on his wrist and drank the last of his coffee.

'So now you've finished with Yuko, do we get some time together?' he said.

'Yes,' said Josie. 'We do. But we've got to hurry. Courtesy of Yuko we're going to the AKB48 show and it starts in thirty minutes.'

They left the cafe and walked down a side street to the Chuo Dori, the pulsating heart of Akihabara. Jostling little shops emitted a cacophony of jingles, slogans and mysterious bleeps, narrow staircases led to upper floors crammed with a bizarre mix of soft toys, dolls, figures and costumes, cellophane-wrapped volumes of manga and every essential for the *otaku* geek lifestyle. Filling the shops and pavement and spilling out into the road were the Akihabara crowd; overwhelmingly young, single minded and pursuing their latest obsessions. Josie dodged through the crowd, avoiding the girls dressed in tiny frilly skirts, over the knee socks and Minnie Mouse shoes, with pink bows in their hair, who were handing out flyers for maid cafes, and the geeky young men with technology-obsessed eyes whose electronic girlfriends, cuter and more accommodating than the real thing, were always available at the touch of an iPhone button.

'Aren't we going back to the AKB48 cafe?' said Dave, thudding down the street like an English oak among the swaying willows of geek city.

'No, the theatre's not there, it's in the Don Quijote building,' said Josie. 'Look, here's the entrance.'

She ducked into a narrow entrance and onto an escalator that was rapidly filling with people.

'The theatre's on the eighth floor,' she said. 'It's not very big.'

'Oh look,' said Dave as they passed the fourth floor. 'They sell maid uniforms here. Maybe I should get you one.'

Josie looked at the little frilly dresses and tiny aprons on the racks.

'Don't even think about it,' she said. 'Not if you value your life.'

The sixth and seventh floors were given over to rows of video gaming machines. The noise they made was deafening, but the players who sat glued to the wide screens seemed oblivious.

At the eighth floor Josie showed their tickets and was issued with a pair of identity bracelets that allowed them inside. The majority of the audience seemed to be single men, many in their forties and fifties, who were clearly committed AKB48 fans. There was just a scattering of girls and families with children.

The show was entertaining, though not intellectually challenging. It consisted of the AKB48 team of the day appearing in a variety of costumes ranging from school uniforms to tartan suits and guardsmen's jackets, all with short frilly skirts, singing bubblegum-style J-Pops and performing simple dance routines while the audience clapped along. The girls were like Lolita fantasies come to life – with their long tousled hair and huge heavy-lashed eyes, they looked like they'd just stepped out of a manga frame. Josie wondered what Dave made of them. Maybe he harboured a secret desire for Japanese child-women like these. She covertly watched him out the corner of her eye. He seemed to be enjoying himself, clapping along to the pounding beat with the rest of the audience.

What does Dave really think of Japan, Josie wondered. Is he only here because I'm here, or would he have come here eventually by himself? Come to that, what am I doing here? I know I love being in Japan and want to stay here for a long time, but does that mean I've decided to make it my home? Not go back to London and my family one day?

Suddenly a wave of homesickness swept over her, a deep longing to stand outside a pub on a Friday night with a giant glass of warm white wine and a gang of mates screaming and laughing, to eat chicken tikka and drink Cobra beer, to go shopping down Catford Broadway on a Saturday afternoon and call in at her mum's on the way home for a cup of tea and a Jaffa cake. I've been away too long, she thought. If I go home now, will I feel like a foreigner in my own city? Will I long for green tea and raw fish and steamed buns?

At the end of the show all the girls lined up to high-five the audience as they filed out. Dave thanked them in English with every sign of enthusiasm. Maybe he really does like them, Josie thought as they walked back to Akihabara station, feeling all too conscious of her height, the size of her nose and the non-swishiness of her hair.

'Would you like to go out with an AKB48 girl?'

she asked Dave.

Dave stopped and turned to face her. He put a hand on each of her shoulders and looked straight into her eyes.

'No,' he said. 'And if I ever catch you with your hair in bunches, I'll cut them off. With a giant pair of scissors. Got that?'

Josie laughed with relief.

'No chance,' she said. 'I'm too big for the kawaii look. Though it suited Yuko, don't you think?'

'Yes, but then she's so fake that being a fake little girl must come naturally to her.'

'You think she's fake?'

'From her boots to her hair bobbles. And I'll tell you something else. I couldn't understand what she was saying, but I understand body language alright. And she was telling you a pack of lies.'

*

Josie got up early the next morning and crept out onto the balcony with her phone without waking Dave. It wasn't that she was trying to keep it from him, but she didn't think any purpose would be served by letting him know she was still trying to track down the elusive bag. She found the piece of paper where she'd scribbled down Eriko's number and tapped it into the phone, crossing her fingers that Eriko was an early riser. She heard the phone ring at the other end and then a voice answered.

'Oh, is that Eriko?' she said. 'It's Josie Clark

here.'

There was a muffled sound of voices and a pause and then Eriko said, 'Oh, Josie. It's good to hear from you. What can I do for you?'

'Well, you remember you suggested I should ring when we met at the unveiling.'

'Yes, yes of course I remember. We must get together. There's something I want to tell you but I can't talk just now.'

'Oh, okay,' said Josie, wondering what it was that was stopping her. 'Great, I'll wait to hear from you then. By the way, do you know if Mr Ando's messenger bag has turned up yet?'

Silence. Then Eriko said, 'What do you mean?' in a strained voice.

'You know, the one he had with him when we went to the castle. Brown leather, rather nice, with a shoulder strap. I wondered if it had turned up at Ando Investments.'

'I told you before, I haven't seen it. And it hasn't turned up anywhere. It's lost, or stolen, more like.' Eriko's voice rose. 'If you hear anything about it, I'd be glad if you'd let me know. It had important documents in it.'

'Right, yes, of course I will. Sorry to have disturbed you so early in the morning.'

'That's okay. I'll be in touch and we'll set something up soon. Maybe we can meet up at the weekend or something.'

'Suits me,' said Josie, though she wasn't sure what Dave would say. She'd have to cross that bridge when she came to it.

After Eriko rang off Josie stood on the balcony thinking, though it was chilly out there and she only had her dressing gown on over her pyjamas. Something wasn't quite right about Eriko's reaction when Josie asked about the bag. And whose was the voice she'd heard in the background?

She stepped back inside the flat, still lost in thought, to find Dave looking at her with sleepy eyes.

'Oh, you're awake,' she said.

'Who were you talking to on the phone?' Dave said in a strange, cold voice.

'Nobody special. Just someone I promised I'd ring.'

'At six o'clock in the morning?'

'People get up early here.' It sounded unconvincing even to Josie, but she didn't want to get into another argument about Matsuyama.

Josie—' Dave stopped.

'What is it?'

'Josie, you would tell me if there, well, if there was anyone else, wouldn't you?'

'What are you talking about? There's nobody else. Don't be so silly.'

'Okay,' said Dave. 'Have it your own way.'

He got up and went to the bathroom for a shower while Josie cleared the bedding and packed it away. She could hear the shower running but Dave wasn't singing the way he usually did. He must have got up on the wrong side of the bed, she thought. He'll cheer up later.

TWELVE

'Are you sure you'll be okay tonight?' said Josie, pausing outside the Marunouchi North exit from Tokyo station and pulling Dave to one side to let the herd of commuters on their way to their offices in Otemachi thunder past. 'You know the way? Shibuya station is a bit of a maze but it's all signposted in English so you shouldn't have any trouble.'

'Of course I'll be okay. I'm all grown up so you can stop behaving like my mother. I can get myself across Tokyo on my own. I've got the Google map app on my phone and you and Yoshi's numbers on speed dial. Plus, if I get lost I can ask someone to help me out.'

'If you do get lost...' said Josie. Dave rolled his eyes.

'If you do get lost, look out for a Koban. They're little police stations with maps on the wall, they have them everywhere. The police just love giving directions, that's what they're there for.'

'Okay, if necessary I'll ask a policeman. Now are

you happy?'

'Yoshi's going to meet you at six. You follow the signs for Hachiko Square as you come out of the station. Just wait and he'll come and get you.'

'It's fine, don't worry.'

'I'll be round at Keiko's if you need anything.'

'I won't. Stop worrying.'

'And you'll be alright on your own today?'

'Yes, I'll be alright. You go off to work and forget about me. I'm going to do the tourist trail – Imperial Palace, Ginza, Kabuki-za, all that stuff you've seen a million times.'

'Okay. You know you can always ring me if you need to.'

'I won't need to. I'll see you tonight. Late.'

Dave took a quick look around, saw that no one was looking and gave her a quick kiss. Then he strode off, swinging his backpack onto his shoulder as he went.

Josie watched until he was out of sight but he didn't look back. He's going to be fine, she thought. He'll have a great day being a tourist and then Yoshi will take him out for a proper boy's night out. Much more fun than if I'd gone along too. And he'll never find out that I've lied to him about going round to Keiko's and I'm actually going to meet Mr Mori.

All the same, she felt a nagging sense of guilt all through the day and jumped every time her phone rang, thinking it might be Dave to say he'd found her out. At five she shut down her computer and rang Keiko.

'I'm just leaving work now,' she said. 'Tell me what you're going to do this evening so I can get my story straight in case Dave asks.'

'I'm making beef *tataki*,' Keiko said. 'Which, as you know, is my speciality, so you're really missing out not being here. Then I'm going to watch a DVD of the latest Takashi Miike film. Which would have been a lot more fun if we'd watched it together.'

'Stop trying to make me feel guilty,' said Josie. 'I feel bad enough about this already.'

'Why don't you just tell Dave the truth?' said Keiko. 'It'll turn out badly if you lie to him, you know that.'

'It'll be aright. I just don't want to get into a row about all this Matsuyama business, that's all. It's no big deal and I don't want it spoiling Dave's visit.'

'Don't you think Dave's bright enough to spot something's going on?'

'It'll be fine, honestly. Just back me up about tonight.'

Josie hung up and hurried out of the office to get the metro to Jimbocho.

Mr Mori had suggested meeting in Jimbocho. She wondered if that was where he lived. Although it wasn't far from Otemachi, it was a part of Tokyo she had never been to, and she was a bit nervous about finding the place where Mr Mori had suggested they meet, a second-hand bookshop called Shimizu's Books.

She took the Hanzomon line to Jimbocho, chose the exit that came out at the junction of Yasukuni

Dori and Hakusan Dori and walked a little way along before realising she was going in the wrong direction. But she had time to spare and wasn't sorry to get a look at the neighbourhood, which was modern and airy, lined with boxy glass skyscrapers which all seemed to harbour secondhand bookshops on their ground floors. On an impulse she ducked into one. It was selling old film magazines and books, illustrated with black and white photos of the film stars of the fifties, whose names meant little to Josie. The next shop she tried specialised in travel books, some of them with sepia photos that had been hand-coloured in lurid pinks and greens.

She went back out into the street and looked around her with new eyes. Now she knew where to look, she could see that there were more secondhand shops tucked away down dark passages and up narrow stairs. All of them seemed to have the same attitude to stock control – cram as much in as you possibly could and leave it to the customers to snake their way between the shelves to discover that special edition they were searching for. The shops at street level had dump bins of cheap books outside that Josie felt oddly tempted to riffle through in search of a bargain.

Back on Yasukuni Dori she headed south and soon found what she was looking for. Mr Mori had said Shimizu's Books was easy to spot and now she realised why; though all the other buildings in the street were tall glass blocks, Shimizu's Books was housed in a building that seemed to have been left behind by the nineteenth century. It was built of warm red brick, three stories high and the width of two shopfronts, and it was topped with a classical pediment that wouldn't have looked out of place on the Parthenon. The windows were, inevitably, stacked floor to ceiling with books; old, musty volumes with titles in spidery writing that Josie struggled to read. Grey-haired men with studious expressions were riffling through dump bins outside.

She stepped gingerly inside and made her way through the towering stacks. At the back of the shop a small space had been cleared, giving just enough room for an old-fashioned desk with a pile of papers and a calculator. Next to it, on an ancient swivel chair, sat a worn-looking man in his fifties with his shirtsleeves held in place by old fashioned clips above the elbow. He looked up as Josie approached. His face was weary but his eyes were kind and Josie took a liking to him straight away. He was talking to someone who had his back to Josie, who turned at the sound of Josie's footsteps. It was Mr Mori, but his face seemed softer than she remembered it, as though being on familiar ground had enabled him to relax and had eased the tense lines from his forehead.

'Sso, you found it,' he said. 'I told you it was easy. You can find me in Jimbocho most evenings, either here or in the beer hall around the corner, discussing the elussive first edition of *Botchan* that will one day make my fortune. But Mr Shimizu here' – he indicated the proprietor who smiled indulgently – 'will no doubt spot it before I do and make his fortune instead. It's a cut-throat business, the ssecondhand book business.'

'I didn't know you collected secondhand books, Mr Mori,' said Josie.

Mr Mori looked at his companion, who seemed to know what was coming.

'Mr Shimizu,' he said. 'Would you describe me as a ssecondhand book collector?'

'No, Mr Mori. You buy and you sell, but you don't collect. Books don't stay with you, they fly from your hands like fluttering doves.'

'Like fluttering doves,' said Mr Mori, obviously pleased with the simile. 'They rest briefly in my dovecote and then they are gone. Pouf!'

He made a gesture of releasing a bird into the air. Mr Shimizu smiled and nodded and pretended to try and catch the elusive birds.

'So do you have your own shop?' said Josie, fascinated by the idea of books passing through Mr Mori's hands so quickly.

'Not exactly. More a... a ressting place for tired doves.' He smiled at the joke and Mr Shimizu smiled too. 'Maybe one day I'll let you come and see it.'

'Did Mr Ando ever go there?' said Josie.

A shadow fell across Mr Mori's face.

'Don't let's talk about Mr Ando here,' he said. 'We'll go to the beer hall if you want to talk about him. Will you come too, Mr Shimizu?'

'You go on,' said Mr Shimizu. 'I'll close up here and join you in a minute. Order me my usual.'

Mr Mori led the way back along the narrow

passage through the book stacks out into the street and down the side road that ran along the side of Shimizu's Books. The roar of the traffic quickly faded as they walked, soon reaching a beer hall with tables outside made of steel beer barrels and ivy tumbling down over its facade. Dimly, behind the ivy, Josie made out a sign that said *Craft Beer Market* in yellow lettering.

'You can get a beer and a curry and a ssalad for a thousand yen here,' said Mr Mori. 'In the summer we like to sit outside but it's too cold for that today.'

Inside there were rows of wooden tables and chairs, and a cheerful atmosphere as local office workers stopped in for a beer after work. Here and there were older men on their own. Mr Mori noticed Josie looking at them.

'Collectors,' he said 'After one particular kind of book, an author perhapss or a whole genre that's caught their imagination and now they're on the trail. There's nothing like the thrill you get when you track down a book you've been after for years.'

'Why don't they just go online?' said Josie.

Mr Mori laughed, a strange wheezy laugh.

'They have lots of secondhand books for sale online,' said Josie. 'I've seen them. You can find pretty much anything you want there.'

'Oh, ssuch a joke,' said Mr Mori, his hissing Tokyo accent becoming more pronounced as he laughed. 'Online? The books that are ssold online are common or garden editions, easy to find. There's no pleasure in that. It would be like your arissstocrats hunting a fox that sits quietly in the field waiting to be found. No, what we collectors want is rarity – we pursue the books that there is never a whissper of online, ones that you can only get a whiff of secretly in special places where connoisseurs drop hints to people they trust.'

'Connoisseurs?' said Josie.

'People like me,' said Mr Mori. 'People who are discreet.'

'Did you mean what you said about looking for a first edition of *Botchan*?'

'No, that was by way of being a joke. Nowadays books like that are all in museums. Sometimes there are rumours that one has become available, but it always turns out to be just a rumour.'

'But if one did turn up?'

'Then it would be very valuable indeed.'

'And the person who found it would come to Jimbocho to find a buyer?'

'Yess. Not to Mr Shimizu's shop. There are other places where rare books change hands. I couldn't take you to such places – you would cause too much disquiet, a young foreign lady like you with eyes that ssee too much.'

Josie didn't know whether to be disappointed or flattered. She looked at Mr Mori and just caught a glimmer of satisfaction in his eyes. He's playing me along, she thought. But I'm not that easily led.

Mr Mori saw the change in her expression and understood the reason.

'Don't be offended,' he said. 'I'm not trying to

mock you. Let's order ssomething to eat and wait for Mr Shimizu to get here. Then I'll talk to you about Mr Ando and his interest in books.'

The waiter, a cheery young man in a white shirt and jeans with a long apron tied around his waist with string came to take their order. They both ordered curry and salad and beer, the waiter seeming to know which of the many beers on display Mr Mori wanted without having to ask. Mr Mori ordered a beer and curry for Mr Shimizu too and again the waiter knew which beer without having to ask.

When the waiter had gone, Josie said, 'I've been talking to Yuko.'

'And how is she?'

'She's pretty upset. Someone attacked her boyfriend, Jiro, a couple of nights ago and stole his keys, then ransacked his flat.'

Mr Mori looked startled.

'Attacked him? Why?'

'We don't know. But Yuko thinks it's to do with what happened in Matsuyama. She thinks whoever attacked him was looking for something.'

'What does she think they were looking for?' Mr Mori glanced around the room warily as he spoke, as though he thought that Jiro's attacker might have followed them in.

'The messenger bag Mr Ando was carrying when he was killed. It's disappeared, you know.'

'Why should anyone think that Jiro had it?' Mr Mori said.

'I don't know. Yuko thought maybe you had told

them he had.'

Mr Mori looked towards the bar as if impatient for his beer to arrive. He picked up a spoon from the wicker basket of cutlery and absent-mindedly tapped it on the table. Then he realised what he was doing and put it back again.

'Yuko is a ssilly girl,' he said. 'You can't trust anything she says.'

'Yes, but on the other hand, the bag's missing and someone must have it. I've been trying to remember where everybody was and what they did after the accident. To see if I can work out who could have got hold of it.'

'And can you?'

'Not really. I know you were the first on the scene, apart from the couple who found him. Did you see what happened to it?'

'No. Maybe they took it.'

'The couple, you mean? But they had nothing to do with it.'

'How can you be so sure?'

'Well, that was what Hina said. And anyway I saw them in the keep afterwards and they didn't have it.'

'Maybe ssomeone hid it. They might have planned to come back for it later.'

Josie tried to remember if there had been anywhere where a bag might have been hidden, but she couldn't come up with anything.

Mr Mori saw the hesitation in her eyes.

'You don't really know, do you?' he said.

'I know where the bag was,' said Josie. 'Mr

Kimura told me Mr Ando left it on the bench in the keep. So anyone could have taken it. Even you.'

Mr Mori recoiled as though she'd hit him.

'Don't say that. Not even here. It could be dangerouss.'

'Why would it be dangerous?'

'Don't pretend to be ssimple when you are not. Someone is willing to kill to get their hands on that bag. Jiro was lucky that all they did was search his flat. It could have been a lot worse. And he is just an innocent bystander, like me. But it is the innocent bystanders who get hurt, and that's why your blundering quessstions frighten me.'

'Who do you think attacked Jiro, Mr Mori? Are you afraid they're after you too?'

The waiter arrived with their beers and curries before Mr Mori could reply. They both drew back as the waiter put the plates and glasses on the table. It was the first time Josie realised that they had been leaning forward and whispering like conspirators.

The noise of a chair scraping back beside her made her turn, to see Mr Shimizu had arrived.

'Just in time,' he said, taking his plate of curry from the waiter and reaching for the cutlery basket.

Mr Mori picked up his spoon and attacked his curry. Josie tasted her beer. It was from the Echigo Brewery in Niigata, though the label bizarrely showed two bearded old men in Tyrolean hats drinking from curly drinking horns. But it was good, clean tasting and strong, and went perfectly with the curry.

As she ate she watched Mr Mori and Mr Shimizu.

Up until now she hadn't liked Mr Mori very much; his constant prying and endless questions had irritated her and his tendency to turn up and listen to a good part of your conversation before you'd realised he was there had led her to think of him as creepy, an impression reinforced by his hissing accent, that made him sound like an old time villain. But now he was with Mr Shimizu he was different. He chatted and laughed, and his guard seemed to drop so that he became ordinary and unthreatening.

They finished their curries and Mr Mori called for another round of beers. He sat back and contemplated Josie with what looked suspiciously like a twinkle in his eye.

'You sseem to be taking quite an interest in our dear departed Mr Ando,' he said. 'How much do you know about Ando Investments?'

'I know it's a bit, well, unusual. Not as big as people think it is.'

'That's right,' said Mr Mori, 'It's not as big as you might think. And its business is not quite as you might think either. Despite what Mr Wada would have you believe.'

'So is Mr Wada the business genius behind the company? Or was it Mr Ando who ran it? And who's going to take it over?'

'I think you'll find that whatever happens, it won't be Mr Wada who gets the company.'

'How can you be so sure?'

'Because I know how Ando Investments really workss. And Mr Wada doesn't.'

Mr Mori smiled, a satisfied smile with a hint of triumph in it that made Josie uneasy.

Mr Shimizu, too, looked nervous and touched Mr Mori's sleeve as though to warn him against saying any more.

Mr Mori took another draught of beer and signalled to the waiter for another round.

'Don't you think—' said Mr Shimizu hesitantly, but Mr Mori cut him off.

'I was always closer to Mr Ando than Mr Wada was. Who was it who went on the haiku trip with him? Not Mr Wada. Who used to ssit drinking beer with him here? Not Mr Wada.'

Josie's uneasiness grew. This was a side of Mr Mori she hadn't seen before. She turned to Mr Shimizu.

'Did you know Mr Ando too?'

'Yes, I often used to join the two of them for a beer. Mr Ando was a charming man. A little imprecise about details sometimes, but always a pleasure to spend time with.'

'Was he interested in books too?'

'Interested, yes,' Mr Mori cut in. 'Knowledgable, no.'

'I thought he used to have a bookshop himself. In Saitama,' said Josie.

'A neighbourhood bookshop selling romances and thrillerss,' said Mr Mori. 'With a big section for magazines at the front where all the local teenagers stood and read the magazines without buying them. No wonder he never made any money.'

'But I thought he was well off? That he set up Ando Investments with his own money?'

Mr Mori opened his mouth to give a cutting reply, but Mr Shimizu caught his eye and shook his head.

'Mr Ando came into some money,' Mr Shimizu said. 'That's how he could set up Ando Investments. Nobody knows the details.'

'Did it have anything to do with Matsuyama?'

'Ah, you are too quick,' said Mr Mori. 'It did have something to do with Matsuyama. Matsuyama, home of haiku and wealth.' He spilt some of his beer on the table and the waiter hurried across with a cloth to mop it up.

'Let me tell you about Mr Ando and Matsuyama,' Mr Mori went on, brushing aside Mr Shimizu's attempts to distract him. 'Mr Ando has been visiting Matsuyama for quite some time now. His visits are very disscreet. Sometimes he goes in order to write haiku. Sometimes he goes to visit the Dogo hot spring. Sometimes he goes to visit the Ishite temple. Sometimes he goes alone and sometimes with other people. But always he goes to Matsuyama.'

'Does he – did he – have some connection there? Family or something like that? Or business associates?'

'Not business. But family, yes. Mr Ando's mother came from Matsuyama, and when his father died she went back to Matsuyama. She died many yearss ago, but still Mr Ando goes on visiting Matsuyama.'

Josie was baffled. What was Mr Mori trying to tell her?

'Why did he go? And who knew about it?' she said.

'Yes, exactly, who knew?' said Mr Mori. 'Some of the people on our trip knew. Others did not know, but ssuspected. And some did not know and did not suspect.'

'So where does the bag come in? And why should anyone think that Jiro had it?'

Mr Mori pushed away his plate and stood up. Mr Shimizu stood up too, picking up the bill from the table.

'I have to go,' said Mr Mori. 'I can't ssay any more. I've said too much already.'

He walked unsteadily towards the door, with Mr Shimizu supporting him. Josie followed them, but once they got outside Mr Shimizu turned to her and said, 'I'll look after Mr Mori. Such a pleasure to meet you. Do please call in at my shop whenever you're in the area.'

He bowed, and he and Mr Mori headed off along the street away from the metro station.

THIRTEEN

'You want to do what?'

Ken stared at Josie across the desk. She tried to make her face look normal, as though what she had just suggested was perfectly reasonable if not downright ordinary.

'I want to get Mr Wada on his own and ask him what he was doing in Matsuyama the day Mr Ando died. And I want you to help me do it.'

'You do realise that being Ando Investments' client relationship officer means that it's my job to keep them happy? Make things easy for them and help them to get the assistance they need from AZT? Not go round accusing their directors of funny business possibly extending to murder.'

'I'm not going to accuse him of anything. I just want to ask him a perfectly reasonable question.'

'Your perfectly reasonable question could sink my promotion prospects.'

'I won't involve you. Nobody need know you had anything to do with it. I just need you to tip me off when Mr Wada's going to be here and I can get to talk to him. At the end of a meeting when everyone else has left, something like that.'

'You're mad.'

'Please, Ken. I really need to do this. You want to find out what happened to Mr Ando, don't you?'

'Mr Ando had an accident, that's what happened.'

'You know that's not true.'

Ken ran his hands through his hair in exasperation and then realised what he'd done and got out a comb and combed it flat again.

'Please,' said Josie. 'Just this once.'

Ken sighed and pulled up his diary on the laptop in front of him.

'We've got a regular meeting scheduled for this Thursday,' he said. 'My boss will be there, and if you do anything while he's in the room, I'll kill you. I'm not going to admit to having told you anything about it, but it's in standard meeting room seven and it's due to finish at eleven-thirty.'

'Bless you,' said Josie.

*

She didn't feel quite as confident when Thursday came and she found herself loitering in the corridor outside meeting room seven. What on earth was she going to say to Mr Wada? And what was there to stop him just brushing her off and walking out, or, even worse, complaining to her boss?

She jumped as a meeting room door opened, but it

was further down the corridor. A group of men came out talking among themselves and swept down the corridor to the lift, almost knocking her over as they went past. None of them apologised. They obviously thought she was just an office lady waiting to clear the empty cups and tidy the room ready for the next meeting. The usual unthinking sexism, but at least they'd given her an idea. She looked into the little kitchen area at the end of the corridor, which was mercifully empty, and grabbed a tray. Now she was as effectively hidden as if she had put on a cloak of invisibility – just an office lady at work.

The door of meeting room seven opened and a man Josie recognised as working in Client Relationship with Ken came out. Josie took a deep breath and walked confidently but deferentially into the room and started busying herself with the empty cups. She saw Ken's eyes widen at the sight of her, but then he studiously turned away. His boss was chatting amicably to Mr Wada. Both of them laughed and then Ken's boss looked round and spotted Josie.

'I have another meeting following straight on from this one so I hope you don't mind if the office lady shows you out,' he said. 'We'll see you again next month.'

'That's fine,' said Mr Wada, putting his papers into his briefcase and turning to Josie, who kept her head down and her back to Ken's boss. She put down her tray, opened the door and stood holding it open, bending her knees to disguise her height. Mr Wada went through without a glance at her, and Josie followed him out.

As they waited for the lift she decided to seize her chance.

'Actually, Mr Wada,' she said. 'I'm not the office lady. I'm Josie Clark – we met at Ando Investments, at the unveiling of the plaque to Mr Ando. Do you remember?'

'Of course I remember. How are you?'

'Fine, thanks. I've been hoping to get a chance to talk to you. I wanted to ask you something about Ando Investments, if you don't mind.'

Mr Wada's eyes narrowed warily but he nodded.

'We could go and sit in the lobby – there's plenty of room there and we won't be disturbed,' said Josie.

They took the lift to the ground floor. AZT had a entrance area of a size that befitted one of the largest insurance companies in Japan. Its airy openness was filled with the glow of the morning sun that made the cream leather sofas gleam and the glass tables, each bearing a small pot of purple orchids and a selection of that morning's papers, twinkle like jewels. It was almost deserted; there were just a couple of dark-suited visitors leafing though the papers as they waited to be collected and a uniformed delivery man handing over a parcel at the desk. Josie looked around and chose a couple of sofas facing each other in a quiet corner in the shadows, away from the bank of lifts. Mr Wada sat down on one sofa and Josie sat facing him.

'Well, Miss Clark,' he said with an attempt to appear relaxed that didn't fool Josie for a minute, 'I didn't expect to see you again so soon. I didn't realise you took such an interest in our little company's affairs.'

'I'm very interested,' said Josie. 'After all, wasn't that the point of our trip to Matsuyama? So we could all get to know each other and work more closely together?'

'Of course it was,' said Mr Wada. 'It's just unfortunate that the trip turned out the way it did. We all miss Mr Ando a great deal.'

'Yes. I didn't have much time to get to know him but he struck me as clever and sociable. Just the kind of person you want at the head of a company.'

Mr Wada nodded.

'Is there any news about who's going to take over?' said Josie.

'Not yet. But our board meets next week so there should be an announcement soon after. Is that what you wanted to ask me about?'

'Well, actually, it's more to do with the Matsuyama trip. You see, I knew when I saw you at the funeral that I'd seen you somewhere before but I couldn't think where it was. It wasn't until we met again at the unveiling that it came back to me. It was in Matsuyama. At the castle that day. I saw you in the castle grounds after Mr Ando fell.'

There was silence. Mr Wada looked at her with his eyes bulging, making him look even more like a pug than ever.

'What?' he said finally.

'I saw you at Matsuyama castle,' said Josie. 'And I

thought I'd ask you what you were doing there. And whether you know anything about what happened to Mr Ando's messenger bag. The one he had with him that day. It wasn't found at the castle after the accident.'

Mr Wada laughed, a short gruff laugh.

'You're mistaken,' he said. 'I wasn't in Matsuyama that day. I was in Tokyo. I had an important meeting that afternoon. I don't know anything about the bag.'

'But I saw you, and I've got a good memory for faces. You could easily have gone to Matsuyama that morning. It's not a long flight – easy to do in a day trip. Business people do it all the time.'

'Look here, Miss Clark. I think you should be very careful what you accuse people of.'

'I am being careful and I'm not accusing you of anything. I just asked you what you were doing there.'

Mr Wada licked his lips and glanced around. Nobody was within earshot. He stared at the purple orchid on the table as if it could help him decide how to answer. Josie stayed silent and waited. Mr Wada looked up and met her eyes.

'Well, actually, yes, I was there that day,' he said. 'It was perfectly innocent. Mr Ando asked me to come down to pick something up. He said you were all going to be at the castle in the morning and I should come and meet him there and he'd give it to me then.'

'What was he going to give you?'

'He didn't say.'

'But whatever it was, it was in the bag?'

'I suppose so. As you say, the bag can't be found.'

'What did you do when you realised Mr Ando had had an accident?'

'I thought, in the circumstances, it was better if I stayed out of things, so I just caught my flight back to Tokyo. It would only have complicated matters if I'd got involved and had to explain what I was doing there.'

'Does anyone else know that Mr Ando asked you to go down to Matsuyama?'

'No. It was confidential.'

'Alright,' said Josie. 'By the way, there's one other thing. Do you know anything about rare books?'

'No,' said Mr Wada loudly. 'I don't know anything about rare books. I'm an investment strategist, that's all. I don't have anything to do with the clients. I don't even know who they are. It's no good asking me about the books. I don't know anything.'

He stood up and almost ran for the exit. Josie let him go; she'd got what she wanted – Mr Wada's precipitate flight was rock-solid confirmation that she was onto something. Why else should he be so rattled by what should have been a perfectly innocent question? All he had to do was say no, but instead he'd suddenly gone into a complete panic. Why did he say it was no good asking him about *the* books? And what did Ando Investments' clients have to do with it? Josie wasn't sure, but the explanation that was forming in her mind was starting to feel more and more right, and it led straight back to Mr Ando's mysterious trips to Matsuyama and the missing bag.

*

Josie walked into Veloce and looked around, thinking at first that Jiro wasn't there. Then she spotted him, sat in a corner with his back to the door and his head turned away. She realised why when she sat down opposite him and put her glass of iced latte down on the table with a bump. He looked up, revealing a ripe black eye on the side of his face he'd been trying to hide.

'That looks painful,' said Josie, shrugging off her coat and putting it over the back of her chair. 'Whoever did that meant business. Do you have any idea who it could have been?'

'No, they jumped out at me from the side and hit me, hard. I fell down and put my hand up to my eye. I could feel it was bleeding and it hurt like hell. I couldn't think of anything else. I got the impression whoever it was had a scarf over their face, but that was all. They grabbed my keys from my jacket pocket and ran off. It was all over in less than a minute.'

'So what did you do then?'

'I looked for my phone to call for help, but they'd taken that too. So I headed for the nearest police station. It took hours to give a report and by the time I got home they'd been through everything.'

'How did you get into your flat?'

'The caretaker let me into the building, and went up to my flat with me with his spare key.'

Jiro took a sip of his tea, made a face and reached for a stick of sugar. He looked sick and sorry for himself. Just the moment to catch him off guard.

'Jiro, last time I talked to you, you told me a story about you and Yuko, but it wasn't true and you and I both know it. I want to know what really happened in Matsuyama, and what you did with the bag.'

Jiro opened his mouth to protest but Josie looked him in the eye and he sank back in his seat again.

'I should have known people would find out,' he said. 'If I'd realised this was going to happen I'd never have gone along with it.'

'Gone along with what?'

Jiro hesitated.

'If I tell you,' he said. 'You won't tell Yuko you got it from me, will you?'

'Of course not,' said Josie.

Jiro pushed his tea away and lit a cigarette. Josie wondered how deep his loyalty to Yuko ran – skin deep, probably, about as far as hers to him.

'Are you actually going out with Yuko, or is that just a story?' she said.

'We were going out. Sort of. I thought we were, anyway. I'm not sure that she did, any more. I never understood why she was interested in me, but then I realised she just wanted someone to do things for her and keep quiet about it.'

'She asked you to come to Matsuyama, didn't she?'

'Yes. She said there was something going on, something to do with the company, and she didn't want to be left out. She got herself on the trip and told me to come down after her but to stay out of sight. I didn't know what she'd planned. The last thing I expected was what happened to her father. She said she had nothing to do with it and I think I believe her, but sometimes I wonder. I mean, why did she ask me to go to Matsuyama in the first place?'

'So what happened the day Mr Ando was killed? What did you do?'

'I was hanging around at the castle, down by the gate, waiting to meet Yuko. She suddenly appeared, in a terrible rush, and gave me this leather bag. She'd had it hidden in her rucksack. She said there was something important inside. She said she'd found it and it was essential that nobody knew she had it. She told me to take it back to Tokyo and wait for her at the airport and give it to her there. So I took it and waited for her like she said.'

'So Yuko has it?'

'Er, no. I took it to Tokyo like she said. But then that guy who was on the trip came along and said Yuko couldn't be seen meeting me and that I should give him the bag and he'd give it to Yuko for me. I thought Yuko must have sent him. How else would he know about the bag? So I gave it to him.'

'What did Yuko say when you told her?'

'She was mad as anything. Said I was incompetent and she couldn't imagine why she'd picked me for a simple job that anyone with a basic modicum of intelligence could do. That was when I realised she wasn't interested in me at all – she was just using me, playing me along, and I'd fallen for it. After all, why would someone rich and pretty like her go out with an ordinary bank clerk like me? I was a fool to think she liked me.'

Jiro looked almost as if he might cry. Josie felt sorry for him, but not so sorry that she was going to sit there and commiserate. After all, he had been stupid enough to give the bag to 'the guy on the trip' so Yuko had some justification for her anger.

'This guy on the trip,' she said. 'Do you mean the little guy with the hissy Tokyo accent?'

'That's the one. If you're after the bag, he's the one you need to ask, not me. Tell that to whoever whacked me over the head and get them to lay off me.'

*

Back at the office Josie picked up the phone and rang Mr Mori's number. No wonder he had been so alarmed at what happened to Jiro. He must have known that whoever had searched Jiro's flat knew the bag wasn't there and would be back on the trail by now. And the trail led to Mr Mori. In fact, a lot of trails led to Mr Mori. He was obviously more in Mr Ando's confidence than anyone, and her visit to Jimbocho suggested that it was more than a coincidence that Ando Investments had a bookcase full of rare books and a lot of clients who knew more about books than the average financial investor. But what Josie couldn't make out was what Mr Ando's trips to Matsuyama were for. She just knew it had something to do with the books.

Mr Mori wasn't answering his phone. She tried ringing through to the finance section at Ando Investments. After a long delay someone answered and said Mr Mori wasn't in and they didn't know when he'd be back. They didn't sound very interested and Josie was afraid to push it any further. No sense in giving the impression she was desperate to talk to Mr Mori, even though she was. Instead she asked to be put through to Eriko.

Eriko's crisp voice answered the phone and Josie hesitated for a minute. Then she said, 'Hi Eriko, it's Josie. I hadn't heard from you and I wondered...'

'Oh, yes, Josie, I'm glad you called. I was just about to ring you as it happens. Are you free tomorrow? If you are, could you come to Yokohama? There's someone there I want you to meet.'

'Tomorrow's Saturday,' said Josie, wondering what she would say to Dave. 'Yes, alright, I can make some time then.'

'Good. I'll email you the address and instructions on how to get there. Would three o'clock suit you?'

'That's fine,' said Josie, feeling a lot less confident than she sounded. She wondered whether to ask Eriko if she knew where Mr Mori was, but something stopped her. After all, just because she couldn't get hold of him didn't mean there was anything wrong, and he wouldn't be very pleased if she raised a hue and cry and he was just off on some business of his own. She resolved to give it another twenty-four hours and then get hold of Mr Shimizu if Mr Mori hadn't turned up.

FOURTEEN

'So I thought today we could go down to Yokohama,' said Josie, trying to sound as if she'd just had a bright idea. 'There's plenty to do at the harbour and it's so nice to be by the sea. We could go round the Nippon Maru – it's a ship, fully rigged like the Cutty Sark, though not as old. And we could have a late lunch in Chinatown. It's the biggest Chinatown in Japan and the food's amazing.'

'Whatever you like,' said Dave, rolling over and almost kicking over the little table with Josie's laptop on it. 'Just come back to bed for a bit first. I've hardly seen you this week and now it's the weekend I expect to get your full attention. Starting now.'

Josie laughed and snuggled back under the covers with him. For a while she even stopped worrying about Ando Investments.

It was late morning before they finally got up. Josie started to bundle up the bedding to restore the room to some sort of order, but Dave stopped her.

'We're going to be out all day,' he said. 'And

when we get back we'll be going straight to bed. Leave it as it is.'

Josie hesitated.

'I'll just hang the duvet over the balcony to air,' she said. 'It's not going to rain today, and it needs freshening up.'

She went out onto the balcony, ashamed to see that all the balconies already had duvets hung over them, and many had washing hung out to dry as well. She felt an immediate twinge of guilt at being such a bad housekeeper. I'm getting Japanese standards, she thought. Back when I lived in a student house in London I never bothered about making the bed, and nor did anyone else.

She took her phone out of her pocket and tried Mr Mori's number. Still no reply. It just went straight to his voicemail and she'd left enough messages now asking him to call her back that there was no point in leaving any more. She was tempted to try ringing Shimizu's Books, but decided to wait a bit longer. Maybe Mr Mori would ring her back later in the day.

She closed the sliding window and joined Dave, who had taken a couple of cans of coffee out of the fridge. He handed her one and they drank them quickly before setting off for the station arm in arm.

'I can't believe it's only a couple of days to Christmas,' Josie said, looking up at the clear blue sky and bright sunshine. 'Are you looking forward to it?'

'Of course I am,' said Dave. 'Though I'm not looking forward to going back to Australia afterwards.'

'Let's not think about that. Let's just think of the good time we're going to have on Christmas Eve. I've booked us into this fabulous restaurant in Ginza. It's Italian, and they have a man with a guitar who comes round and sings Italian songs at the tables.'

'Is he Italian?'

'No, of course not. He's Japanese, but he gets the Italian flavour really well. And they put a red rose by your plate and serve Italian wine. It's so romantic.'

'Sounds it,' said Dave. 'Should I go down on one knee and propose?'

'You don't have to go that far,' said Josie, laughing, though she was surprised when Dave didn't laugh along with her. I hope he's not starting to feel bad about having to go back to Australia, Josie thought, feeling guilty that she hadn't spent every moment that he was in Japan with him. But she had to go to work – that couldn't be helped – and it was unlucky that this Matsuyama business had blown up just at the same time. She wondered if she should have put Mr Ando's death out of her mind while Dave was visiting, but how could she have done that? She was involved, whether she liked it or not. And Dave didn't want to hear about it, so it was better not to tell him too much. Like this trip to Yokohama. They could have a good time together and then she would just take half an hour or so to go and see Eriko and this mysterious person Eriko wanted her to meet. Dave would hardly notice she was gone. It would be fine.

They got to Yokohama at midday, and strolled down from Sakuragicho station to the harbour. Josie relished the fresh breeze that blew in from the ocean, carrying with it the salty scent of the sea. Across the sparkling water loomed the tower of the Yokohama Grand Intercontinental Hotel.

'There's a fabulous view from the top of the hotel,' Josie said. 'We could go up to the top and have cocktails, if you like.'

Dave looked at around at the happy crowds of tourists that thronged the park and the grassy roof of the Minato Museum.

'Maybe later,' he said. 'When it gets dark. Let's stay outside. There's a great view of the ship from here.'

They joined the crowd on the grass and sat staring out over the bay and the tall rigging of the Nippon Maru. Dave seemed pensive and Josie hesitated to mention her planned side trip to see Eriko. Maybe after lunch would be a good time. She surreptitiously checked her phone to see if she'd missed a call from Mr Mori. Nothing.

Dave seemed to look at her oddly as she put the phone away.

'I was just checking Keiko hadn't rung,' she said.

'Keiko,' said Dave. 'What made you think she was going to ring you?'

'Oh, I don't know. She sometimes does.'

'Did you two have a good time together the other night when I was out with Yoshi?'

'Yes, great, thanks. We watched a DVD. Takashi

Miike's latest.'

'Oh. What's it called?'

What's it called, thought Josie desperately. Keiko never mentioned that.

'Oh, I don't know. I didn't notice the title.'

Dave nodded as though what she'd said confirmed something. Josie felt uneasy but decided it was best not to go on digging herself deeper into a hole.

'Shall we head back into town and find somewhere for lunch?' she said.

Dave paused as though he'd meant to say something else. But then he grinned his usual grin and said, 'Yes, let's do that. You promised me the best Chinese food in Japan, so lead on.'

They headed back into town again, towards one of the colourful gates, lavishly decorated and topped with curvy gold tiles, that marked the entrances to Chinatown.

Josie glanced at Dave to see if he was impressed.

'Just like Chinatown in London,' he said.

'Except that in Japan the streets are clean and there aren't any drunk football fans,' said Josie.

'Whoa there! I'm not criticising Japan, you don't have to jump down my throat.'

'Sorry. Of course you weren't. And I miss London really. However much I feel comfortable in Tokyo, London's my home city and always will be.'

'So you think you might come back some day?' said Dave, with a note of hope in his voice.

'Someday,' said Josie, turning away so as not to see the light in his eyes die.

They walked on in awkward silence, peering at the *show window* displays outside the restaurants. A *show window* was a convenient feature of Japanese life; restaurants had hyper-realistic plastic models of their dishes made and displayed them in the window so you could decide what you liked before you went in. In a place like Yokohama, where non-Japanese-speaking foreign tourists were common, it was a necessity.

'That one,' said Dave suddenly. 'It's got whole crabs, look.'

'Crab it is,' said Josie, leading the way inside.

The restaurant was cool and dark after the brightness of the street. It was decorated in traditional Chinese style, with ornate red and gold panelling.

They were shown to a large round table with a metal plate in the middle that rotated when you pushed it. Josie ordered the crab set lunch with fried rice and stewed vegetables. She picked up her chopsticks; they weren't the short pointed Japanese chopsticks she was used to but the thicker, longer square-ended Chinese sort.

'I learned to use chopsticks in a Chinese restaurant in Beckenham with chopsticks just like these,' she said nostalgically. 'I tried to get my mum to go there, but she wouldn't touch foreign food. Said you couldn't be sure what was in it. She was fine with a good curry though.'

The waiter came back, piled the table high with dishes of crab and gave them each a pair of crackers and a finger bowl. They were silent for a while as they concentrated on extracting the juicy crab meat from the pile of crab legs in front of them.

When it was all gone Dave sat back and spread his arms out across the back of the booth.

'Now I need to relax,' he said. 'Somewhere with coffee.'

'There's a Starbucks just down the road. You can get a coffee and then I... I could just pop off and see a friend. She lives in Yokohama and she's always saying I should come and see her so I thought...'

'I'll come with you,' said Dave.

'Oh, no need for that. I'm literally just going to say hello. It won't take long. You have your coffee and take it easy.'

A look of pain crossed Dave's face.

'Josie,' he said urgently. 'Do you have to do this?'

'I'm only going to be gone for half an hour or so,' said Josie. 'Honestly, you'd think I was going to the North Pole.'

'You know what I mean.' Dave looked down at the table. 'You know what you're doing.'

'It's only half an hour,' said Josie, feeling uncomfortable but not knowing how to get out of it.

Dave slumped down in his seat.

'Do what you want,' he said dully. 'I know I can't stop you.'

Josie hesitated but then left him there. She could make it alright with him later. She just had to go and see Eriko now.

The address Eriko had given her was mercifully not far from the centre of town. It was in a concrete apartment block, probably dating from the 1980's, old by Japanese standards. The paving stones in the courtyard were uneven and there were children's toys scattered about and lines of nappies on the washing lines. It seemed like an odd place for Eriko to live. Josie would have figured her for a smart high rise with a gym in the basement. Maybe Ando Investments didn't pay as well as she'd thought.

She rang the bell and Eriko buzzed her in through the faded wooden doors into a lobby with a worn carpet that smelled of disinfectant. Josie got the lift to the seventh floor where Eriko was waiting in the corridor for her. She led the way into her apartment.

'Can I get you anything?' she said. 'Some tea?'

'That would be great, thanks,' said Josie, looking around the flat in surprise. It wasn't much bigger than Josie's, though there was a door that looked like it led to a separate bedroom. It was sparsely furnished with well-worn furniture and there were some children's toys on a shelf and a glittery mobile hanging at the window. Pinned to a cork board were a collection of children's drawings. Eriko saw her looking at them.

'My son did those,' she said.

'I didn't know you were married,' said Josie unthinkingly.

'I'm not.'

Josie was taken aback. She knew about the strict Japanese attitude to having children outside marriage. If girls got pregnant they had abortions; they didn't bring up children by themselves. She'd never imagined Eriko to be the sort of woman who would defy convention like this. She seemed far too organised and ambitious to do anything that might impede her career, and simply having a child could put an end to a woman's advancement in Japan, let alone being a single mother.

'No one at Ando Investments knows. I've told everyone here that I'm a widow, otherwise I would never have got this flat.'

'Of course I won't say anything,' said Josie. 'Where's your little boy now?'

'He's asleep in the bedroom. He's the person I wanted you to meet.'

Eriko went into the tiny kitchen to make the tea.

Josie sat down and studied the room. There were some children's picture books, a big television and an iPod dock next to it. Out on the balcony were some geraniums, still in flower even this late in December, and a couple of duvets hanging over the rail to air. Just a normal flat where normal people lived. So why did it make Josie uneasy? Maybe it was just that it wasn't what she'd expected, not the kind of place she'd imagined Eriko would live in. Though, if she had a child, her life must be very different to the life Josie had thought she lived. No it was something else. It was that Eriko had a whole side to her life that Josie knew nothing about. And that it included a man that Josie knew nothing about as well.

Eriko came back with a pot of green tea and two cups. She poured out the tea, passed Josie a cup and sat down on a sagging armchair.

'It's good of you to come all this way,' she said.

'No problem. I was coming to Yokohama anyway.'

'Not many people know about Hiroshi. In fact, nobody knows. The people round here don't know where I work and anyway, they mind their own business. I prefer it that way.'

'What happens to Hiroshi while you're at work?'

'One of the women in this block takes care of him for me. She has a couple of kids of her own.'

'What about when you were away in Matsuyama?'

'I managed to make some arrangements. Does it matter?'

'No, of course not. I'm sorry,' said Josie, trying to find a tactful way to ask about who Hiroshi's father was, but not succeeding. She wondered if it was anyone she knew. For an awful moment she thought it might be Mr Wada and then started hoping desperately that it wasn't.

'I asked you to come here because of what happened in Matsuyama,' said Eriko. 'And to tell you about Hiroshi.'

'Yes,' said Josie. 'Go on.'

Eriko didn't reply straight away. Instead she stood up and walked to the window and stood looking out. With her back still turned to Josie she said, 'How much do you know about Mr Ando?'

'Mr Ando? Not very much. I'd never met him before the Matsuyama tour. He seemed like an interesting person, I'd have liked to have got to know him better. I know he used to run a bookshop in Saitama before he started Ando Investments.'

'What about his wife?'

'His wife? Only that they've been married a long time and Yuko's their only daughter. Mrs Ando didn't make a huge impression on me in Matsuyama, to be honest.' Josie carefully failed to mention that she'd met Mrs Ando since then. Somehow she felt that wouldn't go down well.

Josie's answer seemed to please Eriko.

'You're right,' she said 'Mr Ando was very special. His wife's completely different. She's cold, unfeeling and obstinate. She's been a complete drag on him since he became successful.'

'I don't think she enjoys the change success has brought,' said Josie. 'Aoyama and the money. It doesn't appeal to her very much. It suits Yuko though.'

'Yes, it suits Yuko. Yuko would be very upset if the money dried up.'

'Is it going to dry up? Now Mr Ando's dead, I mean.'

'It could. It depends what happens about Ando Investments. Whether it can keep going or not.'

'Surely it's in safe hands with Mr Wada? They say it's his investment strategy that made it successful in the first place.'

Eriko laughed.

'There's a lot more to Ando Investments than you think,' she said. 'It can't last long without Mr Ando, not the way it works at the moment.'

'So how does it work at the moment? Does it have something to do with the books?'

'What do you know about the books?'

'I know Mr Ando was interested in rare books, and that a lot of his clients were too. Is that what keeps Ando Investments going? Mr Ando's book collecting friends?'

'Yes,' said Eriko. 'You could say that.'

'But it's not the whole story?'

'No, it's not the whole story. But it's enough.'

'So why did you ask me to come today?' said Josie, tiring of Eriko's air of mystery.

'You asked me on the phone if I'd seen Mr Ando's bag. Well, I haven't. But somebody's got it and it's vitally important that it's found.'

'There's something special in it, isn't there? Something valuable.'

'Something very valuable. Something worth more than the whole of Ando Investments. Whoever gets hold of it can live in luxury for the rest of their lives.'

'How do you know about it?'

Eriko paused.

'Mr Ando told me,' she said, in an unnaturally firm voice. 'The night before he died.'

'Was that why you wrote that haiku? The one that caused all the trouble at the haiku session?'

'That's right. I wanted to warn Mr Ando, but it backfired.'

'Warn him of what?'

'Warn him that someone was after the bag. That's why he kept it with him when we went to the castle. To keep it safe.'

'Mr Wada said Mr Ando had asked him to come

down to Matsuyama to pick up something important. Was that whatever was in the bag?'

'Did he? Well, he was too late. Someone got their hands on the bag when Mr Ando had his accident.'

'You still think it was an accident then?'

'I don't want to think of the alternative. But I need to find the bag. Mr Ando promised it to me. He said if anything happened to him, I was to have it.'

'When did he say that?'

'What does it matter when he said it?' said Eriko. 'Why do you always have to know when things happen? Don't you believe me?'

'Of course I believe you,' said Josie, privately wondering whether she did or not. Eriko seemed to share a talent for histrionics with her arch-rival, Yuko.

Eriko seemed to sense Josie's doubt. She came and sat down beside her and looked her in the face, challenging Josie to look away.

'You have to believe me,' she said. 'Even though you don't want to. And I have to trust you, even though I don't want to.' She paused. Then she stood up and said, 'Come and see my little boy.'

She led the way to the bedroom and opened the door. Josie followed her and peered in. Asleep in bed with the covers thrown back and his arm around a Miffy toy was a little boy of about three years old. His black hair was ruffled and Eriko reached down and smoothed it before tiptoeing out of the room and softly closing the door.

'Hiroshi means everything to me,' she said. 'And I'm all he's got now. That's why I need to find the bag. Mr Ando promised it to me. It's for Hiroshi's future.'

Josie felt a penny slowly begin to drop. Hiroshi; that was Mr Ando's first name, she'd seen it on the plaque. And there was no sign of a boyfriend or anyone else living in the flat. How stupid she'd been!

'Mr Ando is Hiroshi's father, isn't he?' she said, and Eriko nodded.

'So you can see now why I have to find the bag. And why you have to help me.'

'Eriko,' said Josie. 'Just tell me. What's in the bag?'

'A book. A rare book. So rare that nobody even knows it exists.'

FIFTEEN

Josie hurried back to meet Dave, her head in a whirl. If Mr Ando had a son with Eriko, all the relationships she'd thought she understood were different. If Mrs Ando knew – she cursed herself for being so stunned by Eriko's announcement that she failed to ask this basic question – then she had a motive to kill her husband. A very strong motive. And so did Yuko. No wonder Yuko had been so keen for Josie to ask awkward questions about what had happened to Mr Ando's bag. She needed to get to it before Eriko. But Mr Mori had got there before either of them. And what had happened to him? Josie felt cold at the thought of all the time she'd wasted ringing him up and getting no reply. She should have tried to find him right away. Now it could be too late.

She continued to worry about Mr Mori all the way back to the Starbucks down the road from the restaurant where she'd left Dave. She felt as though hours had passed since she'd left him there, though when she looked at her watch she saw it had been not much more than three quarters of an hour. She didn't know what to say to Dave about her visit to Eriko. It would be hard to pretend that it had just been a lighthearted visit to a girlfriend as she had suggested, but on the other hand she didn't feel up to confessing to Dave what her real motives had been and how things had turned out. Fortunately he didn't ask her anything about it, just picked up his rucksack and followed her back to Sakuragicho station.

They sat in silence on the train back to Tokyo, each wrapped up in their own thoughts. Josie's mind bounced from Mrs Ando to Yuko to Eriko and back again. What was the real situation between them? Had Eriko been telling the truth about her relationship with Mr Ando? Presumably – Josie couldn't think why she should lie about it. How far would Yuko go to get her hands on the book? Surely she didn't care so much about money that she'd push her own father off a veranda to get more of it. And Mrs Ando – what did she know, and what might she have done about it? She was a strong determined woman, quite capable of taking matters into her own hands if she felt the situation justified it.

After a while it occurred to Josie that Dave had been unnaturally quiet. It wasn't like him to be so gloomy.

'Is anything the matter?' she said. 'Did the crab disagree with you?'

'Nothing disagrees with me, not even goat curry. You know that.'

'So what is it then?'

Dave looked at her intently.

'You mean you can't guess?'

'You're not cross because I went off to see my friend and left you on your own?'

'No, I'm not cross, as you put it, about that. I'm fed up with you telling me stupid lies and thinking I'm not going to catch you out.'

'Oh,' said Josie. 'That.'

'Yes, that,' said Dave savagely.

'Okay, I know I haven't been very open with you about it, but you were so down on me about asking questions about this Matsuyama thing that I thought it was better not to mention it. It was Eriko I went to see this afternoon. You know, Mr Ando's assistant.'

'Don't give me that,' said Dave. 'You can't expect me to believe you're still obsessing about that stupid trip and whether that guy fell or was pushed. And even if you are, why would you lie to me about it?'

'Well...' said Josie, thrown off balance by his unexpected response.

'Josie, stop trying to distract me. You know what this is all about.'

Josie's mind went blank. If this wasn't about Matsuyama, then what was it about? Seeing her face, Dave grimaced and said, 'Who is it you know who lives in Yokohama? Someone you know well, see all the time, see too much of in my opinion.'

Josie thought hard.

'You surely don't mean Ken?' she said.

'Yes, I do mean Ken. You went off to see him this afternoon, didn't you? You got me down to

Yokohama on some stupid pretext just so you could slope off and spend some time with him. God knows what you were doing.'

'How can you think that?' said Josie. 'I wouldn't do that to you. What sort of person do you think I am?'

'I don't know what sort of person you are any more. We hardly ever see each other. I thought things were fine when you came over to Australia, but I suppose that was just because you didn't have any other distractions around. But since I've come to Japan I've felt like you don't have time for me any more. You're always at work or saying you're with Keiko when I know full well you're not. That night you sent me off with Yoshi, what was that all about? I rang Keiko and asked to speak to you and she gave some pathetic excuse that didn't fool me for a moment. You were off somewhere seeing Ken, weren't you? I wouldn't mind so much if you didn't lie to me about it and expect me to believe you. You must take me for a fool.'

'Whoa, where did this all come from?' said Josie, feeling her face get red as the anger rose up inside her. 'How long have you been thinking this? Going round suspecting me and not saying anything? What kind of relationship do you think this is? If you've got issues, I expect you to tell me about them, not sulk in a corner like some six year old.'

'You're a fine one to talk about six year olds, when you've been telling me stupid lies and expecting me to fall for it.'

'Look, Dave, once and for all, I am not seeing Ken. Alright?'

'No, it's not alright. You need to grow up. I'm not some toy you can pick up when it suits you and forget about when there's something more interesting going on. Take me seriously or forget about me. It's your choice.'

Josie sat in silence, too stunned to reply. She'd known Dave was prone to jealousy – there'd been one or two incidents when they were at uni that had taught her that – but this accusation was so bizarre, so unrelated to anything in the real world, that she just couldn't deal with it.

As she sat there, their train drew into Tokyo station. Dave got up.

'You think about it,' he said. 'And let me know when you're ready to be honest with me. Because, until you are, I don't see any point in us talking any more.'

He grabbed his coat from the rack and put it on.

'Where are you going? What about Christmas Eve?' Josie called after him, but he just shouldered his way through the line of people waiting patiently to get off the train and disappeared into the night.

He's mad, thought Josie. He's gone completely off his trolley. Me and Ken? How could he! If that's what he thinks, let him go. He'll come back when he's come to his senses.

She got off the train and wondered what to do. She didn't feel like going back to her empty flat where the bed they had left unmade that morning would mock her with its promise of good times lost. She thought angrily of the way Dave had dismissed her investigations into Mr Ando's death as too trivial to serve as an explanation for her absences. It's not trivial, she thought. It's important and nobody else is troubling themselves over it, so I've got to. And if I find out what really happened down in Matsuyama then Dave will have to admit he was wrong.

She left the station and wandered along the street, not knowing where she was headed, her mind seething, until she realised she'd walked nearly to Yurakucho station. The tall, knife-shaped silhouette of the International Forum rose up in front of her and she went into the paved tree-lined courtyard that separated the two halves of the building and sat down on a bench under the trees to think.

It was beginning to seem that everyone on the haiku tour had known what was in the bag and why it mattered. Everyone except Josie. But now she was beginning to understand. Mr Ando went to Matsuyama regularly, so Mr Mori had said, and Josie was pretty sure he went there to pick up rare books. Then when he got them back to Tokyo they were sold, to secretive collectors who didn't want anyone to know what they were doing. How would that work? Through Ando Investments, of course. Ando Investments' clients weren't ordinary investors at all – they were rare book collectors paying for the books Mr Ando supplied. Ando Investments' whole investment strategy was a sham; they made their profits from books, they just couldn't admit it.

But where did Mr Ando get the books, and why were they shrouded in such secrecy? And, if the investment strategy was fake, surely Mr Wada must have been in on the deception. He could hardly have been duped by Mr Ando into thinking the profits really were the result of his canny investments. Was that why he'd gone down to Matsuyama? Because he knew about the book?

Josie couldn't work it out. She wondered whether to go and see Mr Tanaka. He could always help her see her problems clearly and work out what to do. But she hesitated. If she went to Mr Tanaka, she knew she'd end up telling him what had happened with Dave, and she didn't want to do that. Besides, there was only one person who she was sure could make sense of it all for her – Mr Mori. But he had vanished. She got out her phone and tried his number again, though she knew it was pointless. He wasn't answering.

It was chilly on her bench. Now the sun had gone down and a chill wind had sprung up it felt wintry. People hurrying past were wearing padded coats and scarves and Josie regretted having gone out into the sunshine so uncaringly that morning in a light coat. She felt in her pocket for gloves, but there was nothing there except the receipt for lunch from the Chinese restaurant.

She looked up the website of Shimizu's Books on her phone and got the number, but when she tried it there was no reply. She'd left it too late; Mr Shimizu had left for the night. There was nothing to do but wait until morning and contact him then. She'd go out to Jimbocho and see him, that was best. If anybody knew where Mr Mori was, he did. She tried not to let the growing sense of fear take over. She would find Mr Mori. He would explain everything. Dave would come back. It would all be alright.

*

She slept badly, haunted by dreams of Eriko and Dave together in Eriko's flat in Yokohama, laughing at her, and of Mr Mori behind a sheet of glass mouthing some words to her that she couldn't understand. It was a relief to wake up to a grey, cloudy day and eat a solitary breakfast with the bedding neatly stowed away.

She wondered where Dave had spent the night and what he was doing with himself this morning. She wanted to ring him but was too proud to make the first move. Besides, she had something to do today and she didn't need Dave's help to do it.

She wanted to set out for Jimbocho first thing, but she knew the shops there were not likely to open much before eleven on a Sunday. She tried Shimizu's Books' number but, as she expected, there was no reply. She filled in time, going out to the convenience store on the corner to buy milk and canned coffee and a bacon-and-egg Danish pastry for breakfast. She ate slowly with her eyes on the television, not taking in anything it said. At last it was time to go; she put the empty coffee can in the recycling bin and shrugged on her padded coat, checking that her gloves were in the pocket. She didn't intend to end up freezing like she had the night before.

Jimbocho was quiet when she got there, with that Sunday morning quietness that's the same in cities the world over. The bare trees that lined the Yasukuni Dori stood like sentinels and cars drove past slowly, their drivers' faces relaxed, not tense as they would be on a weekday. A group of young men, heading for one of the secondhand magazine shops by the look of them, came out of Family Mart with cans of hot coffee and walked down one of the side streets to drink their coffee and smoke out of the wind.

Josie looked down towards Shimizu's Books. The bargain bins outside were in place, which meant it was open, but there didn't seem to be any customers as yet, and the interior was dark as though not fully ready for business. Josie pushed open the glass door, relieved to find it unlocked, and walked in through the tall shelves to the little desk at the back.

Mr Shimizu was nowhere to be seen. Instead an elderly woman with grey streaks in her hair sat in his place, reading the Sunday paper. She glanced up briefly at Josie and went back to her paper.

'Er,' said Josie, wondering how to begin.

The woman turned the page of her paper. *Man on Death Row gets Reprieve after Fifteen Years*, said the headline.

'Er,' said Josie again, a bit louder this time.

The woman looked up at her.

'All the books are on the shelves,' she said.

'Fiction this side, non-fiction that side, alphabetical order of author's name. Large books on the shelves at the back. If you're looking for something special you can ask.'

'No,' said Josie. 'It's not about a book. Actually, I was looking for Mr Shimizu.'

'He's not here today.'

Josie's heart sank.

'Do you know where I could find him?'

The woman looked doubtful.

'Please, it's important. It's not about books. It's a personal matter. Look, I work for an insurance company.'

Josie got out her AZT business card and handed it over. The woman studied it intently and then grudgingly picked up the phone.

'Mr Shimizu's coming,' she said after a short conversation.

'Thanks,' said Josie. 'I'll wait outside.'

The street was beginning to come to life now. Other shops were opening up and more customers were appearing, to riffle through the dump bins or vanish into the dark interiors. Josie walked up and down, feeling the chill of the morning air but not wanting to wait inside the shop with the taciturn old woman. After ten minutes of this, to her relief, she saw Mr Shimizu hurrying down the street towards her.

'Mr Shimizu,' she called. 'It's Josie Clark. We met the other day, with Mr Mori.'

'The foreign girl, isn't it?' said Mr Shimizu. 'I

remember you.'

'I was trying to get hold of Mr Mori but he's not answering his phone and nobody seems to know where he is. I thought you might be able to help.'

'Mr Mori goes his own way. He isn't answerable to me.'

'Yes, I understand that. But this is different. He hasn't been seen for several days, not even at his office, and he's not answering his phone. I'm worried something's happened to him.'

'Why should something have happened to him?'

'Mr Mori has a bag. It belonged to Mr Ando and it went missing down in Matsuyama. A lot of people are looking for it and I'm afraid, if they've found out that Mr Mori has it, he may be in danger.'

'What's in this bag?'

'A rare book. A very valuable rare book. Valuable enough to kill for.'

Mr Shimizu got out an ancient mobile phone with a cracked screen and scrolled through a short list of numbers till he found the one he wanted. Josie could hear it ringing unanswered.

'You see?' she said. 'He's not answering his phone and no one has seen him. I'm really worried. Please can you give me his address?'

'He doesn't live far from here. It's strange that he doesn't reply – he always picks up for me, whatever he's doing. Maybe we should go round there now and see if he's there.'

Josie felt a wave of relief flood over her. She suddenly felt convinced that, if they went to Mr

Mori's flat, they would find him there and there would be a simple reason for his not answering his phone. It would all be alright.

Mr Shimizu set off down the side street where the craft beer hall was. He walked past it to the next corner where he turned left and headed up a long street that stretched away into the distance. It was quiet except for the sound of birdsong and the distant revving of a motorcycle engine. There was a tang of pine needles in the air, reminding Josie painfully that it was Christmas Eve, and she still hadn't heard from Dave after their quarrel the night before. She wondered if the dull ache in her chest was to do with that or the returning fear that something terrible had happened to Mr Mori. Perhaps it was both. At any rate, her life, which had been going so well only a few days ago, was now in tatters, and she had to admit she had only herself to blame. Why hadn't she been open with Dave about what she was up to, instead of all that stupid secrecy that made him think she was carrying on behind his back with Ken? It wouldn't have hurt her to have come clean, even if he hadn't been keen on her trying to find out about Mr Ando. Now everything had gone wrong and she didn't know how to put it right.

She hurried to catch up with Mr Shimizu, who moved surprisingly fast for a man of his age. It was a good thing she did, as he suddenly turned and dived down a little narrow side street. The new glass skyscrapers gave way to the tiny crowded buildings of old Japan – a little traditional restaurant, closed and shuttered, a grocer's selling a few green vegetables in boxes, a ramen house with a sign for mah jong in the window above. Mr Shimizu passed them without pausing but stopped when he reached an anonymous-looking concrete building with an ancient air conditioning unit screwed precariously to the front wall.

'Mr Mori's flat is just down the street,' he said. 'But I want to call in here first. It's…it's, ah, it's a sort of annexe for Shimizu's Books. It's just possible that Mr Mori is here.'

He fumbled in his pocket and got out a jingly set of keys. Choosing one, he inserted it with difficulty into the faded door. There was a small window next to the door but the blind inside it was down and, from the number of spiders diligently building their webs across it, had been that way for some time. Mr Shimizu had to give the door a good push to move it and it slid open with a rattling noise which sounded like gunfire in the quiet Sunday morning street. It was dark inside and the air smelled musty.

Josie followed Mr Shimizu down a long shadowy passageway, vaguely aware of tall bookshelves on either side of her. At the end Mr Shimizu fumbled for a light switch and clicked on a light. Its dim glow showed a book-lined passage ahead of them and another off to the side.

'Mr Mori,' called Mr Shimizu, but there was no reply.

Mr Shimizu walked down the side passage and Josie followed him, curious to see what was there.

She found that what she had taken for a passage was one side of a large room with six or seven tall bookshelves running right across it at intervals that just left enough room for one person to walk between them. It must extend along the back of the other buildings on the street, as it was far wider than the narrow frontage Josie had seen as they came in. Mr Shimizu walked methodically to the end of each bookshelf, peered into the far recesses and then went around the end, back up the other side to the passage where Josie stood and did the same with the next one.

'It's a bit of a rabbit warren, I'm afraid,' he said when he'd finished them all. 'We use it to store our excess stock. And Mr Mori keeps some books here sometimes.'

'His "resting doves"?' said Josie.

'That's right. That's why I thought he might be here, but I was wrong. Not unless he's in the office.'

He opened a creaky door to reveal a square room with a desk and chair. There was nobody there and the dust on the desk suggested it hadn't been disturbed in months.

'I hardly ever come here,' said Mr Shimizu. 'I don't move the stock very often. Business isn't that good at the moment.'

He closed the door again, returning the office to its dusty stillness. Josie walked down the side passage and peered down at the rows of books. The dim light didn't reach right to the end of the shelves and some trick of the light made her imagine that something moved in the gloom. Something small and scrabbly.

'Watch out for the mice,' said Mr Shimizu. 'I try to keep them out but it's a losing battle.'

Josie hurried after him, back to the door and the comforting daylight, hoping that when he said mice he meant mice and not something larger.

Mr Shimizu locked the door again, a worried expression on his face. They walked further along the narrow street but passed no one. Most of the little shops and restaurants still had their shutters up. They could have been a million miles from the clean modernity of the Yasukuni Dori.

'Down there,' said Mr Shimizu. 'In that block of flats with the glass doors. That's where Mr Mori lives.'

Josie stared down the street towards the block, an old brick building that had clearly seen better days. Mr Shimizu was walking more slowly now as though reluctant to arrive and confront whatever was waiting for them in Mr Mori's flat.

'How are we going to get in?' said Josie.

'I have a spare key. Mr Mori left it with me so I could feed his cat when he was away.'

'Mr Mori has a cat?' said Josie.

'You didn't think Mr Mori cared for anything, did you?' said Mr Shimizu, and Josie felt guilty that he had guessed what she was thinking. 'But he cared for his cat. She was a street cat, a kitten from an abandoned litter, but the others all died. She was a skinny little thing and she used to hang around my shop looking for scraps. Mr Mori took a liking to her and took her in. That was a good few years ago now.'

Mr Shimizu pushed open the worn door into the small block of flats. The wind whistled down its concrete corridors, open to the air, and the ancient lift clanked towards them when Mr Shimizu pressed the button as though on its last legs. There was just room for two of them inside it and it took an age to stagger up to the fifth floor with them on board.

Mr Shimizu led the way down the chilly corridor to a door at the end. He knocked and called Mr Mori's name. There was no reply from inside, and no sign of life from any of the neighbouring flats. Mr Shimizu grunted and fished out his bunch of keys again. He selected the biggest and oldest key and inserted it in the lock.

He had to give the door a hearty shove to get it open. The room beyond was in darkness and smelled of old books and neglect. Mr Shimizu called Mr Mori's name again. There was no reply, but this time they could hear a faint mewing coming from behind a closed door.

Mr Shimizu looked at Josie. She nodded and, summoning up her courage, stepped inside the flat.

SIXTEEN

It took a few moments for Josie's eyes to get used to the dark. The curtains were drawn but they were old, a faded shade of green, and some light filtered through, giving the room a feel of being underwater. The ancient kitchenette was clean and tidy, the sink empty and dry, pots and pans stowed out of sight and china neatly stacked in a glass-fronted cupboard. But the living room beyond was a different story. It had been ransacked.

Mr Mori had clearly been an avid book collector. The room was lined with bookshelves and a reading lamp conveniently placed next to a cosy chair spoke of evenings spent poring over first editions. But someone had shattered the peace of the room, hurling books down from the shelves and kicking a footstool out of the way so that it lay overturned on the faded rug.

Josie picked up a book from where it had fallen under the chair. She tried to straighten its bent pages but when she closed it she saw its spine had cracked under the force with which it had been thrown. It seemed to be an old children's book, with colour illustrations of little girls in kimonos and boys in sailor suits.

Mr Shimizu was riffling helplessly through the books scattered around the room.

'I remember this one,' he said, picking up a book and lovingly restoring its torn paper cover. 'Mr Mori bought this from me years ago, not long after we first met. It's not particularly rare but he was fond of the author. He was putting together a collection of his complete works. He only needed two more. They would have been worth much more as a set.'

He put the book back on one of the now-empty shelves, where it sat forlornly, and started poking about among the chaotic piles, looking for its companions.

Neither Josie nor Mr Shimizu mentioned the closed door which must lead to the bedroom, although the mewing they had heard when they first opened the front door was coming from there and was getting louder and more frantic. They were both mesmerised by the destruction spread out before them and the terrible tale it told. But finally Josie straightened up and made her way across the room, stepping carefully over the strewn books, took hold of the door handle and turned it. As she pushed the door open a ball of tabby fur hurtled past her and out the main door into the fresh air. Josie felt inclined to follow it as the smell that came out of the closed-up room told its own story.

She looked round at Mr Shimizu who nodded to her to go in. She didn't much want to, but it was what they had come for and it was better to get it over with.

The bedroom, like the living room, was in chaos. The only difference was that there were fewer books so the sense of a whirlwind having passed through was lessened. Again the curtains were drawn, and the darkness had a sinister air, a foreboding sense that it hid what they had come to find. There was an old-fashioned wardrobe along one wall which had been opened up and the clothes flung on the floor. Underneath them Josie could make out the outline of a futon with a bean-bag pillow and a duvet roughly pulled up over the shape of a body. Even in the darkness Josie knew that the stains on it must be bloodstains.

Gingerly she reached out and twitched back a corner of the duvet. Mr Mori lay underneath, one side of his head a dark shapeless mass. Josie dropped the duvet and turned away. Mr Shimizu had already retreated back to the living room where he stood twisting his hands together with an expression of anguish on his face.

'What shall we do?' he said as Josie came out of the bedroom, closing the door carefully behind her.

'Ring the police,' she said. 'It's for them to deal with now, not us.'

Mr Shimizu nodded.

'What about the books?' he said.

'We shouldn't touch anything. It needs to be exactly as it was when we came in.'

They both looked at the book Mr Shimizu had put back on the bookshelf, solitary and accusing. Slowly Mr Shimizu reached out and dropped it back onto the chaotic pile on the floor.

'Do you think they found what they were looking for?' he said.

'I can't tell,' said Josie. 'But I somehow suspect not. Mr Mori knew they were likely to come looking. I don't imagine he left it lying around for them to find. I think he hid it somewhere else, but I don't know how we're going to find out where. Perhaps we never will.'

They tiptoed out and closed the front door behind them. Mr Shimizu leaned against it and took great gulps of fresh air. It must be awful for him, Josie thought, to find his friend dead and his books in such chaos. I wonder what will happen to it all now? Did Mr Mori have any relatives to leave all this to or will it just be thrown out like worthless junk? And what about the flat and that poor cat? What's going to happen to her?

She looked around and spotted a huddled shape in the far corner of the balcony.

'Poor thing,' said Josie. 'She must be starving. Goodness knows how long she's been locked up in there.'

'I can't take her,' said Mr Shimizu. 'She'll have to fend for herself, or find someone to take her in like Mr Mori did.'

Josie looked at the pathetic frightened animal.

'What's her name?' she said.

'Rin. It's a pretty name isn't it? She's a pretty cat and good natured too.'

'Rin,' said Josie. As she spoke the cat looked up at her and mewed piteously.

Josie bent down and stretched out her hand. Rin sniffed it gingerly. Josie wished she had something to give the poor starved cat but all she had was a bottle of Evian water. She poured some into her hand and held it out. Rin lapped it up gratefully and allowed Josie to stroke her head and then to pick her up.

'I'll take her with me,' she said. 'Will you ring the police and tell them about Mr Mori? Here's my number if they need to get hold of me.'

Mr Shimizu took her proffered card and nodded, then waited while she tucked the cowering cat inside her jacket and got back in the clanking lift. As the lift began its descent she saw him pull his mobile phone out of his pocket and begin to tap out a number.

She walked back to Jimbocho station as quickly as she could. Fortunately Rin seemed to have settled down in the warmth of her coat and kept calm and quiet until Josie got back to her own flat again. Josie put a bowl of water on the floor, which the cat lapped up, and then hurried out to the convenience store to buy cat food and a bag of cat litter. Rin greeted her enthusiastically when she got back and gobbled down two tins in rapid succession.

Josie made herself a cup of tea and sat on the sofa, where Rin came to join her.

'You were pretty hungry, weren't you?' said Josie, rubbing Rin's ear as the cat purred. 'You'd been locked up in that flat with no food for quite a time.'

She thought back. She'd tried to get hold of Mr Mori on Friday, but they said he hadn't been into work that day. That suggested he might have been dead since Thursday night. Josie had spoken to Mr Wada on Friday and to Eriko on Saturday. Neither of them seemed to be hiding a guilty secret, but then, if you were a double murderer you'd presumably got past the stage where you gave yourself away by your agitated behaviour.

Yuko hadn't been in touch for a while, but then, after Jiro had confessed about the book, she probably didn't think there was much point. And Yuko had known from the start that Mr Mori had the bag. As for Mrs Ando... Josie had no idea what, if anything, she knew.

Josie suddenly felt very tired. Rin had curled up on her lap and gone to sleep, and Josie lay back too and let her mind wander over the events of the weekend. It had all been rather too much. First the fun of the trip to Yokohama with Dave, then the strange interview with Eriko and Dave's unexpected outburst. And now finding Mr Mori's body. She tried not to think about that, although she knew the image of his battered head would haunt her for the rest of her days. Who could have done such a thing? Mr Mori was sly and morally dubious, but he'd never done any real harm and he certainly wouldn't hurt a fly. Who could be so desperate for money that they would do that to a harmless old man?

And what exactly had they been looking for? A

rare book, Josie knew that much. What was it, and where could it be now? It was the key to everything, and she was pretty sure that the murderer was still out there looking for it. Who else might they kill in order to get it?

The room was warm and Rin's weight on her lap was oddly comforting. Josie found herself drifting off to sleep, to dream confused dreams of monsters with knives pursuing her though darkened rooms as Mr Shimizu struggled after her with a dozen cats in his arms and Dave called to her from somewhere very far away that she couldn't reach.

When she woke it was late afternoon and the sun was low in the sky. Rin had settled herself in a furry ball in the corner of the sofa and just purred briefly when Josie stroked her. Josie put some more food in her bowl and opened the sliding door to the balcony a sliver so Rin could get out to her litter tray, then picked up her phone and tapped Yuko's number. When Yuko answered, Josie said,

'Are you at home?'

'Yes, why? What's this about?'

'I'm coming over to see you – I want to talk to you about your father. And this time I don't want you telling me any more of your stories. I want the truth.'

There was silence at the end of the phone. Then Yuko said, 'Okay, I'll be here.'

Josie slipped on her coat and went out quietly so as not to disturb Rin. On the train she texted Dave: *So sorry about what happened yesterday. I can explain everything if you come to the restaurant tonight.*

Don't make me spend another Christmas Eve alone. Love Josie. She added the directions to get to the restaurant and sent it off.

Yuko was waiting for her when she arrived at the house in Aoyama and let her in straight away. In the failing light the spare elegance of the room was cold and unwelcoming; even when Yuko turned on the lamps they didn't give a warm orange glow but a cold white light that made it seem like they were preparing for an interrogation.

Which I am, in a way, thought Josie, as she sat down opposite Yuko. I'm not leaving here until I get some answers, some real answers, and Yuko knows that.

'Is your mother here?' she said.

'No, she's gone to see a film with a friend. They won't be back until later this evening.'

'And are you planning to go out with Jiro, seeing as it's Christmas Eve?'

'Jiro? No. That's all over. There was never anything to it anyway. He was just useful, but now he's not useful any more.'

Yuko's face in the glare of the lamp was ugly. Looks like he dumped her, thought Josie with a certain sense of satisfaction.

'I want you to tell me about your father,' she said.

'You know all there is to know about what happened.'

'I don't mean about Matsuyama. I mean about him, his family, his background. His hobbies and interests.'

'You mean the books,' said Yuko wearily.

'Yes, I mean the books. And other things too. Let's start at the beginning. Where was he born?'

'Here in Tokyo.'

'But his mother was from Matsuyama?'

'Yes. She went back there when his father died. He used to visit her, but when she died he kept on going down there. That was about the time he started Ando Investments.'

'And before that he ran a bookshop?'

'Yes, in Saitama City. But just an ordinary one, not rare books or anything. He sold it when he started up Ando Investments.'

'But he kept going to Matsuyama. What did he do there?'

'I don't know. He didn't have a girl there or anything, I'm sure of that. But he was very secretive about it. One thing though, he always went to see Mr Mori when he came back.'

Josie thought for a moment.

'What did your grandfather do for a living?'

'He ran a bookshop too – my father inherited it. But his father was a farmer, just outside Tokyo. They say he made a lot of money.'

'From farming?'

'Not from farming. From the war. Towards the end Tokyo was on its knees. Half of it had been firebombed and there was no food to be had anywhere. Rich people went out into the country with everything they owned and bartered with the farmers for food. The farmers could demand anything they liked – it was pay or starve. People traded valuable kimonos, jewels, anything they had, just for enough food to keep them going for a few days.'

'Anything they had... including rare books?'

'I suppose so.'

'Did your grandfather inherit everything?'

'Yes, but he was ashamed of what his father had done. He said he didn't want to profit from other people's misery. He sold the farm and used the money to buy the bookshop.'

'But he kept the books?'

'As far as I know. I never saw them and the family didn't talk about them.'

'But when your grandfather died and your grandmother moved back to Matsuyama, she would have taken the books with her?'

'She might have. I don't know.'

Josie stopped and thought. A picture was forming in her mind of how it might have gone. The old farmer, selling his food at exorbitant prices; the rich family, trading in their priceless book collection for a fraction of its worth. And then the farmer hiding away his loot, waiting for better times when its value would appreciate again and he could sell. Perhaps waiting too long, dying before he could turn it to profit and then his son refusing to have anything to do with the tainted riches. So the books stayed hidden, first in Tokyo and then in Matsuyama until Mr Ando inherited them.

Josie wondered if Mr Ando had struggled with his conscience before selling the books. He must have known how his father had felt about them. Maybe he thought of trying to find the family that sold them and returning them, but after all it was a long time ago and there was no record of who it might have been. No way to trace them and make amends. And the books, sitting there in their hiding place in Matsuyama, rotting away, seen and appreciated by no one. What had happened to make up Mr Ando's mind?

'Yuko,' said Josie. 'When did your father met Mr Mori?'

'I don't really remember.'

'Was he an old friend?'

'Not that old. I don't remember him when I was growing up. He started coming around when I went to university, so it must be eight or nine years ago now.'

Eight or nine years ago. Just before Ando Investments was set up. Started with the proceeds of the bookshop sale, but then drip fed with great tranches of money – money that came from the hidden Matsuyama books, brought back by Mr Ando and sold to rich collectors that Mr Mori brought in. Ando Investments' success wasn't founded on Mr Wada's famed investment skills, but on lies and deceit and the suffering of a forgotten family who had sold their birthright for enough food to stay alive.

Josie looked at Yuko. How much had she really known about what her father went to Matsuyama for? He'd tried very hard to keep it secret. That supposed interest of his in haiku – was that real or was it just a story, designed to explain his frequent Matsuyama trips? And why, on this last trip, had he decided to invite the AZT contingent to join him? Was it because he was frightened?

Yuko looked at her watch and got up.

'I don't mean to hurry you,' she said. 'But I do have a date. I'm not going to sit at home by myself on Christmas Eve.'

Josie stood up too.

'Thanks for letting me come,' she said. 'By the way, did your mother know the truth about your father's Matsuyama trips?'

'You'll have to ask her that. She doesn't confide in me.'

'I will,' said Josie. I'll ask her as soon as I can, she thought. If she knew about the books, and that Mr Ando was planning to leave her for another woman, then it's pretty clear what might have happened that day in Matsuyama.

She walked slowly to Omotesando station. It was dark now, and the crowds were out, amongst them dozens of couples on their way to restaurants for a romantic dinner. Josie hoped very much that she was too, and not heading for the humiliation of a solitary meal in a restaurant filled with couples who would know only too well that she had been stood up on the most romantic night of the year.

She checked her phone as the train sped towards Ginza. No message from Dave. She hoped he'd seen her text, and that he'd cooled down enough to give her another chance. This time she wouldn't make the mistake of lying to him. She'd learned her lesson about secretiveness.

At Ginza station the crowds were thick and it took

her an age to get out of the station and head down one of the narrow back streets behind the Chuo Dori, where the evening shopping frenzy was in full swing, to the Italian restaurant where she'd booked a table. She reached it at ten past seven. Late. She hoped Dave hadn't come at seven, seen she wasn't there and gone away. She held her breath and pushed open the door to the restaurant.

SEVENTEEN

The restaurant was busy. Couples sat at little tables decorated with trails of ribbon with the promised red rose beside each girl's plate. The waiter led her through the narrow passage between the chair backs of happy couples to a table tucked away in the corner. Perfect, Josie thought. Quiet and secluded, just the place for a romantic meal. There's only one thing missing. Dave.

She sat down disconsolately and picked up her red rose. She had been so happy when she first found this place and decided to book it for Christmas Eve. She'd been lucky to get a table; even booking months in advance it was already almost full. She thought back to the Christmas Eves of previous years, when she'd studiously avoided going out, knowing that if she did the sight of so many romantic meals would make her feel even more lonely. It was hard, making a new life in a different country by yourself. She'd been lucky, making new friends, finding a good job and a flat that wasn't too expensive. She'd got what she wanted; the only thing missing was Dave. And now she'd had the chance to make it work with him again and she'd blown it by her own foolishness.

The waiter handed her a menu and left one on the empty plate opposite her.

'Would you like a drink while you wait for your companion?' he said. 'Pink champagne with a strawberry in it?'

'I'll wait, thanks,' said Josie, unable to face drinking pink champagne by herself. She was afraid she would burst into tears at the first sip.

She looked around the room – every other table seemed to have two glasses of pink champagne on it, every other girl was dressed in their party best and smiling sweetly at their beau. She was the only one on her own, plus she'd been so busy she hadn't even remembered that she was supposed to dress up. She was still wearing the jeans she'd put on that morning, the jeans she'd been wearing when she and Mr Shimizu found Mr Mori's body.

Perversely, the thought made her giggle hysterically. I bet nobody else here found a dead body this morning, she thought. And I bet they didn't adopt a cat either. Or have a final bust-up with their boyfriend last night. In fact, I can't imagine anybody else in the entire world behaving as stupidly as I've been doing recently.

She called the waiter back.

'I will have that pink champagne,' she said. Might as well go the whole hog now she was here; drink the champagne, eat the 'romantic night' pasta and the tiramisu and then go home and cry herself to sleep.

The waiter came back with two glasses of champagne, placed one carefully in front of Josie and the other at the empty place opposite her, beamed and left. Josie looked at the second glass. Oh, well, she could always drink two.

She picked up her glass but then realised to her horror that the guitarist, who had been serenading the other tables, was heading in her direction. This I can't bear, she thought, looking round wildly for an escape route. But as she tried to get to her feet, two strong hands bore down on her shoulders.

'Not leaving me already are you?' said a welcome voice. 'I know I'm late, but at least give me a chance to drink my champagne before you run for it.'

'Dave!' said Josie, 'I thought you weren't coming.'

'Not coming? On the most romantic night of the year?' Dave picked up his glass and, with a twinkle in his eye, clinked it against hers. 'Happy Christmas Eve. Now try and look a bit happier while this poor guy sings his song. You look like a wet weekend in Birmingham.'

Josie smiled and drank her champagne as the singer crooned his way through *O Sole Mio* in Japanese and the waiter brought little dishes of seafood salad.

'I'm so glad you're here,' she said when the singer had finished and been politely applauded. 'I can't tell you what kind of day I've had. And anyway, where on earth have you been? I've been worried sick.'

'No you haven't,' said Dave calmly, wolfing down

his salad and gesturing to the waiter to bring a bottle of wine. 'You never worry, that's what I like about you. I bet you've been off doing something so exciting you didn't even have time to change.'

He looked at her old jumper pointedly and Josie felt herself redden.

'All right, yes, that's exactly what I have been doing,' she said. 'But it's not been much fun. Poor Mr Mori is dead.'

'I'm sorry,' said Dave. 'I know how you must feel. You were getting to like him, weren't you?'

'Yes, I suppose I was. But that's not all. I was the one who found the body.'

'Today?'

'This morning. It was awful.' Josie suddenly felt as though she might start crying. Dave reached across the table and took her hand.

'Hey, now,' he said. 'Don't let it get to you. You're tougher than that.'

Josie blinked back the tears. Dave was right; she was tougher than that.

'Tell me what you've been doing,' she said. 'Where on earth did you spend the night?'

'In a hotel next to Tokyo Station. It was okay, and they spoke enough English for me to get a room. I spent the evening drinking in the hotel bar and went out like a light when I got to bed. Then this morning I got up and went out for a wander around Tokyo on my own. It gave me time to think and I realised how stupid I'd been. I don't really think you've been up to anything with Ken. It was just that I could tell your mind was on something else and I resented your not telling me about it. I want you to share things with me, not bottle them up and treat me like a stranger.'

'I'm sorry,' said Josie. 'It's just I was afraid you wouldn't approve of what I was doing and would tell me to stop.'

'I wouldn't dare,' said Dave, laughing. Then he leaned across the table to kiss her, oblivious to who might see. 'Let's just put it behind us, shall we? You can tell me all about what you're up to and I promise I won't try and stop you. Deal?'

'Deal,' said Josie, wondering where to start.

'But first, let's do the romantic Christmas Eve thing. I can see the waiter heading this way with our wine and pasta. Strictly neutral conversation until dinner is over, okay? Then you can spill the beans.'

They stuck to Dave's suggestion and found themselves reminiscing about the old days in London when Josie shared a flat in New Cross with a girlfriend who obsessed about mice in the kitchen and Dave lived with five other men in a house like a tip in Peckham.

'We never ate like this in those days,' said Dave, contemplating the tiramisu, which, in true Japanese fashion, was a tiny work of art decorated with sparkling heart-shaped sweets and a loveable santa figure. 'It was fish and chips or an Indian takeaway, and a kebab on Friday nights after the pub. And you got a proper facefull, too. The trouble I have with Japanese food is, it's all too delicate and tiny. I need man-sized food.'

Josie laughed. She was too happy Dave was back to start the kind of mock-fight that tended to characterise their conversations. Instead she said, 'Shall we skip coffee? I could make us some when we get home instead.'

'Suits me,' said Dave, signalling to the waiter to bring the bill. 'I think it's time we moved on to more in-depth romance than you can go in for in a restaurant.'

On the train back to her flat Josie rested her head on Dave's shoulder and listened while he reminisced about family Christmases when he was a child. The wine had relaxed her, taking away the tension and the pressure of the day, leaving her calm and mellow. Dave seemed to understand how she felt; when they got home they made love gently and soon fell asleep.

She woke late the next morning, refreshed but with a returning sense of things weighing on her mind. Dave was still asleep, but as she jogged his arm he flung it out sideways, disturbing Rin, who had crept under the duvet during the night. Rin screeched and leapt away to cower in the corner, spitting. Dave shot straight up in the air.

'What's going on?' he said. 'What happened?'

'Nothing,' said Josie. 'I forgot to tell you, I have a cat now. Meet Rin.'

'Rin? That's an odd name.'

'No, it's quite a common name for a cat. It means...well, it means lots of things. A bell, or something beautiful.'

She held out her hand and Rin slowly emerged

from her corner and crept into bed with them.

'She was Mr Mori's cat,' said Josie. 'She's homeless now so I thought…'

'So you took her in,' said Dave. 'It'll be nice for you to have a cat. Company for when I'm not around.'

Rin snuggled under the covers and began to purr, a small, fierce sound – the purr of a cat that knew the chill of nights on the street and didn't intend ever to go back there.

Over breakfast Josie gradually told Dave the story of her investigations, starting with her first conversation with Yuko at the house in Aoyama, which seemed like an age away, and ending with the visit to Eriko in Yokohama.

'So that's where you were,' said Dave. 'Why didn't you just say?'

'Sorry,' said Josie, restraining herself from pointing out that it was Dave's objection to her getting involved in another murder investigation that had led to her secrecy in the first place. Sometimes it was better to quit while you were ahead.

Instead she went on to describe the events of the previous day. Dave's face clouded as she talked about finding Mr Mori's body, but he didn't say anything until she finished.

'And now what?' he said. 'So far as I can see, you've discovered that a lot of people had a motive for bumping Mr Ando off, and that the book they're all after is still missing. Where are you going to go from here?'

'I don't know,' said Josie. 'I don't think whoever killed Mr Mori found what they were looking for in his flat. He was far too canny a man to have hidden it anywhere so obvious, especially after what happened to Jiro. So it must be somewhere else. All we have to do is work out where.'

'Not too tall an order then,' said Dave. 'All we need to do is think like a Japanese rare book collector with a cat and a tendency to find out more than was good for him and we're home and dry.'

He picked up Rin, who graciously allowed him to scratch behind her ear.

'We've already got the cat,' Dave said. 'So the rest should be easy.'

Josie looked at Rin.

'I wonder why Mr Shimizu didn't want her,' she said. 'After all, he was Mr Mori's friend and he used to look after Rin when Mr Mori was away.'

'He was probably afraid she'd damage his precious books,' said Dave.

'It didn't seem to bother Mr Mori. But then, he probably didn't keep his really valuable books at home. I expect he kept them in Mr Shimizu's home for tired doves.' She stopped. She'd forgotten about Mr Shimizu's hidden book storage place.

'Where's that?' said Dave, putting the cat down on the sofa, where she trod in a circle and settled down to sleep.

'It's near Mr Mori's flat in Jimbocho. It belongs to Mr Shimizu but he said Mr Mori kept some of his books there. Oh, I'm so stupid! It's obvious that's where Mr Mori would hide the Matsuyama book. Mr Shimizu must have known straight away. We've got to get down there.'

'How do we get in?' said Dave. 'You'll need a key.'

'We can get it from Mr Shimizu. His shop's just around the corner.'

'But it's Christmas Day,' said Dave. 'All the shops will be shut.'

'No they won't. Don't be fooled by all the decorations and Christmas carols. This is Tokyo, remember? Today's a normal trading day. I'm only off work because I took the day off specially so I could spend it with you. Otherwise I'd be sitting at my desk in Otemachi like everybody else.'

'Let's go, then.'

*

By the time they got to Jimbocho it was lunchtime and the bookshops were full of customers browsing though the racks. Shimizu's Books was busy but Mr Shimizu wasn't there. The same woman Josie had seen the day before shrugged her shoulders when they asked where he was.

'He hasn't been in today. I'm not surprised, either. Did you hear about what happened to poor Mr Mori? Found dead in his own flat with his head bashed in. They reckon it was a robbery gone wrong. Mr Shimizu found him, had to get the police in and everything. Terrible business.'

Interesting, thought Josie. The woman didn't seem to know that she'd been with Mr Shimizu when Mr Mori's body was found.

'Not to worry,' she said, as calmly as she could. 'We can come back another day. If you see him, tell him we called in about a book and we'll come back.'

She grabbed hold of Dave and dragged him out of the shop.

'She hasn't seen Mr Shimizu today,' she said. 'I bet he's round at the book storage place, looking for the missing book. Come on.'

She led the way down the backstreet to the book store. It looked unpromising; it was dark and shuttered and didn't look like there was anyone inside. Josie peered though a chink in the blind but could see nothing. There was no bell so she hammered on the door, but nobody came.

'If he's in there, he's not going to let us in,' said Dave. 'He doesn't want to be disturbed, does he? Especially not by us.'

'He's going to let us in alright,' said Josie. 'Because I'm not going to leave him in peace until he does. He's soon going to realise that letting us in is the easier option.'

She started to hammer on the door and shout Mr Shimizu's name. Dave joined in until they were kicking up quite a racket.

'Shh,' said Josie. 'I think I heard something.'

They paused. A faint voice inside said, 'Alright, alright, I'm coming. Stop your noise.'

There was a sound of bolts being drawn back and

then the door opened to reveal Mr Shimizu, wearing an old-fashioned brown apron and with dust all over his hands.

'Oh, it's you,' he said. 'You'd better come in.'

Josie followed Mr Shimizu into the dark corridor with Dave behind her, inserting his big frame with difficulty into the narrow space between the groaning bookshelves. Mr Shimizu headed down to the corner where he'd said Mr Mori kept his books. There were signs that the rows had been recently disturbed; there were piles of books on what little floor space remained, and half a bookshelf was conspicuously empty.

'You've been looking for it, haven't you?' said Josie.

'Looking for what?'

'The book that whoever searched Mr Mori's flat didn't find. You guessed it would be here.'

'Yes, I guessed it would be here, but I guessed wrong. There's nothing here. I've checked every book he had. They're all part of his normal stock. He didn't hide it here, that's the truth of it.'

'What did he say?' said Dave, who had been looking from one to the other as though trying to fathom out the meaning of the Japanese through sheer force of will.

'He said the book's not here. He says he's searched and he can't find it.'

'Well, we'll just have to search again, won't we?'

'It's difficult when you don't know what you're looking for. Searching for a rare Japanese book among a lot of other rare Japanese books? I don't think we're going to get very far with that.'

Mr Shimizu watched them with interest.

'Is he your husband?' he said to Josie. 'Tell him I've done the best I can for you. I didn't mention to the police that you were there when we found the body. I've kept you out of it. You should be grateful.'

'Did you tell the police about the missing book?' she said, and when Mr Shimizu looked guilty, said, 'I thought so.'

'There was no reason to complicate things,' said Mr Shimizu. 'The police have enough on their plate without that. And I thought I'd find the book here.'

'You're taking a huge risk. If you found it and the killer knew you had it, you could end up like Mr Mori.'

'And what about you? Aren't you doing just the same thing?'

'Yes, but..' Josie stopped. She'd been going to say, that's different, but of course it wasn't.

They stood in silence for a moment. Then Josie said, 'Okay, if it's not here, then Mr Mori hid it somewhere else. I bet there's something here that will lead us to it. You looked at all the books, but did you search behind them on the shelves? There could be something hidden that you overlooked because you thought you were looking for a book.'

'There's nothing, I told you.'

'What about in the office?'

There's nothing in there. Just the desk and Mr Mori's stock book.'

'Let's have a look,' said Josie, marching back up the passage to the office and pulling out the drawer of the desk. Inside was a stock book and an old bunch of keys. Josie stared at them, defeated. Either Mr Mori had outwitted them, or the book had been in his flat after all and the killer had got what they came for.

She picked up the bunch of keys. Keys, she thought. Keys to what? She riffled though them.

'Are these Mr Mori's keys?' she said to Mr Shimizu.

'Yes, he's always kept them here. They're just a spare set of keys to his flat and my shop.'

'What about this one?' said Josie, picking out a small key with an official-looking number on it.

'That one?' said Mr Shimizu, staring at it. 'I… I don't remember that one.'

'It looks like the key to a locker,' said Josie. 'The sort of left-luggage locker you get at stations. Or airports.'

Dave picked up on the change in her tone of voice. He looked at the key with light dawning in his eyes.

'Have we found it?' he said.

EIGHTEEN

Josie wrestled with the key ring, trying to get the locker key off, but her hands were trembling so much with excitement that she just fumbled at it. Dave reached over and took it from her.

'You see, I have my uses,' he said, sliding the key expertly off the ring.

Mr Shimizu stared at them.

'Do you know where the locker is?' he said.

'Not exactly,' said Josie. 'But I bet it's at Haneda airport. That's where Mr Mori got the bag from Jiro. He probably knew it was too dangerous to take it back to his flat. Putting it in a left luggage locker was his best bet – the key would be easier to hide than the bag or even the book, and he could go back when all the fuss had died down and pick it up. I bet he had a buyer for it all lined up – all he had to do was deliver.'

Dave broke in impatiently.

'I don't know what you two are discussing, but can we stop standing around chatting and do something?

There's a killer out there looking for the bag and we've got the key to it – literally got the key. I heard you mention Haneda Airport – if that's where we need to go, then let's get going.'

Josie nodded and translated what he had said for Mr Shimizu.

'Your husband's right,' he said. 'You should go without delay.'

'Come with us, Mr Shimizu,' said Josie. 'You won't be safe if you stay here.'

'No thanks. I would have liked to have found my old friend's book, but I'm too old to go chasing around town with a murderer on my tail. I'm going back to my own shop on Yasukuni Dori and staying there. Nobody's going to come and murder me there – far too public. Let me know if you find the book.'

'Give me your mobile number,' said Josie. 'We need to stay in touch.'

She tapped the number into her phone and then turned to Dave and switched into English.

'Mr Shimizu's not coming with us. But he's okay with us taking the key, so let's go.'

*

As they set off Josie thanked her lucky stars that it was Haneda Airport they were headed for, not Narita. Narita was an hour's train ride from Tokyo station but Haneda was close in – just a fifteen minute trip on the express monorail from Hamamatsucho. But that was once they got to Hamamatsucho, which took longer than Josie expected, so it was mid-afternoon when they finally joined the stream of passengers getting off the monorail at Haneda.

'Where's the best place to start?' said Dave.

'Well, when Mr Mori met Jiro he'd just arrived on a plane from Matsuyama, so the domestic arrivals hall is our best bet. All the coin lockers are numbered so all we need to do is find the block where the numbering matches up with the key.'

It turned out to be easier said than done. Coin lockers were spread around the airport in a haphazard way. Just when they thought they'd found the right block the numbering would run out before it reached the number on the key and they'd have to start again. They drew a blank on the arrivals floor and on the departures floor above it.

'Now what?' said Dave.

'There's more lockers on the basement level, where the monorail station is,' said Josie, looking at the airport guide she'd picked up. 'It has to be there. We've looked everywhere else.'

'I don't want to slow you down,' said Dave. 'But it's been a long time since we last ate anything. Couldn't we take a break and come back to this?'

'There's only the basement floor left,' said Josie, though she was uncomfortably aware that her stomach was rumbling too. 'It won't take us long to check there. Then we'll get something to eat.'

There were three banks of coin lockers on the basement floor. They started with the one at the far end, by the escalator from the north arrivals hall, but drew a blank. Nothing in the central bank either. That just left the one below the south arrivals hall. Josie worked her way along the rows.

'Ninety-two, ninety-three, ninety-four,' she muttered, reaching the end of the row and turning the corner, fully expecting to find that she'd reached the end of the numbering. But there was another small row of lockers tucked away in the corner that most people probably never realised were there. Josie's heart skipped a beat.

'Ninety five, ninety six, ninety seven... Ninety seven! That's it!'

She squatted down in front of the locker (it would be on the bottom row) and put the key in the lock. It turned easily. Taking a deep breath she reached inside and pulled out... Mr Ando's messenger bag.

'This is it!' she said. 'We've found it!'

'Open it up.'

'I'm not sure I can. It's got a combination lock on it.'

'I've got a case with a combination lock,' said Dave. 'And I've never bothered to reset it from the factory setting. Too much trouble. It's one of those things you keep promising yourself you'll do but then you lose the instructions and you don't want to risk locking yourself out. Try just setting it to all noughts. Always works for me.'

Josie did as he said. With a click the bag opened.

Inside was a couple of dirty shirts, shoved in higgledy-piggledy and beginning to smell distinctly ripe. Underneath them was a parcel. A small, book-shaped parcel wrapped in thick paper and tied up with string.

'Do you think this is it?' said Josie, hesitating with the parcel in her hand.

'There's only one way to find out. Look inside.'

'Right,' said Josie, taking a deep breath and fumbling with the knot of the string. It was the tough kind of string, made from twisted paper, and it had been knotted firmly and tightly; the more she fiddled with it the tighter it got.

'Oh, for Pete's sake,' said Dave. 'Don't you have some scissors or something?'

'No, only a pair of nail clippers.'

'Well try those.'

Josie scrabbled around in her handbag, eventually coming up with a novelty-sized pair of nail clippers that she'd got free in a Christmas cracker one year. Dave looked at them in disbelief.

'Is that the best you can do?'

'Yes, it is, as a matter of fact,' said Josie, feeling her temper rising. 'If you can do any better just say so.'

'Sorry I spoke. You're the one with the lethal weapon – unsheathe it.'

Josie slid the edge of the clippers under the string and managed to get them to chew their way through it. She tore it off and carefully undid the thick paper. Inside was a book. She stared at it, trying to make out the unfamiliar characters on the cover.

'It's a book of Basho's haiku,' she said breathlessly. 'Do you think this is it?'

Dave looked at it dubiously.

'Well, actually...' he said.

'I know. You're going to say you can't read Japanese so you've got no way of telling,' said Josie.

'No, I wasn't going to say that. I was going to say... Well, doesn't it look in surprisingly good condition for a rare book that's been hidden since the war? No grime, no ragged corners. In fact, it looks in mint condition.'

Josie stared at the book for a long moment.

'You're right,' she said. 'It looks brand new.'

She opened the book and checked the copyright page. It said *this edition published 2013*.

A wave of disappointment swept over her. The book was worthless. It was a modern edition that you could buy anywhere for a few thousand yen. All the excitement drained out of her and she rocked back on her heels and sat down on the cold hard airport floor. The book tumbled from her hands into the mess of old shirts in the bag.

Dave picked it up. He looked at the date on the copyright page and put his hand on her shoulder.

'I'm sorry, Josie,' he said. 'We got so close.'

'It must be in there somewhere, said Josie, throwing the shirts onto the floor and feeling around inside the bag.

'Tell you what,' said Dave. 'Let's go and get something to eat. We're both tired and hungry. Putting something in our stomachs will set us up and you'll be able to work out what to do next.'

Josie nodded and got to her feet. She wrapped the

book up again in the paper and put it in her bag. She piled the shirts back in the messenger bag, threw the chewed-up piece of string in after them, and put it back in the locker.

'Food,' she said. 'I feel like I haven't eaten in a week.'

They headed back to the main concourse and took the escalator up to the restaurant area. Josie stared vacantly up at the floor after floor of shops and restaurants, unable to focus on anything, until Dave said, 'What about that one on the next floor? It's doing a Christmas special – chicken nuggets and strawberry cake. It is Christmas Day after all.'

Josie nodded and they took the escalator up to the next floor. The restaurant had been fitted out in dark wood with banquette seating like a nineteenth century European cafe. Josie stared into space while they waited for their food to come, while Dave checked the emails on his phone and whistled a tuneless whistle.

They ate in silence. The chicken nuggets weren't very good, but at least they were hot and came with cardboard cups of thin french fries. The strawberry cake was better – moist yellow cake covered in a storm of whipped cream with fresh strawberries all over the top. Slowly Josie began to feel better as her thought processes returned from their state of frozen despair.

'Well, at least we got Christmas dinner Japanese style,' said Dave.

'In an airport cafe,' said Josie. 'I'm sorry. I didn't mean Christmas Day to turn out like this.'

'A mad race round Tokyo in pursuit of a missing book and an unidentified killer?' said Dave. 'I'm glad. If you'd planned it like this I'd have had serious doubts about your sanity.'

Josie grinned.

'I'll make it up to you. We'll have a quiet New Year's Eve. Just you, me and the telly. Promise.'

'And Rin.'

'Oh, yes, and Rin. You don't mind about her?'

'Whatever you want. I'm past complaining.'

The thought of Rin reminded Josie of Mr Mori.

'Do you think,' she said, 'that Mr Mori knew about the book in the bag? That it wasn't the real one, I mean?'

'I don't see what you're getting at. If Mr Mori knew it wasn't the real book, why did he get the bag from Jiro and hide it at the airport?'

'Well, I was thinking. The book must have been switched at some point before the bag was put in the locker.'

'Someone took the real book out of the bag and put this one in its place, you mean?'

'Maybe. If that's what happened, then only three people could have done it; Yuko, who had the bag first, Jiro who brought it to Tokyo, and Mr Mori, who got it from Jiro when he got to Tokyo.'

'Assuming Mr Mori put the bag in the locker before he left the airport, that sounds about right.'

'Right then. We can't ask Mr Mori about it because he's dead, but we do know that his flat was thoroughly searched by the killer and Mr Shimizu's been through everything in the book storage place and not found anything. So the chances are he didn't have the real book.'

'Fair enough. Go on.'

'I'm inclined to rule out Jiro too. He's not the brightest spark and I can't see him coming up with the idea of switching the books. He didn't even know what was in the bag when Yuko gave it to him, so he could hardly have had a spare book to hand to make the switch. And anyway, the killer searched his flat too and didn't find anything.'

'Right. So that leaves Yuko. I wouldn't put it past her. She's a devious one.'

'She is. But I doubt that she'd have had the time to get the other book and make the switch before she handed the bag over to Jiro in Matsuyama. I think she's telling the truth about just grabbing the bag opportunistically.'

'Then how could the switch have happened?'

'It didn't. The book in the bag was always the wrong book. Mr Ando put it there himself.'

'Now you've lost me.'

'Look, think about what was going through Mr Ando's mind. He'd gone to Matsuyama to get the last of his grandfather's books, the most valuable of them all, and it made him very nervous. Maybe he had reason to think someone knew about the book and was out to get it. So he does everything he can to confuse this person. First of all, he sets up a haiku tour with a lot of people from AZT on it to make it difficult for anyone to get him on his own. Then he arranges for Mr Wada to come to Matsuyama so he can give him the book to take back to Tokyo while Mr Ando carries on with the tour.'

'But he didn't give the book to Mr Wada.'

'No, Mr Wada came too late. And something made Mr Ando realise that he couldn't wait for Mr Wada, he had to find another way to hide the book.'

'You mean it could still be in Matsuyama?'

'No, the whole idea was to bring it to Tokyo where presumably a buyer was waiting to take it off his hands. Somehow he must have sent it by another method. All we have to do is work out what it was.'

They sat in silence while Josie racked her brains. There was something at the back of her mind, something that had seemed trivial at the time but was actually crucial, if only she could remember what it was.

'I think this is a two slices of strawberry cake problem,' Dave said, signalling to the waiter.

Josie let her mind run back over all the things that had happened since they got back from Matsuyama. She hardly noticed the waiter bring two more slices of cake and started eating mechanically when Dave put a slice in front of her. Then she stopped, fork half way to her mouth.

'I've got it,' she said. 'I know how he did it. And I know where the book is now. Oh, clever Mr Ando! None of us suspected.'

'Suspected what?' said Dave.

'Hina,' said Josie. 'Hina's got the book.'

NINETEEN

Josie pulled out her phone and scrolled down to Hina's number, praying she'd still be at the office. She waited, listening to the phone ringing at the other end until, with a ping, the ringing stopped and Hina answered.

'Hina, it's Josie Clark from AZT. I know this might sound like a strange question, but do you have anything that belongs to Mr Ando?'

There was a pause at the other end. Then Hina said, 'Well, yes, actually. As a matter of fact, I do. How did you know?'

'Just a lucky guess,' said Josie. 'Is it at the Haiku Country Tours office?'

'Yes, it is,' said Hina. 'It's here for safe keeping.'

'And you're at the office now?'

'Yes, I'm working late on the end of year figures.'

'Then can we come and see you about it?'

'Right now?'

'Yes, right now. It's important.'

'Alright. I don't suppose my boss will mind.'

'We'll get there as soon as we can,' said Josie and broke the connection.

'So where are we off to now?' said Dave.

'The Haiku Country Tours office in Shinjuku. That's where Mr Ando sent the book. Come on.'

They headed back down to the monorail platform and leaped onto a Haneda Express train just as the doors were about to close. Josie found the trip agonisingly slow, though they hurtled through the stations without stopping. At last the shining expanse of water at Tennozu Isle came into view.

'Come on,' Josie said, leaping from her seat as the train drew into Hamamatsucho. 'We can get the Yamanote line to Shinjuku from here.'

The train to Shinjuku was packed. They straphanged the whole way there with more and more people piling in until it seemed like all the air had been squeezed out of the carriage leaving only human bodies jammed tightly together behind. Luckily, half the carriage got off at Shinjuku and Josie and Dave found themselves carried along on the wave.

Hina was waiting for them when they got to the Haiku Country Tours office. Josie introduced Dave, then Hina took them into the meeting room they had used on Josie's previous visit, which now looked quite different, with every available surface covered in open box files, piles of dog-eared letters, bulldog-clipped invoices and an old-fashioned mechanical calculator with a handle that you pulled to perform the calculation. It was like a trip back to the twentieth century.

'Sorry,' said Hina, pushing a pile of papers to one side and pinning back a lock of hair that had fallen over her face. 'We're not very up to date here. We've gone on doing things the same old way for so long now, it just seems less trouble to carry on than to try and bring it all up to date. I do have a computer I take on trips with me, but my boss likes the accounting done on paper. Sit down and tell me why you're here. You said it had something to do with Mr Ando's property?'

'Yes,' said Josie. 'I don't know the details, but I think he asked you to look after something for him down in Matsuyama. A book maybe?'

'Yes, he did. But it wasn't just one book. And he didn't exactly ask me to look after it.'

'Tell us what happened,' said Josie.

Hina hesitated. 'I don't want to break any confidences,' she said.

'You can't break Mr Ando's confidence now he's no longer with us. And I'm sure he'd have wanted you to tell me. There was something he was trying to hide and if we're not careful whoever it was he was hiding it from will get hold of it, and then all his precautions will have been wasted. So really, you owe it to him to tell me, so I can help you protect it.'

'Oh,' said Hina. 'Well I suppose... If you really think—'

'I do,' said Josie firmly.

Hina looked hesitantly at Dave. His bulky presence seemed to reassure her.

'Wait here a minute,' she said. 'I'll go and fetch

it.'

They sat down on a couple of the wooden chairs. Dave's creaked alarmingly.

'She's going to get it,' Josie whispered to Dave. 'This time I really think we're on the right track.'

After a few moments Hina returned. She was carrying a box, large enough to hold a dozen books, covered in stickers from Kuroneko Yamato, the universal delivery service.

'This is what you meant, isn't it?' said Hina.

'Er, yes,' said Josie, disconcerted. 'Tell me how you got it.'

'It happened the first night in Matsuyama. You remember, the haiku reading ended unexpectedly early and everyone went off on their own. I had some work to do back in my room and when I finished I came down again, planning to take a walk. I ran into Mr Ando in the hotel foyer. He had a big bag of books with him and said he wanted to send them back to Tokyo.'

'Did he say where he'd got them?'

'He said he'd been to a bookshop in town. He's a great bookworm. Apparently he used to have his own bookshop.'

'Yes, Mrs Ando told me about that,' said Josie.

'Well, Mr Ando said he could never resist buying books but he didn't want Mrs Ando to know because she always told him off. She said he had enough books already and they didn't have room for any more. So then he asked me if he could have them sent to Haiku Country Tours for him to pick up, so that

Mrs Ando wouldn't know he'd bought them. Of course I said yes.'

'And then what?'

'Then I went out for my walk and Mr Ando arranged at the hotel desk for Kuroneko Yamato to pick up the books.'

'So you never actually saw the books?'

'No. I didn't wait around to see. It was none of my business.'

Dave, who had been listening intently as though he could somehow wring the meaning from the unfamiliar words by sheer force of will, suddenly shifted in his chair and Josie took pity on him and translated the conversation so far.

'So he sent a load of books,' Dave said. 'Do you think they're all rare and valuable?'

'No,' said Josie. 'I think he did exactly what he told Hina – went out and bought a load of books at an ordinary bookshop. But then, before he sent the box to Tokyo, he took out one of the books and put it in his messenger bag, and put the rare book in the box with the others. It was the perfect cover – and, for once, not even Mr Mori knew what he'd done.'

'But how did you know he'd sent them here?'

'I remembered when we came here before for a meeting, Hina said she had something belonging to Mr Ando that she needed to ask Mrs Ando about. I didn't pay much attention at the time. But then it came back to me and I realised what it meant.'

She turned back to Hina and switched into Japanese again.

'What did you do when the box arrived?'

'Well, by then poor Mr Ando was dead. I didn't know what to do in the circumstances. I didn't want to burden the family with any more problems, so I just put the box away safely to give to them when the funeral was over and things had settled down. But then my boss said that maybe we shouldn't do that. He said maybe there were books in there that Mr Ando didn't want his wife to know about, and that was why he had the box sent here.'

'Books Mr Ando didn't want his wife to know about?' said Josie, wondering for one wild moment whether Hina's boss had guessed what was hidden in amongst the books Mr Ando had just bought.

'You know,' said Hina. 'Gentlemen's books.'

'Oh,' said Josie. 'I see what you mean. So did you look inside to check they were alright?'

'No, of course not,' said Hina. 'We didn't have the authority. We put the box in a safe place while we thought what to do. And then I'm afraid, we've been so busy we didn't do anything about it.'

'Can we open the box now?'

Hina recoiled in horror.

'I couldn't let you do that,' she said. 'It's not my property. It belongs to Mrs Ando now.'

Josie felt like she'd just run into a brick wall. They'd got so close, she could hardly bear not to open the box and see what was inside.

Dave saw her reaction and looked at her enquiringly.

'It's Mr Ando's box but she won't let us open it,'

said Josie. 'Because it doesn't belong to us.'

'Sounds perfectly reasonable,' said Dave. 'Have you explained to her why we want to look inside?'

'Not yet. I'll try that.'

She turned back to Hina.

'You see, the thing is,' she said. 'We think that maybe Mr Ando's falling off the veranda wasn't an accident. We think he might have been pushed.'

'Pushed?' said Hina. 'Who would do such a thing?'

'I don't know. But I think whoever it was, was after a valuable book that Mr Ando had. And I think Mr Ando knew that, and he hid the book in the box of books he sent here, so that the person shouldn't get it.'

Hina looked at the box of books, as though she hoped to see through the thick cardboard to the books beneath.

'In that case,' she said. 'I must get in touch with Mrs Ando right away and tell her I have the box.'

'Oh,' said Josie. 'I'd rather you didn't do that, at least not right now.'

'Whyever not?'

'Well, because it's just possible that Mrs Ando is the person Mr Ando was frightened of.'

'Then what shall we do?'

'We can't leave the box here. It's too dangerous. Someone else might put two and two together the way I did. We need to put it in a safe place. Can you let me take it back to AZT?'

'Well,' said Hina. 'It would have to be officially

received and accounted for. Can you stamp the official seal of your company on a receipt?'

'No,' said Josie. 'But I know someone who can.'

She got out her phone and rang Ken's number. When he answered she said, 'It's Josie. I need your help. Are you still at work?'

'Of course I'm still at work. I'll be here until ten tonight, as you well know. Junior client support staff don't get to go home at a civilised time like foreign assistants with jammy jobs in Corporate Support.'

'Actually, I'm on leave today,' said Josie. 'But it doesn't feel like it. I've done enough running around Tokyo today to last me a lifetime.'

'What are you up to now?' said Ken with a note of resignation in his voice.

'I'm at Hina's office.'

'What are you doing there?'

'I came because she's got a box of books that Mr Ando sent from Matsuyama. I don't want to leave it with her because I'm afraid that whoever killed Mr Ando might come looking for it, so she's agreed that I can take it back to AZT for safekeeping. But she won't give it to me without an officially stamped receipt, and I know you've got a company stamp so I wondered if...'

'If I'd drop everything and come over there and do it for you?' Ken finished the sentence for her.

'Well, yes.'

There was a long silence at the other end of the phone. Then Ken said, 'I don't why I let you drag me into these messes of yours. If I do this for you, do you promise it will be absolutely the last time you ever ask me anything like this ever again?'

'I promise,' said Josie. 'Honestly. I wouldn't ask you if it wasn't an emergency.'

At the other end of the phone she could hear Ken talking to someone else in the office. She held on. Finally he came back.

'I've explained that there is a bit of a crisis at Haiku Country Tours to do with our visit to Matsuyama and I have to go and sort it out. So I'll be with you in thirty minutes with a bit of luck. Hang on.'

Josie pressed the end call switch on her phone.

'Ken Ueda's coming over with the company stamp now,' she said to Hina, who nodded.

'I'll get the papers ready,' she said.

Josie turned to Dave.

'Er, I've had to ask Ken to come here. He's bringing the AZT company stamp so Hina will give us the box.'

'Ken? Isn't there anyone else in your entire organisation you could have asked?'

'Well, no, actually, there isn't. And anyway it's time you two met and you stopped being so stupidly jealous.'

'I am not stupidly jealous,' Dave began, but stopped himself. 'Hey, it's Christmas Day,' he said. 'Let's not quarrel. Let's just find a piece of mistletoe to stand under.'

Josie looked around the dusty, paper-filled office.

'That may have to wait,' she said.

'I'll get you some tea, shall I?' said Hina.

Time dragged by. Hina brought them the inevitable green tea and then went back to work on the accounts. The room fell silent apart from the steady clicking of Hina entering figures into the ancient calculator and the whirring sound as she pulled the handle. Distantly the sounds of Shinjuku at night reached them – a booming base line from the ghetto blasters in the square outside Shinjuku station where the kids gathered to dance, the occasional burst of chatter and laughter from passing groups on their way to the restaurants and clubs in Kabukicho. Josie looked at her watch; eight o'clock. It felt much later, as though the day had gone on forever.

Josie let her mind drift back to Haneda airport, to the morning when she'd first met Mr Ando and the other tour members. She'd liked Mr Ando so much – he'd been full of life, his eyes lighting up as new ideas chased themselves across his mind, and he leapt to catch hold of them before they vanished. Even his inaccurate grasp of facts and his tendency to misquote the great poets to an almost criminal extent had been endearing. She felt a wave of anger against the person who'd deprived her of the chance to get to know him better. No doubt he'd had his faults – presumably he hadn't been much of a husband if he'd gone off and had a child with Eriko. If he'd lived, would he have started a new life with her and his baby son, or would he have stayed with Mrs Ando and Yuko? Josie saw for the first time how crucial the answer to that question was. What would he have done with the money from the book? Would it have been Mrs Ando and Yuko or Eriko that he chose?

There was the sound of feet on the stairs outside and Josie looked up as Ken appeared. Hina got up to greet him, and then laid a set of Haiku Country Tours headed papers on the table next to the box of books.

'This is the receipt for the box,' she said. 'You need to stamp each copy here, here and here.'

Ken got out the company seal, a small wooden stamp with AZT inside a circle incised into one end, and stamped the papers Hina put in front of him. She gave him one copy and put the others carefully in her file.

'That's all done,' she said. 'You can take the box away, but AZT guarantees its safety until it's delivered to Mrs Ando.'

'Thanks, Ken,' said Josie. 'I owe you one.'

There was a pause as Ken and Dave looked at each other.

'Er, Josie,' said Dave. 'Shouldn't you introduce us?'

He held out his hand to Ken.

'I'm Dave, Josie's boyfriend from England,' he said. 'Pleased to meet you. *Hajimemashite. Yoroshiku onegaishimasu.*'

Ken's face lit up in a huge grin.

'Dave!' he said. 'I'm so pleased to meet you at last. *Dozo yoroshiku onegai-itashimasu.*'

He gave a deep bow.

Dave sketched a bow back and grinned too.

'He's okay. Looks like a decent bloke. Not at all

what I expected,' he said.

Typical, thought Josie. Now he's actually met him, I suppose Ken is going to be Dave's new best friend. I know him. He'll get an idea into his head about someone and nothing will shake it until he actually meets the person and suddenly everything is sweetness and light and he denies it's ever been any different. She tried to feel cross, but a sneaking feeling that this was one of the things she liked about Dave prevented her.

'I don't want to press you,' Ken said. 'But now we've sorted out about the box it would help if you could bring me up to speed on what this is all about.'

'It's about Mr Ando. The whole haiku trip to Matsuyama was a pretence. He arranged it to hide the fact that he was getting his rare books from there. And that's why he was killed.'

'Whoa, slow down,' said Ken. 'Start at the beginning and spell it out to me.'

'I suppose it all starts with the books,' said Josie. 'Mr Ando's grandfather got hold of some rare books during the war – he got them for almost nothing when a rich collector traded them for food. Mr Ando's father inherited them, but kept them hidden because he was embarrassed about not having got them legitimately. Then Mr Ando's mother took them to Matsuyama, and when she died Mr Ando started going down to Matsuyama to collect them, one or two at a time so as not to arouse suspicion. But somebody got to know about it, and Mr Ando was afraid. So, when he went to get the last book, the most valuable one, he arranged for us all to go on the haiku tour as a kind of protection.'

'But what did he do with these books?'

'He sold them secretly via Mr Mori and his contacts in the rare book trade. They used Ando Investments as a cover. That's why Mr Mori supposedly worked for Ando Investments even though he didn't know the first thing about finance. Mr Mori did the deals and the money stayed in the company, disguised as investment profits, until Mr Ando was ready to draw it out. He probably paid Mr Mori an inflated salary for his services.'

'So you're saying that Ando Investments is a sort of giant money-laundering operation?'

'That's exactly what I'm saying. But someone found out about it. Mr Ando knew he was in danger, so after he picked up the last book he hid it in a box of other books and had it sent to Hina. Then he pretended the book was in the messenger bag he took to Matsuyama castle, thinking that someone would steal it there. He even left it lying around in the castle keep to make it easy for them. Perhaps he thought he'd be able to catch them out, come back in from the veranda suddenly and catch them in the act. What he didn't realise was that whoever it was, was prepared to kill for it.'

Ken looked stunned.

'So now you see why I need you to take the box back to AZT where it'll be safe,' said Josie.

'Fine,' said Ken, hefting the box of books off the table. 'I'm on my way.'

Josie hadn't realised until then that she'd been holding herself rigid with tension. She let it ease out of her body. The box was safe.

Then her phone rang. She looked at the display and saw Mr Shimizu's name.

TWENTY

'Mr Shimizu,' Josie said, feeling guilty that she hadn't given him a thought since they'd left him that morning to go to Haneda airport. 'I'm so sorry I haven't been in touch. It's a long story, but I think we've found the book.'

'What book is it?'

'Oh, er, well, I haven't actually seen it yet. But we know where it is and it's safe, that's the main thing.'

'Good. But I wasn't actually ringing about that. I've had a phone call and I wanted to let you know about it.'

'Go on.'

'It came through at Shimizu's Books. It was a woman who said she was looking for a rare book and that Mr Mori had been helping her. She wanted to know if I knew anything about it because she hadn't been able to get hold of him. Of course, I had to tell her what had happened. She was very dismayed. She said the book was important – a birthday present for her husband, she said, and she needed it right away.

Mr Mori had told her he'd managed to get hold of it but she didn't know where it was now.'

'What did you say to her?'

'Well, I wanted to help her. It was her husband's birthday after all. So I said Mr Mori might have left it in our book store and if she told me what it was I could go and look for her. She was very grateful.'

'Mr Shimizu,' said Josie, a sick feeling starting in the pit of her stomach. 'You're not going to go to the book storage place to look for it are you?'

'I've already been, but I couldn't find it. So I rang and told her and she said she'd like to come and see for herself. She said she knew exactly what it looked like and she'd be able to pick it out straight away. So I agreed she could come over and I'd meet her there.'

'Mr Shimizu,' said Josie. 'Don't go. It's too dangerous. You don't know who this woman is.'

'Oh yes, it's alright. She gave me her name and her phone number and everything. Her name's Kobayashi. She sounded very nice. It's just that I wanted to let you know. I promise we won't disturb anything.'

'Mr Shimizu,' said Josie. 'Wait right where you are. We're coming straight over. We can be with you in half an hour. Just don't do anything until we get there.'

'Oh,' said Mr Shimizu. 'Only it is rather urgent.'

'Yes, but please wait. We'll get there as fast as we can.'

Josie dropped her phone back in her bag and turned to Dave.

'I don't know how to tell you this,' she said. 'But we're going back to Jimbocho. Right now.'

*

I'm so sick of trains, thought Josie, as they waited on the Shinjuku Line platform for what felt like the thousandth train trip that day. And I don't think I'll be going back to Jimbocho in a hurry when all this is over either.

She looked across at Dave who gave her an encouraging grin and squeezed her hand.

'It won't take us long to get there,' he said. 'Don't worry.'

Josie nodded.

'The train is about to arrive. It's dangerous, so please stand back behind the yellow line,' said the announcer, using the humblest word in the Japanese vocabulary for 'arrive', as though the train was going to creep modestly into the station rather than hurtle along the track towards them. They lined up obediently opposite the markings that told you where the doors would be and stood to the side as the passengers got off. The train was emptier now the main rush hour was past and the carriage was silent as the few occupants bent in concentrated attention over their mobile phones.

'Do you think this woman could be the one who killed Mr Ando?' said Josie, knowing what the answer was but torturing herself by making Dave say it.

'It's possible. Well, actually, it's more than possible, it's pretty likely.'

'I know. Who else would turn up with a story like this? And who else would be in such a hurry? Birthday, indeed! I'm surprised Mr Shimizu fell for that.'

'Did he tell you what kind of voice the woman had? Old or young?'

'I didn't think to ask. I wish I had now. It would have given us some idea who we're dealing with.'

Josie thought about who it could be. Mrs Ando, Yuko, Eriko. One of those three.

'At least we know it isn't Mr Wada,' she said. 'But I was pretty sure of that in any case. He was just part of the window dressing at Ando Investments. His famous investment strategy was nothing special in the end. All he had to do was make it look as though Ando Investments was legitimate. He didn't actually have to make a profit at all.'

'Sounds like a great job. I wonder what he'll do now?'

'Well, I can't see the board agreeing to let him run the company. Not once it comes out what's really been going on.'

The train pulled into Kudanshita, the stop before Jimbocho. Josie had been there once, in cherry blossom season, to walk along the path by the old Imperial Palace moat and look at the great billows of cherry blossom reflected in the water, and the colourful paddle boats floating past filled with happy sightseers.

'This is the strangest Christmas Day I've ever had,' she said, feeling weariness creeping into her bones. If only she could stay on this warm, comfortable train and not have to think about books or murderers ever again.

The siren that heralded the closing of the doors sounded and the train pulled away.

'Next stop's ours,' she said, pulling herself to her feet and going to stand by the doors ready for them to open. Dave came and stood beside her and when the doors slid back they leapt off and headed for the Yasukuni Dori exit.

'We'll start at Shimizu's Books,' said Josie. 'If we're lucky Mr Shimizu will be there waiting for us.'

They sped down Yasukuni Dori but even from a distance it was clear that Shimizu's Books had closed up for the night; the bargain book bins were nowhere to be seen and the windows were dark. They tried the door and shouted but nobody came.

'He's gone to the book storage place,' said Josie. 'Come on.'

They raced down the side street, past the beer hall, where groups of diners sat around the long wooden tables with glasses of beer in their hands. It looked warm and cosy and Josie would have given anything to have gone in and joined them. But she gritted her teeth and ran on past.

It was gone nine o'clock and, though the streets were well lit and a full moon shone, it felt cold and dark after the brightness and warmth of the train, with a hint of frost to come. Christmas weather; a time to be at home with mistletoe and mulled wine, not racing through empty streets in search of a murderer.

The book store, when they reached it, was dark and shuttered. Even the industrious spiders seemed to have crept off into hidden corners, leaving their webs deserted.

'Do you think Mr Shimizu's inside?' said Dave, looking at the deserted-looking shop and the silent street.

'I don't know, said Josie. 'I'm ringing his mobile but he's not replying.'

'So what do we do?'

Josie tried the door. It didn't open, but it did move slightly, as though it was only on the latch, not fully locked.

'Mr Shimizu,' she called. 'Mr Shimizu, are you in there?'

They waited, but there was no reply. A dog barked somewhere off in the distance and they both jumped.

'We'll have to break in,' she said. 'Do you think you can get the door open?'

Dave looked at the door.

'It's open an inch or so already,' he said. 'If I can get my fingers round the edge I can force it back.'

He worked his fingers into the gap, took a deep breath and then gave a sharp tug. The door rattled back and slammed into the far side of the frame.

'All part of the service,' Dave said, standing back to let Josie go first. She peered down the corridor. All was dark and silent.

'Mr Shimizu?' she called, stepping inside and

starting to make her way down through the shelves of books.

There was a rustling sound from deep among the stacks. It stopped, as though someone had moved and then held their breath.

'Mr Shimizu, it's Josie. Are you there?'

Silence.

Dave was crammed into the narrow passage behind Josie. He tapped her on the shoulder and gestured to her to let him go first. Josie shook her head. Whatever or whoever was waiting among the silent books, it was her problem, not his. She reached for the light switch but nothing happened when she clicked it. Either the bulb had failed or someone had taken the precaution of removing it. There was nothing for it but to go ahead in the dark.

Josie took out her phone and set it to torch mode. It cast a thin beam of light ahead of her as she crept along the passageway toward the shadowy bookshelves.

She remembered the layout from her previous visit – the long rows of bookshelves that didn't quite stretch to the far wall, so you could dodge round from one aisle to the other without having to come back to the main corridor where she and Dave now stood. The door to the office at the end of the passageway stood slightly ajar but Josie couldn't see inside – the beam of her makeshift torch didn't reach that far. What to go for first, the bookshelves or the office?

'You stay in the doorway and make sure no one gets past you,' Josie whispered to Dave. 'I'm going to check out the office and then work my way along the bookshelves.'

She began to creep along the passage towards the office door, shining her light down between each of the rows of bookshelves as she went. But the light only extended about half way down the silent rows, leaving the far ends in darkness.

She reached the office door and cautiously pushed it open with her foot. At first she thought there was nobody inside, but then she saw a foot protruding from under the desk and heard a muffled groan.

'Mr Shimizu,' she said. 'Mr Shimizu, it's Josie. Are you alright?'

Mr Shimizu groaned again and sat up. Josie helped him up into the chair.

'You'll be alright,' she said. 'You're hurt but I don't think it's too bad. I'm going to leave you here for a bit while I go and see if there's anybody else around. Do you understand?'

Mr Shimizu nodded and then groaned again. He put his hand to his head and looked at it in disbelief as it came away sticky with blood. Josie fished out a clean tissue and wiped some of the blood away. There was a gash on the back of his head but it wasn't deep and the blood was already starting to dry.

'She hit me,' Mr Shimizu said disbelievingly. 'How could a nice woman like her do that?'

'You saw her then?'

'Yes, she was waiting for me outside. She said she needed to get the book and it wouldn't take long. So I let her in.'

'Did you recognise her?'

'No, but then I didn't meet any of the people Mr Mori dealt with. He liked to keep things discreet.'

Josie got a fresh packet of tissues out of her bag and started to wipe the rest of the blood from his head. But then she heard another sound from the book stack. A rustling noise, like she'd heard before.

'I'll be back,' she said, handing Mr Shimizu the rest of the tissues. 'Stay here.'

She crept back along to the book stack nearest the door. She could see Dave waiting in the doorway, his bulk filling the tiny doorframe. She gave him a wave and then peered down the dark tunnel between the towering stacks.

'Come out,' she shouted. 'I know you're in there.'

Silence. Just the odd little rustle again.

'Right, I'm coming in after you,' she said, starting down the narrow space next to the first row of bookshelves. But before she could reach the end there was an ominous creak as the shelf at the far end wobbled and tipped forward, emptying its cargo of books onto the floor with a crash. She jumped back out of the way, coughing from the cloud of dust that blew up, and retraced her steps to the main passageway. She paused and listened. All was quiet.

She moved on to the next row of bookshelves and started to creep along it, more cautiously this time. As she neared the end the next stack toppled, sending its books crashing to the floor. It was closer this time, so close that several of the books bounced painfully off her shoulder before hitting the floor; whoever was pushing the stacks had clearly got better at judging where Josie was. Not a good thought.

Josie crept back to the main passage as quietly as she could, rubbing her shoulder where the books had struck, and stopped to listen. She thought she could hear someone breathing heavily but it was impossible to pinpoint where the noise came from. She decided on a change of tactics, skipping one row of books and darting down the next. She was rewarded by a quick glimpse of a white face in the darkness before whoever it was ducked behind the end of the row and out of sight.

'You can't go on doing this,' Josie shouted. 'There's only so many bookshelves in the place. Come out now.'

Silence.

Dave shouted from the doorway, 'Do you want me to come and help you?'

'No,' Josie shouted back. 'You stay where you are. She's not getting out of here and it's your job to stop her if she tries.'

'Right you are,' said Dave. Josie could hear his feet scrape on the wooden floor as he braced himself for any impact.

She crept as quietly as she could along the passage, trying not to give away which row of books she was going to choose, trying to outguess the person at the other end of the stacks. But whoever it was, they were too quick for her; as she tiptoed down the last row the shelves behind her started to topple, blocking her exit. And then the books above her began to fall. She threw up her hands to protect her head but the books rained down on her and she fell to her knees, feeling books crash down onto her back as pain stabbed her shoulder and arm. She knew she had to do something fast, or the killer would be on her.

'Listen,' she shouted. 'The book you're looking for isn't here. Mr Mori didn't hide it here, he didn't even have it. Mr Ando sent it back to Hina's office the night before he died. She's the one who's had it all along. You're looking in the wrong place.'

Silence.

'It's hidden now, somewhere you'll never find it. But I can get it for you,' shouted Josie. 'It's what you wanted, isn't it? The last book. The one worth more than all the others put together. You can be rich for the rest of your life on what that book will sell for. But you can't get it without me.'

A little rustle in the distance. Was Josie imagining it, or did the person's movements seem less assured than they had done? As though they weren't sure whether to believe her?

She just needed one more thing to convince them. One more piece of information that showed she knew what she was talking about. If only she'd been able to get a look at the book, so she could show that she really did know what it was. She thought desperately. The book they'd found in the messenger bag in the coin locker had been a modern edition of Basho's poems. It was possible that Mr Ando had put it there on purpose – as a clue, or maybe even just as a joke. Josie decided to take a chance. She didn't know much about Basho, but his most famous haiku had stuck in her mind.

'Listen,' she called. 'Listen to this and you'll know I'm telling you the truth.'

She took a deep breath and said, '*An old quiet pond, When a frog jumps into it, The splash of water.*'

Long pause. Then the person at the other end of the book stack appeared and began making their slow way over the piles of fallen books. It was still too dark to see who it was and Josie hesitated to shine the light of her torch directly in the person's face. But as they got close Josie could see who it was and the knowledge filled her with a deep sense of sadness. The last person in the world she had wanted to see.

Eriko.

TWENTY ONE

They met in standard meeting room seven at AZT on the last day of the year, the remaining participants of the haiku tour. It had been Mr Tanaka's idea – that they should all come together this one last time.

Mr Tanaka sat at one end of the table with the box Mr Ando had sent to Haiku Country Tours, its Kuroneko Yamato labels and packaging still untouched, on the table in front of him. Mr Kimura sat in the centre of one long side of the table, his long face looking particularly serious. Next to him sat Ken Ueda, his pen poised ready to take notes, and Josie, with her arm in a sling. Ranged down the other side were Mrs Ando, Yuko and Hina. At the far end of the table, at a slight but respectful distance, sat Mr Shimizu, the gash on his head almost healed.

The office lady wheeled in a trolley of cups of green tea and little plates of soft sticky *mochi* and handed them round. Nobody said anything until she'd gone. Then Mr Tanaka cleared his throat and said,

'Well, first of all I'd like to thank Mrs Ando for

allowing us all to be present when she opens the box her husband sent from Matsuyama before his unfortunate demise. As we now know, his death was not the accident we all believed it to be but murder. Eriko Ono is in police custody and, I understand, has made a full confession. Once again I must express our sincere condolences to the Ando family on their unfortunate loss.'

He bowed to Mrs Ando and she bowed in return. She looked less grim than she had the day Josie met her at the Aoyama Flower Market Tea House, as though finding out the truth about her husband's death had given her some release. It gave Josie the courage to ask the question that had been on her mind ever since her visit to Yokohama.

'Er, Mrs Ando,' she said, hesitating as all eyes in the room turned to her. 'I was wondering, if you don't mind my asking, whether you knew about Eriko and her son.'

Mrs Ando nodded, as though she'd expected the question and welcomed it.

'I knew,' she said. 'My husband told me all about it. It was just a silly fling, but Eriko thought it was more than that. She thought he was going to marry her. When he said he'd help support the boy but that was all, she turned against him.'

'So that's when she started going after the book?' Josie said, beginning to see the light.

'That's right,' said Mrs Ando. 'She found out about Ando Investments and where the money really came from, and she worked out that my husband brought the books back from his Matsuyama trips. Mr Mori said she was dangerous but my husband didn't believe him. It was only when we got to Matsuyama and she started to threaten him that he got worried. That's why he hid the book. He knew that was what she was after, but he never thought she'd go as far as murder.'

'What will happen to her little boy now?' said Josie.

'Eriko's neighbour has taken him in,' said Mr Tanaka. 'The one who used to look after him while Eriko was at work. She seems very fond of him.'

'Of course, I will see that his material wants are provided for,' said Mrs Ando. 'He is, after all, my husband's son.'

Josie looked across the table at Yuko. How much of all this had she known? It was impossible to tell. Yuko had no sense of the difference between truth and lies. She said what suited her and hid what didn't; that was how she lived.

'We're fortunate that Mr Shimizu was able to join us today,' Mr Tanaka said. 'He will be able to advise on the value of the books in the box.'

Mr Shimizu got up, bowed and walked along to the end of the table where the box rested. Mr Tanaka picked up a substantial pair of scissors that had been laid ready and handed them to Mrs Ando. She took them and cut through the thick tape that sealed the top of the box. As she opened it up everyone craned forward slightly.

Some crumpled paper that had been used to fill out

the box hid what was inside. Mrs Ando took it out and began taking out the books, one by one. The top layer consisted of modern editions of works by Masaoka Shiki and Kurita Chodo, the two haiku poets most associated with Matsuyama. Below that were books by Basho – Josie recognised the edition of *The Narrow Road to the Deep North* that she had sitting on her shelves at home. And below that... below that was some more crumpled paper and a single book wrapped in thick cardboard.

Mrs Ando took it out; Ken piled the packaging debris back in the box and moved it from the table to the corner of the room. Very carefully, Mrs Ando undid the cardboard cover to reveal a rectangular shape wrapped in silk. It seemed as if the whole room held its breath as she gently unwrapped it.

Beneath the silk was an ancient-looking book. Josie couldn't read the spidery writing on the cover but when Mrs Ando gently opened it and reverently turned the delicate pages, Josie knew what it must be.

'It's Basho isn't it?' she said. 'Mr Ando's favourite poet.'

'Yes,' said Mrs Ando. 'It's his collection of poems, *Shrivelled Chestnuts*.'

For a moment they all sat in silence, staring at the book. Then Mr Shimizu said, 'May I?'

When Mrs Ando nodded, he took the book from her and examined it carefully.

'It's genuine,' he said at last, placing the book reverently back in its silk covering. 'Basho wrote *Shrivelled Chestnuts* in 1683, and it looks like this edition was published not long after that. It's been printed using woodblocks, like the ones they used to make floating world prints. The paper is *washi*, traditional Japanese paper, which is long lasting and doesn't turn yellow with age. It has been bound and sewn in the *fukuro toji* style. It is the most remarkable book that I have ever had the pleasure of holding. Despite its great age it is in superlative condition. There is probably not another like it in the world, not even in a museum.'

'How much is it worth?' said Yuko.

'I can't estimate it. The owner of such a book could name their own price.'

Yuko, her face flushed with excitement, reached out to pick up the book. But her mother's sharp voice forestalled her.

'Leave it where it is,' she said. 'It doesn't belong to us. It came into our family by trickery and exploitation. It belonged to people who traded it for food to keep from starving. We can't profit from such a thing. I will donate it to the National Archive as a gift in commemoration of my husband. I am sure Mr Shimizu will help us to make the arrangements.'

Mr Shimizu bowed.

'But you can't do that,' said Yuko. 'It's worth a fortune! What are we going to live on without it? Now it's come out about Ando Investments and what it was really doing, the company can't carry on. The tax authorities are already sniffing around the accounts. It'll be wound up and we'll be lucky if there's more than a few yen left.'

'I know that,' said Mrs Ando calmly. 'That's how it should be. Everything needs to come out in the open and be put right. The house in Aoyama too, that will have to be sold.'

'Not the house!' wailed Yuko. 'Where will we live?'

'I shall live in our old house in Saitama. That, at least, genuinely belongs to us. And it's where I belong. Aoyama was never the right place for me. All my friends are in Saitama. They'll welcome me back and let me go back to my old life when all of this is forgotten. You can come with me if you like, but you'll have to earn your own living from now on.'

'I'm never going back to Saitama,' said Yuko. 'I'd rather die.'

'Then you must make your own way,' said her mother. She turned to Mr Tanaka.

'Can I leave the book in AZT's custody until we can arrange its transfer to the National Archive?' she said. Mr Tanaka bowed.

'We would be honoured,' he said. 'What do you want to do with the rest of the books?'

Mrs Ando thought for a moment. Then she looked at Josie.

'My husband wanted you to learn about haiku,' she said with a smile. 'Please take these books as the start of your haiku collection.'

'Thank you,' said Josie, wondering where she would put them in her tiny flat but feeling pleased all the same. 'They'll remind me of Mr Ando every time I read them.'

Mrs Ando stood up.

'You'll be very welcome to drop in if you're ever in Saitama,' she said to Josie. 'You're the one who got justice for my husband. I won't forget that.'

Ken stood up too.

'I'll take you down to reception,' he said. 'Yuko too.'

Yuko tossed her head but said nothing.

'I must be off too,' said Hina. 'There's another haiku tour leaving tomorrow. I need to do a final check on the arrangements.'

They filed out and Mr Kimura picked up his papers, nodded to Mr Tanaka, and left too. Only Mr Tanaka, Josie and Mr Shimizu remained.

'May I?' said Mr Tanaka, picking up the Basho book reverently. 'It is such an honour to hold it, even for a moment.'

'I wish Mr Mori had been here to see it,' said Mr Shimizu. 'It would have meant a lot to him.'

They stood in silence for a moment and then Mr Tanaka handed the book back to Mr Shimizu, who wrapped it up again carefully.

'I'll see you out,' said Mr Tanaka. 'Let me know when you've made the arrangements with the National Archive.'

Josie watched them go and then hurried back to her desk and rang Dave.

'It's over,' she said. 'The book was there, just like we thought. It was amazing to see it – it was like Basho was in the room with us. It's going to go to the National Archive, so maybe we'll get to see it again some day.'

'That's great. When are you coming home?'

'Right away. I'm going to take the rest of the day off – after all, it is New Year's Eve.'

'Great,' said Dave. 'Rin and I will be waiting. And don't forget, you promised me a quiet New Year's Eve in front of the telly. Just you, me and the cat, remember? Oh, and a bottle of champagne, please.'

'You're on. I'll pick up the champagne on the way home. And I've written a haiku for you too, just to show I can. Do you want to hear it?'

'Go on.'

'Peaceful moonlit night, It's the turning of the year, Future looking bright.'

Author's note

If you enjoyed this book, I hope you'll like the other books in the Josie Clark in Japan mystery series:

The Tokyo Karaoke Murder – A night at the karaoke goes badly wrong for expat Londoner Josie Clark when she is accused of murder, leaving her just an hour to prove her innocence. Can she do it? (Novelette).

The Cherry Blossom Murder – Josie goes backstage at Japan's unique and spectacular Takarazuka Revue to expose a murderer and save a priceless treasure.

The Bullet Train Murder – When a body is found on the bullet train travelling between Osaka and Tokyo, it's nothing to do with Josie. Or is it? (Coming soon.)

To find out more about the Josie Clark in Japan mystery series, please visit my website, franpickering.com.

If you liked this book, why not add a short review on Amazon or Goodreads? Customer reviews help others decide what to read, and help authors get new readers.

Acknowledgements

Grateful thanks to my beta readers Rodney Pickering, Yannick Pucci and Desiree Erasmus, and to my cover designer, Andrew Brown of Design for Writers.

Made in the USA
Lexington, KY
22 November 2017